AT WAVE'S
END

ALSO BY PATRICIA PERRY DONOVAN

Deliver Her

AT WAVE'S END

PATRICIA

PERRY

DONOVAN

LAKE UNION
PUBLISHING

Published by Lake Union Publishing, Seattle

www.apub.com

Amazon, the Amazon logo, and Lake Union Publishing are trademarks of Amazon.com, Inc., or its affiliates.

ISBN-13: 9781503939387
ISBN-10: 1503939383

Cover design by Diane Luger

Printed in the United States of America

*For my parents,
who first took me "down the shore,"
with love and gratitude*

I am not afraid of storms for I am learning how to sail my ship.

—*Louisa May Alcott*

PART 1: PREDISASTER

1

With Piquant's stainless steel kitchen door propped at exactly the right angle, head chef Faith Sterling could clandestinely scan the entire dining room, which at eleven o'clock on this mid-September weeknight remained two-thirds full. She'd barely left her station at the South Street Seaport eatery all evening, but now, with her final entrées plated and run, she could breathe.

"So I'm reading this magazine," her mother continued.

"Magazine. Got it." Adjusting the phone at her ear, Faith answered absently, intent on interpreting Xander's end-of-night table-hopping. All seemed positive as her boss sipped his ritual armagnac while chatting with the regular at table nine (filet medallions *au poivre*, medium rare), but Faith didn't relax completely until his laughter bellowed over Piquant's piped-in music. *Another successful night,* she thought with relief. Xander had been shrewd to open on the ground floor of the Wall Street residential high-rise, whose wealthy occupants treated Piquant like their local diner, descending from their glass-walled condos almost nightly to dine.

"So what do you think?" her mother asked.

"About what?" Faith had tuned out whatever her mother had been saying.

"About the opportunity, Faith. In the magazine. I think I just might win this one!"

Opportunity. Faith stiffened at Connie Sterling's code word for the contests, sweepstakes and assorted schemes that consumed her. Her code word for *obsession*. Of all people, Faith's single mother should have figured out by now that life rarely offered something for nothing. Faith had survived more of her mother's "opportunities" than she cared to remember. Like the earn-thousands-by-working-at-home offer. Or the no-money-down real estate course for which Connie borrowed some of Faith's summer waitressing money earmarked for college textbooks to purchase the course's CD recordings. Though her mother had promptly repaid the loan, it had still rankled Faith that the recordings sat unopened in the back of a hutch, Connie already seduced by the next sure thing.

Faith had long ago schooled herself to spot the warning signs, horrified that her mother could devote days, weeks, months to obvious scams. Thankfully, before she left for college, she had convinced Connie to take a job in the packaging department at the local food-processing plant. Though she earned only a pittance, her mother at least would qualify for a pension and lifetime health benefits after ten years—a milestone now just months away, to Faith's immense relief.

Faith reminded herself of this approaching stability now, to keep from being too worried about this latest "opportunity," whatever it was.

"You know how these things always end up," Faith said, massaging her lower lip.

"I know. But I feel this one in my bones. If I win this time, I'll never enter another contest again. You have my word. Moon and stars."

Moon and stars—words her mother could take to the bank, Faith thought ruefully, scanning the gradually emptying dining room once more. Her gaze fell on Piquant's entrance, where the appearance of a stocky, balding male prompted the remaining staff to snap to attention— all but Faith, who inched back from the kitchen door a bit.

The late arrival was a building resident and an *NPR*—kitchen shorthand for "nice people get rewarded," or a diner meriting over-the-top

4

service. He asked for Faith each time he dined, ever since she'd impulsively broken her own rule about steering clear of the clientele and trooped upstairs with the staff for a tour of his penthouse.

Knowing her boss would have zero qualms about seating the high-roller regular, even at this hour, her heart sank. And, sure enough, she watched Xander clap the man on the back and steer him to a table, extending her shift and all but assuring she'd have to join him at some point for another round of awkward small talk.

"Sorry, Mom. Big customer. Talk later."

Don't make the mistake of socializing with a customer ever again, she scolded herself, returning to her station. Abandoning the kitchen's protective cocoon made her anxious and vulnerable, like a soldier without armor or an asthmatic without an inhaler. She preferred connecting to Piquant's patrons strictly via the dinner tickets fluttering on her rail like crisp white shirts on a clothesline: table seven's coffee-burnished *magret de canard*, rare and rosy; blue-corn-dusted cobia with zucchini and okra for the gluten-free-by-choice diner at table thirteen; table twenty-one's salmon and quinoa salad, carrot-sesame vinaigrette dressing *SOS* (sauce on the side).

"Very funny," she muttered as Cesar, Piquant's senior server, clipped the NPR's ticket to the rail in front of her, a thick red heart encircling the man's order.

Faith adjusted her beanie and tightened her ginger ponytail before decimating a handful of garlic cloves on a cutting board. Scraping the dice into a sauté pan, she attempted to recall Connie's words: something about a magazine? It was probably just some coupon, she decided. And besides, the odds were pretty much stacked against her mother winning anything at all.

By the time she had goldened the garlic in its drizzle of olive oil and seared the man's chicken paillard and fingerling potatoes to perfection, she had all but forgotten the exchange with her mother. As she bathed the entrée in its fragrant coriander extraction, Faith's breathing steadied, the exercise so meditative she even managed a smile when Xander himself appeared to run the NPR's meal.

Once her boss exited the kitchen, Faith double-checked her station's lineup of essential ingredients and oils and condiments for the next day. Satisfied with her *mise en place*, she grabbed her coat from a hook, about to depart to meet her friend Ellie for a drink, when the door swung back open and Xander reappeared.

"Hey, Faith. Before you go—"

"Don't even say it." Faith dropped her coat onto a kitchen stool. "I know. Somebody wants to pay their compliments to the chef."

2

Beneath the string of bare bulbs, Ellie's haloed solitaire glinted at Faith across the Copper Nickel's high-top like a lighthouse beacon.

"Sorry I'm so late. Blame the NPR," Faith panted, out of breath from her dash down Atlantic Avenue, where she dodged the exuberant throng exiting the Barclays Center in hopes of catching her roommate before last call. Her breastbone burned, a consequence of the fast food fries inhaled on the way over.

"English, please?" Ellie demanded, sliding a beer toward her.

"Sorry. He was a VIP customer. A regular."

"Was he cute? Maybe you should give him a chance."

"Ugh. No way." Faith swallowed a swig of beer.

"Well, if not him, somebody else, then. I'd just like to see you loosen up for once. Have some fun."

"Please. Why is everyone so anxious for me to let loose? I like my life just fine the way it is."

"If you call working around the clock a life."

"I can't help it if I love what I do."

"Then why is it the second someone tries to get close to you at work, you move on to the next restaurant?"

"I do not. I'm just always on the lookout for a better opportunity." *Now who's talking about opportunities?* "Besides, Piquant is the dream job I've been waiting for. I'm not going anywhere."

Faith fervently believed that, having hitched her wagon to her boss's. Xander had managed the first New York restaurant she ever worked in. He had grander aspirations for himself, and was biding his time until he could open his own establishment, he told her the night they met. When he finally acquired enough capital to open Piquant, Faith was the first person he hired for his kitchen.

So what if he had overextended himself a little recently. The cash pinch was simply part of Piquant's growing pains, he explained.

Ellie's fiancé, Dennis, sidled over and draped an arm around Faith. "Tough night, huh?"

"Doesn't matter. It's over now." Faith pressed her hands to her cheeks to cool them. "Can we *please* talk about something else?"

"Of course. Dennis, what do *you* think we should talk about?" Ellie's eyes danced.

"I don't know. What do *you* want to talk about, babe?"

Their coquettish back-and-forth made it obvious the two were bursting with urgent news to share. "Just tell me," Faith pleaded. "You two are adorable, but I've had a crazy night. Let me guess: you finally booked the honeymoon."

"Not exactly." Ellie licked her lips, then slid a paper across the table toward her. "It's more like a *baby*moon."

3

Ellie was pregnant.

Faith squealed and got up to hug her friend.

"See, these are the arms." Ellie stroked the peanut-shaped mass on the paper in front of them.

"That's amazing," Faith murmured, leaning over to examine the whorled image, which was no bigger than a thumbprint. Cocking her head, she found that it more closely resembled a Teletubby than a newborn—a Teletubby that would turn her happy-go-lucky friends into parents, she thought with amazement. As Faith listened to Ellie describe the bliss of hearing her baby's heartbeat for the first time, she tried to visualize her friend balancing an infant on her lap in six months instead of the designer handbag occupying that space tonight.

"What's so funny?" asked Ellie.

"Nothing. Just thinking ahead to this time next year."

"Right. Next year." Ellie grabbed Dennis's elbow and pulled him toward her, her blond head barely reaching his shoulder. "We *should* talk about next year, shouldn't we, Dennis?"

Dennis shoved his hands in his pockets. "Yes. Right. Good idea." He cleared his throat. "Sorry, Faith. No easy way to say this, but there's been a change of plans."

Instantly, the vibe veered from celebratory to serious, like the abrupt *zzz-zzzTTT* of her mother's old turntable needle skidding off a well-worn Carly Simon album and cutting off the music. As Dennis talked, Faith's smile faded, and she rubbed at the anxiety prickling her neck. It now appeared that this baby, this Teletubby, would seriously impact Faith's life as well, altering the game plan she and Ellie had mapped out for Faith to stay on in their apartment until the wedding. In that version, newlyweds Ellie and Dennis would assume full ownership of the well-appointed Park Slope townhouse Ellie's parents bestowed on her at college graduation, while maid of honor Faith moved on to a new domicile.

But as Dennis now explained, this infinitesimal being would force Faith out about five months earlier than anticipated—the five months she needed to replenish her savings after helping Xander out of his credit jam.

Had the couple adhered to their original timetable, Faith could have dug herself out of her financial hole. But without an all-important security deposit in her pocket, she couldn't go anywhere, except possibly to a friend's couch. She'd sleep in Piquant's kitchen before going back to those days.

So even as Faith smiled and nodded at the couple, she couldn't squelch the selfish seed of anxiety germinating in her own gut.

"So are you *sure* you don't mind moving out just a teensy bit sooner? I know the whole Craigslist thing can be a drag." Ellie's brow wrinkled with the question, and Faith noticed for the first time the slight mooning of her face that marked a pregnant woman, as though the life she carried filled her clear up to her cheekbones.

"Of course I don't mind." Faith prayed she sounded sincere. If only a wade into the New York City rental market were her only worry.

Ellie hugged her. "I knew you wouldn't. Didn't I tell you, Dennis?" They planned to convert Faith's bedroom to the nursery, she explained. "Nursery, Faith. Can you believe I'm even saying the word?" As Dennis rubbed his fiancée's back, Ellie further volunteered that their wedding would be postponed until after the baby's birth, when she could squeeze back into the wisp of a designer wedding gown she had her eye on. "I know I'm going to be such a cow at nine months. It runs in my family."

And how *amazing* that Faith would now have not one but *two* very important roles: Ellie's maid of honor *and* godmother to the new baby!

Faith nodded, worrying in what universe her paycheck could cover the costs of Ellie's bridal and baby showers in close proximity. No doubt Ellie and her socialite mother would expect celebrations of a certain caliber. Then there was the worry of wrangling time off from Piquant for both.

Stop being so selfish, Faith admonished herself. Her best friend was going to be a mother, and this was how she reacted? Further plumbing her emotions, Faith realized she felt hurt that her best friend hadn't confided in her about her pregnancy. Until now, they'd told each other everything.

Perhaps there had been signs. Had Ellie offered a lame excuse the last time Faith suggested a girls' night out? She couldn't recall. She only knew that even when there was no food, their fridge always contained an open bottle of pinot grigio, corked with a hideous stopper in the shape of a bride, a wedding favor from a couple who divorced within the year, after the bride's affair came to light.

Forcing a smile, Faith held up her flute for more of the champagne that had materialized after the announcement (with a side of sparkling cider for Ellie).

Perhaps she should take a page from her mother's book and buy a lottery ticket on the way home—anything that might shore up her precarious circumstances now that Ellie quite literally had pulled the rug out from under her.

4

"How's the hunt going, Faith? Got a new crib yet?" Tomas, Piquant's lead bartender, polished another pilsner glass as it came out of the steamer and slid it onto an overhead rack.

"I don't, but my roommate does," Faith joked. Ellie had already registered for dozens of baby items, including a futuristic pod crib with clear acrylic sides that turned into a toddler bed. "This whole apartment thing is stressing me out."

Indeed, in the four weeks since Ellie had announced her pregnancy, Faith had gone through the motions, visiting countless Brooklyn apartments, fudging her financial picture to get by the agents. Meanwhile, the apartment felt less and less her own, especially with the dog-eared *What to Expect When You're Expecting* taunting her from their coffee table.

Faith picked up Piquant's leather cocktail menu and perused its offerings—all ironically named and featuring muddled produce of one sort or another: muddled orange slices and blackberries, even muddled celery. Xander claimed to have foreseen this trend.

Faith felt a bit muddled at the moment—as though someone had taken a pestle to her well-ordered existence. She ran a finger down the list of drinks and paused at the Boxcar, a blend of London gin, Cointreau, fresh lime juice and egg white, reminded of Henry, Jessie, Violet and Benny Alden, the heroes of *The Boxcar Children*, a book series she had devoured as a child. If those young orphans managed to survive in a boxcar, she certainly could blaze a new trail as well. Look at the way millennials had appropriated trailer parks lately.

After setting the menu down, she headed back to the kitchen. Her fatal mistake had been thinking of the apartment as hers, when it had been on loan from Ellie all along (despite the day-to-day details of phoning a plumber or camping out for the cable company usually falling to Faith).

Everything about their place was perfect: its proximity to the 2 train and the ironic Bread & Beyond, purveyor of both tombstones and fresh baguettes, on their corner. And the game-changer: the stacked washer/dryer that ate up precious closet space but saved hours of schlepping.

Sighing, Faith smoothed the front of her double-breasted chef coat and ignited her grill station. The intense dinner crush that followed barely offered a moment to breathe. However, the gods did smile down on her by keeping the persistent NPR customer away for the night. When she finally stepped out back for a break, she saw her mother had called four times, so Faith phoned her back immediately.

"What's wrong? Are you okay?"

"I'm *better* than okay, Faith. I'm fantastic! I *won*. I won the mermaid's purse!"

Faith frowned. Had her mother attended some sort of under-the-sea-themed bazaar? "Cool. But four calls over a pocketbook? I was worried sick you'd been in an accident."

"Pocketbook?" her mother laughed. "The Mermaid's Purse isn't a handbag, Faith. It's a bed-and-breakfast. An actual B and B at the Jersey shore. I'm going to be an innkeeper!"

5

"Wait . . . *what?*" Faith sank onto the picnic bench behind Piquant to digest her mother's announcement. "How in the world did you win a bed-and-breakfast?"

"I entered that contest. In the magazine. I told you."

Magazine. Faith vaguely recalled the reference from their last conversation. "Right. Remind me of the details again?"

"I still can't believe Maeve chose me," her mother gloated.

"Who's Maeve?"

"Maeve Calhoun. The owner of The Mermaid's Purse. She chose my essay out of thousands of entries."

"What was your essay about?"

"Why I would be the perfect candidate to take over her inn. Obviously, I persuaded her. And now I'm going to run a bed-and-breakfast. At the beach!"

Faith kneaded her forehead. "But you don't have any experience. You've never even waitressed."

"I've made beds. And breakfast. And I worked as a hotel maid for a while."

"Motel," Faith corrected. "Which is nothing like an inn. A bed-and-breakfast is much more personal." No doubt her mother's Disneyized vision of innkeeping had everything to do with afternoon tea, chilled pitchers of lemonade, and crumpets consumed on porch rockers, with zero regard to the round-the-clock housekeeping, gardening and dozens more daunting responsibilities and costs that came with the innkeeper title. "So when is all this supposed to happen? Next summer?"

"Why, no. I have to take ownership sooner than that."

"But you can't, Mom. Your job, remember? You're *this* close to getting that pension. That security." In the darkness behind the restaurant, Faith pinched her thumb and forefinger together.

"Well, of course I'm taking my employment into consideration."

Faith sagged against the picnic table in relief. "That's good to hear."

"Just remember, Faith: there are other paths to financial peace of mind."

No. You will not throw away this one sure thing. Glancing at her watch, Faith felt the back of her neck flush with heat, her body's reflexive response to Connie's irresponsible impulses. "I've got to get back to work now. But we need to talk more about this. A *lot* more."

"I agree. That's why I've already booked my flight. I'll see you soon!"

6

Upon returning home from work that night, Faith opened her laptop, found the Mermaid's Purse giveaway online and pored over the details:

After more than two decades of running an idyllic bed-and-breakfast on the Jersey shore, Maeve Calhoun wants to hand over the straps of The Mermaid's Purse to one lucky essay-contest winner.

Lucky, huh? Faith scrutinized Calhoun, a tall, sturdy, pleasant-looking woman with soft white hair, who smiled broadly in front of a charming two-story shingled Victorian. Calhoun held open a wrought-iron gate and carried a gingham-lined basket brimming with muffins, a touch Faith found to be a bit of overkill.

Reading on, Faith learned a number of things about Maeve: that she herself had won the inn in an essay contest twenty-five years earlier; that Calhoun would miss her returning guests, who had become like family; and that selecting exactly the right successor to run The Mermaid's Purse would ease the innkeeper's sadness.

How wonderfully warm and inviting the whole possibility sounded. *Too* inviting. Faith eyed the alluring accompanying images: turquoise surf crashing onto almond sand; candy-colored umbrellas stuck into soft dunes like lollipops; a rainbow of towels spread beneath them. All in all, Maeve had expertly packaged this tempting prospect of beginning a brand-new life at the beach, right down to the golden muffins resting on their gingham bed.

No wonder Connie had entered. The proposal had been designed to seduce someone like her. And as usual, it would be up to Faith to dash that dream.

Scrolling down to the contest rules, Faith learned Connie had paid a one-hundred-twenty-five-dollar entry fee for the privilege of submitting her essay—no small sum to her coupon-clipping mother, Faith thought, massaging her lower lip. Reading further, Faith sucked in her breath: according to the mathematics of the novel contest, her mother's essay had outshone the fifty-six hundred or so other entries Maeve needed to recoup the inn's market value of seven hundred thousand dollars. *That must have been some essay, Mom,* she thought.

The rules also defined the winner's obligations: assume ownership within three months of the contest closing date (her mother *had* been correct on that count); run the property as an inn for at least one year; and allow Calhoun to stay on at The Mermaid's Purse for an unspecified transition period.

For more context, Faith scanned some of the inn's guest reviews, which were mostly positive (although only a handful had been posted recently). The target of some scathing feedback from diners herself, Faith discounted the inn's single vicious review, no doubt planted by a jealous rival.

At that point, Faith closed the laptop in frustration, the clock ticking on her opportunity to influence her mother's decision. She called Connie in the morning, and several times more in the weeks leading up to her arrival, but nothing Faith said dissuaded her from her East Coast trip.

Her mother was coming to Wave's End—with or without Faith's blessing.

7

Why had table eleven chosen today of all days—the day her mother arrived to size up her lottery winnings—to dawdle over dessert? Faith fretted as she drove toward Newark Airport. A brisk autumn breeze swirled through the Zipcar's open windows, its freshness occasionally fouled by factory fumes. Ahead of her, Faith eyed a rare sight: a perfectly spaced queue of departing jetliners dotting the skyline like prayer beads. Where were they headed? she wondered. Having recently paid off the last of her student loans at the ripe old age of twenty-seven, she had yet to treat herself to an extravagant adult vacation—not that this would happen anytime soon.

Driving in the fast lane to make up for lost time, Faith tried hard to imagine that experience. Her only comparisons were discomfiting weekends with her mother at various hotel chains during her teens, enduring punishing time-share pitches in return for their stay. (One time Connie had literally kissed her hard-earned room voucher on their way to the pool.) At checkout, her mother's promotional tote bulged with breakfast buffet booty: cereal boxes, packaged breadsticks, tiny jam jars in foreign flavors like boysenberry. The entire ordeal made Faith cringe with embarrassment.

Even today, the memory made her recoil. For distraction, she turned on the car radio.

"At the moment, US forecasters predict that tropical storm Nadine will make landfall on the East Coast . . ."

Nadine: the name certainly sounded harmless enough, Faith thought, switching the station. She'd had her fill of weather prognostications for the moment. For days, the mere mention of Nadine churned up waves of panic from Cuba to Canada in terms of the impact she *might* have, even though the storm barely rustled Caribbean palm trees currently. Already that morning, Xander had asked Faith to estimate Piquant's frozen reserves as a precaution.

After leaving the rental car in short-term parking, Faith headed toward the arrivals area. For now, her priority was taming the tornado that was her mother. She soon spotted Connie sprinting down the narrow hall, her gray hair flying and her oversized chunky cardigan flapping over her calf-skimming paisley dress, and raised a hand to wave. Seconds later, Faith found herself wrapped in her mother's familiar patchouli-and-warm-wool scent.

"I've missed you so much." Stepping back, Connie smoothed Faith's ponytail, laying it to rest on her daughter's shoulder. "So, how's my little cook doing?"

It's chef, not cook. "Tired. I raced across the river to get here on time."

"Well, we're together now, and that's what counts. And isn't *this* going to be an adventure. I can't wait to show you The Mermaid's Purse." Oblivious to the masses moving around her, she yanked a magazine from her worn leather tote and opened it, the twin turquoise Buddhas dangling from her ears quivering. A glance at the page told Faith it mirrored what she had seen on Maeve's website.

"Not here, Mom. We'll get trampled." Faith took her mother's elbow and steered her toward baggage claim.

"All right." Connie rolled up the magazine. "But you have to admit, it's serendipitous this prize brought me to the East Coast. To *you*." Tapping Faith's arm with the coiled periodical, she stepped onto the down escalator, then turned and smiled up at her daughter. "Now I'll just be two hours away."

"Fantastic. But don't get carried away. We haven't even seen the place."

"I don't care. I can already see myself there," Connie said as they stepped off the escalator. "And it would be nice if you weren't always such a party pooper."

"I'll be the first one to throw a party, once you're officially retired." Faith stopped to consult the arrivals board, then led her mother toward her flight's luggage carousel. *Party pooper.* Her mother acted as if Faith had relished being the buzz kill her entire life, the raiser of red flags, as though she were the parent and not the other way around. Faith had long ago accepted her fate. Connie had barely been out of her teens when she gave birth, and Faith's father hadn't remained in the picture for very long. Her mother had said little about him, other than he had loved Faith very much but couldn't take care of himself, much less a family. End of story.

Nor had Connie's mother been much help. Always restless, Edna Winnick abandoned her daughter and son when her children were teens, lured by Las Vegas's glitter and promise—a broken promise, as it turned out, as the best the Strip offered her was a job at an all-night buffet. Ultimately, Faith's grandmother died a penniless waitress.

Faith had never even met her—the only relic of the woman was a gold locket gathering dust in her own mother's jewelry box.

Yes, Connie had been dealt a crappy hand, Faith thought as the conveyor belt lurched to life, uncomfortable with the resentment she still harbored. And, unfortunately, her mother had become something of a gambler herself, taking risks like the one that brought her to the East Coast today.

This time, she feared her mother had gone too far. She needed to stop her before this Mermaid's Purse situation grew too messy for Faith to clean up.

Still, Connie literally thrummed with excitement over winning, and had come all this way to claim her prize. Trying to summon a little enthusiasm, Faith joined her mother at the luggage carousel and took her arm. "I *am* curious to see the inn up close."

At that moment, Connie spotted her bag and stepped away to grab an oversized tapestried suitcase reinforced with a thick belt of duct tape.

"That's a pretty big bag for a couple of days," Faith said.

A carton similarly swathed in duct tape lurched down the ramp onto the conveyor, and her mother grabbed that as well. "Keep an eye out, Faith. There's three more like that."

"You're kidding, right? Is there anything left in your apartment?" Faith wondered if the compact Zipcar would hold all of her mother's baggage.

"No." Her mother kicked the base of her suitcase. "This is it, Faith. I have a really good feeling about this, and I want to be prepared, just in case!"

8

To Faith's immense relief, Connie confirmed that she hadn't quit her job, but had only redeemed her remaining vacation days for her extended stay. There was still a window of time for Connie to reconsider, to go back to Albuquerque with her pension intact. Not wanting to waste a day, Connie insisted they head straight to Wave's End from the airport.

Despite the fact that her mother hadn't thrown away her chance at stability, as they crested the Driscoll Bridge around four thirty, the mouth of Raritan Bay glistening below them, Faith had the unsettling feeling she was driving straight into the eye of a storm. "Remember, Mom: no matter how great The Mermaid's Purse seems, you promised you wouldn't sign anything until a lawyer looks everything over."

"Yes, Faith. I recall that conversation."

Faith glanced at the back of the Zipcar, loaded with her mother's belongings.

"We're going to need a plan B. In case this doesn't work out."

Connie stretched. "I refuse to think about that possibility."

Once over the bridge, Faith ignored her GPS, leaving the Garden State Parkway and heading east to connect with the coastal road. She had been down this way with Xander a few times last year to scout a new restaurant location, scouring shore towns from the Atlantic Highlands to Cape May. They had not stopped in Wave's End, home to The Mermaid's Purse, however. In the end, Xander dismissed the entire region as foodie Siberia and wound up opening a pop-up patio bar in the Hamptons instead. Maybe that was where her boss had gotten himself into trouble, spreading himself too thin.

The navigation system rerouted, and mother and daughter meandered south, the marzipan Victorians, reproduction streetlamps and quaint tent communities giving way to pizza stands, bars and souvenir shops. They passed clusters of surfers peeling out of wetsuits, leaning dripping boards against their cars.

A block of weather-beaten bungalows and an ornate brick arch marked the town line; on the other side of the arch, the ocean road suddenly widened, as if in deference to the stately mansions studding its curb, their expansive columned verandas and inviting porch rockers facing the sea.

"Hey, look!" Connie exclaimed. "That sign says, 'Welcome to Wave's End.'" As Faith drove, Connie alternated between peering out the car window and consulting Maeve's magazine spread on her lap. "I don't get it. We're at the beach. But I don't see anything that looks like The Mermaid's Purse. Why is it telling us to keep going? I don't trust that gizmo, Faith."

A single lane now, the beachfront road elbowed at a fishing pier, whose clapboard snack stand had been nailed shut for the season. Faith slowed to a crawl, peering at each structure.

"Well, I do. Let's see where it takes us." After a scant two miles, another sign indicated they were leaving Wave's End, and, per the pre-programmed directions, Faith navigated away from the coastline. Out of the corner of her eye, she could see her mother's smile fade as the beach receded behind them.

"Cheer up. I'm sure we're almost there." At the next traffic light, Faith turned left as the system instructed.

"Okay, we should be close now." Connie leaned forward. "Look. Up ahead. There's someone on the sidewalk waving. That must be Maeve." Faith slowed the car at the snowy-haired woman flagging them down.

Behind her, a wall of arborvitaes all but hid a dilapidated Victorian sandwiched between an auto body shop and a real estate office, the latter roped and anchored to resemble a seaside shack.

As Faith pulled to the side of the road, Connie leaned over her for a better look. "That can't be the inn. It looks nothing like . . ." Connie glanced at her lap again in confusion.

"It has to be. Look at that sign on the porch." Faith pointed to the placard hand-lettered with the inn's name. "I think we found your prize, Mom. Welcome to The Mermaid's Purse."

9

Pulling into the inn's driveway, Faith drummed the steering wheel, her worst fears realized. She needed to devise an exit strategy.

"Well, what are we waiting for?" Connie resolutely tucked her hair behind her ears.

"You really want to go in?"

"Of course I do. I won the place, didn't I?"

"So they said. But look at it, Mom. And then look at *this*." Faith tapped the magazine in her mother's lap. "Those pictures had to have been taken twenty years ago. This inn looks nothing like you expected. She scammed you."

"A lovely-looking woman like that would not scam me."

"Of course she would. This is no different from those jacked-up rental ads on Craigslist, with their misleading descriptions and pictures." Faith sat back. "Tell you what: I'll take you back to the city. You can spend a few nights with me, have a meal or two at Piquant. After that, we'll figure out how to get you back home."

"I can't go back to Albuquerque."

"Of course you can. You've got your job there."

"And what do I tell everybody?"

"That you changed your mind. Decided you weren't cut out to be an innkeeper. It'll make a great story."

"Right. Hilarious. *Connie Sterling duped again.* No, thanks." She tossed the magazine into Faith's lap, then opened the car door.

"Mom, wait! Where are you going?" Faith scrambled to catch up with Connie, who strode resolutely toward the inn. Meanwhile, the woman who had waved at them from the sidewalk had disappeared.

Grimly, Faith stood beside her mother, surveying the property. Up close, the wall of trees hid more than The Mermaid's Purse; it also camouflaged the inn's sorry state of disrepair. The shingles on the two-story clapboard building had faded to sea foam, its claret shutters sorely in need of stripping. On either side, overgrown oaks scraped the bed-and-breakfast, begging to be trimmed. And with no front yard to speak of, the inn's nominal front porch, crowded with only two wicker rockers, all but butted up against the busy county road.

Silently, mother and daughter crossed the narrow strip of lawn and climbed rickety steps to the porch, whose floorboards protested under their weight. At the front door, Faith took off her sunglasses and squinted at a wrought-iron mailbox. From its curled and rusted newspaper rack hung a rough, black, pillow-shaped object with hornlike hooks protruding from its corners.

Faith's mother caressed one of the appendages. "Wow. Here it is. A mermaid's purse. This place is named for it."

"How do you know that?" Overhead, the porch-light globe housed a summer's worth of beetle carcasses.

"I looked it up for my essay. Thought it might increase my chances of winning."

"Guess it paid off."

"No need to be sarcastic." Connie pressed the buzzer, jumping at its shrillness.

"Hello-o-o-o!"

Faith and her mother turned to find the woman from the sidewalk grinning at them from the inn lawn. "I'd all but given up on you." She took the porch steps two at a time, a feat for someone Faith judged to be somewhere between seventy and eighty years old.

"I'm Maeve. Maeve Calhoun," she said, extending her hand. "Proud proprietor. For a bit longer, that is. But of course that's why *you're* here, isn't it?" Studying their faces, Maeve tapped her lips with her index finger for a few seconds before pointing at Connie. "It's *you*. You're my winner."

Connie smiled broadly. "Why, yes I am. How did you know?"

"My gut. You look as spunky as your letter."

Way to lay it on. Faith held out her hand. "I'm Faith, Connie's daughter."

"Lovely to meet you." Maeve linked her arm in Connie's. "Are you ready for the grand tour of your new bed-and-breakfast, Connie Sterling?"

Beaming, Faith's mother nodded as Maeve reached for the front door.

"Excuse me, Ms. Calhoun," Faith said. "My mother and I have a couple of questions before we start. There are a few things that don't make sense."

"Now, Faith," Connie chided, "there's no harm in letting Maeve show us around the place. After all, we did drive all the way down here."

"For some fantasy in a magazine."

Maeve patted Connie's arm. "Oh, dear. You must be referring to those photos. I may have been a little younger in those days, but my goodness, young people do it all the time with computer dating, don't they? Put their best face forward?"

Privately, Faith agreed, having encountered frequent credibility gaps herself in that milieu.

"I'll admit it," continued Maeve. "I'm a bit vain."

"Vanity is one thing," Faith said. "But misrepresenting the condition of this place, leading people to believe the inn sat on the water—"

"I never said that. The beach photos simply demonstrated the beauty of the area." Maeve patted the porch railing. "And it's true this old girl has aged a bit, but it's nothing a little tender loving care won't take care of."

"Yes, but there's a price tag attached to that TLC," said Faith. "Let's be honest here, Ms. Calhoun. You should have clarified a few things in your contest."

Frowning, Connie detached herself from Maeve. "Excuse us a moment," she said, pulling Faith to the far end of the porch. "My God," she whispered when they were out of Maeve's earshot. "Will you stop berating that poor woman?"

"I can't help it." Faith glared over her mother's shoulder at Maeve. "She took advantage of you."

"That's a bit harsh. Nobody forced me to write that essay. And since we're here, let's at least take the tour. Maybe she'll give us a free night."

"Are you serious?"

"Just promise me you won't say a word. We'll talk after."

"You swear?"

"Moon and stars."

"Perfect. *Very* reassuring." Sighing, Faith walked back to the innkeeper, who now sat in a rocking chair. "You seem like a lovely person, Maeve. But all I see so far is one gigantic money pit. Money my mother doesn't have. And we haven't even gone inside yet." Faith yelled the last few words to make herself heard over a quartet of Harleys roaring by at that moment.

"You're a wonderful daughter to be so concerned." Maeve got out of her rocker. "I promise you: once you've seen The Mermaid's Purse inside and out, you'll fall in love with her, just as I did." She clasped her hands to her heart. "And afterward, if you truly feel the place isn't for you, well, then, I guess I'll have to move on to the runner-up. Whose essay didn't hold a *candle* to yours, Connie, I have to tell you."

Connie nudged Faith. "Did you hear that?"

Faith rolled her eyes.

"No pressure, I promise." Maeve smiled sweetly. "Shall we go?"

No pressure, my foot. This woman knows exactly what she's doing. Feeling something soft at her ankle, Faith looked down at an overfed pewter Persian winding itself around her leg, fixing her with a copper stare.

"See, even Pixie wants you to stay," Maeve laughed. "She's our little mascot. Been with me since I took the reins of this place twenty-five years ago."

Faith crouched to stroke the cat, which snarled in response.

"Don't feel bad. Pixie just has to get to know you." Maeve knelt and scooped up the cat. Meowing in protest, Pixie leaped from her owner's arms and skittered down the steps, where she disappeared beneath the porch.

"She'll grow on you," Maeve continued. "Just like this inn will. Now, right this way, please."

About to follow Maeve inside, Faith was startled by a male voice booming from behind.

"Excuse me. May I have a moment, ladies?"

Faith turned and found herself staring down the barrel of a camera lens.

"Say cheese, please! We've got to capture this historic moment for posterity!"

Before Faith or Connie could protest, the man's camera exploded in a succession of blinding flashes.

10

"Why, Bruce Neery. You nearly gave us a heart attack. Please don't run that one of me in my apron." Maeve untied her smock and laid it on a rocker. "Bruce owns the *Beacon*, our local paper," she explained. "When he got wind of our winner's visit today, he wanted to take a few pictures."

"Doing a photo essay on Wave's End's newest business owner," explained the burly journalist with thinning, slicked-back gray hair. He pulled a smaller lens from a pocket of his khaki vest and swapped it out with the longer lens.

"It's a little premature for that," Faith protested, even as her mother preened alongside her. Connie could never resist a camera.

"Of course it isn't. I want to capture your first impressions. So who's the lucky winner?" After putting on a pair of glasses, he produced a notebook from a back pocket.

"That would be me." Ignoring Faith's elbow in her side, Connie spelled her last name as he scribbled. "That's right. Sterling. And this is my daughter, Faith. She's a chef in New York."

"Is that right? Hope you're not planning to mess with Maeve's scones," he chuckled. "They're perfection."

"Wouldn't think of it," said Faith. "Anyway, I won't be here."

"Oh, you will. You won't be able to resist Wave's End." He flipped his notebook closed. "Done for now. I'll stop back later for the rest of the story."

"Sorry about that," Maeve said once Bruce had gone. "It's a small town. News travels fast."

As fast as Maeve could alert the newspaper to their arrival, Faith thought, following her into the front hall's half darkness. There was something off about the reporter's appearance, Faith thought, wrinkling her nose—as off as the inn's mildewed air that even Maeve's strategically placed room fresheners failed to mask.

"This salon is our common area. Guests love to sit in here and read after the beach," Maeve said, leading them into a long, dark living room. Heavy velour sofas faced a stone hearth, and sickly philodendrons hung from macramé hangers. A thick armoire housed a dated television set, and a pile of well-worn women's magazines sat on a coffee table. Faith glanced at the top one, the previous year's Christmas issue. When she pointed this out to her mother behind Maeve's back, Connie only frowned and shook her head.

Next came the dining room, which echoed the salon's dated décor. A half-dozen rattan tables for two or four were set with plastic lace tablecloths and bud vases of tired-looking silk daffodils. "Over there is where we put out our meals." Beneath a bow window, a trestle table had been laid with a Bundt cake under a glass dome and a sweating decanter of ice tea.

"Looks very inviting," observed Connie.

"We do our best to make our guests feel at home." Crossing her arms, Maeve looked out the window. "Not like that fussy new hotel by the water. Imagine, expecting guests to dress for dinner at the *beach*!"

"Hasn't she ever heard of the Hamptons?" Faith whispered behind Maeve's back, to which Connie twisted an imaginary key at the corner of her mouth.

Ignoring her, Faith asked to see the kitchen.

"Straight through there, my dear."

Faith walked through the swinging door Maeve held open for them, and for the first time since arriving at the inn, she perked up. Despite its outdated appliances and badly chinked porcelain farm sink, the sun-soaked, airy kitchen was a chef's haven, with broad, spare counters uncluttered save for a stand-up mixer and ceramic canisters labeled *Flour*, *Sugar*, *Coffee* and *Tea*. Its creamy vanilla walls offered a reprieve from the inn's ubiquitous floral wallpaper, and a weathered farm table occupied the heart of the room. "My work table." Maeve slapped its worn top. "Don't know how many scones I've rolled out here over the years. Must be a hundred thousand by now."

Faith ran her hand over the wood's pocked history. "It's beautiful."

"My mother's. It came with her from Ireland. She left it for me, along with her scone recipe. Reminds me of her every day. You're lucky you still have yours."

Before Faith could respond, Maeve held open the swinging door again.

"Next stop is the upstairs."

Back in the front hall, the pair followed Maeve up a grand staircase whose faded floral carpet was threadbare in spots.

At the top, Faith peered over the banister at the lower level, taking in the building's Victorian details: decorative trim, broad bay windows, asymmetrical room shapes. For all its disrepair, the bones of the inn were lovely. Someone with the right vision and an unlimited budget could work magic. Unfortunately, that person wasn't her mother.

Moving on to the guest accommodations, Maeve opened a door into the room captioned "Shabby Chic" on the contest website. In reality, worn-out furniture overpowered this tiny chamber, which reeked of mothballs and offered barely enough space to walk around the tarnished brass bed, neatly made with a clean but faded spread.

"Very nice," Connie managed, following Maeve and Faith into the tiny fuchsia en suite bathroom, its stall shower so narrow an average man would have difficulty lifting his arms overhead.

They'd find another suite like this one down the hall, Maeve said. (Faith raised an eyebrow at the word *suite*.) Additionally, there were two single and two double rooms that all shared a large bath with a tub—six rooms in total, Faith tallied. That was a lot of people sharing one bathroom.

"No shower?" Connie asked a moment later when they gathered around the original cast-iron claw-foot tub.

"Of course there is." Leaning into the tub, Maeve produced a coiled rubber attachment connected to the faucet. "This does the job nicely. And being at the shore, guests prefer the outside shower. There's nothing like rinsing off under a blue sky." Maeve promised to show them that feature later in the tour.

Faith had had enough. Leaving Maeve and Connie to debate the merits of baths versus showers, she wandered downstairs and back outside. Following a brick walkway that wrapped around the inn, she soon encountered the touted exterior shower. Its spring door hid a vinyl shower curtain hemmed with mold, and a plastic caddy containing a splintered bar of soap and half a bottle of shampoo whose label the sun had faded white.

Unimpressed, Faith let the door fall shut, then jumped at the sound of hammering overhead. She headed to the backyard to investigate, where she found a ladder leaning against the inn and a man atop it, his back to her as he wrangled a large sheet of plywood.

"Do you need a hand?" she called.

"No, thanks." When he turned to answer, Faith took a step back, surprised to see Bruce Neery again, his mouth full of nails, and a leather tool belt over his photographer's vest.

"What are you doing?" she asked.

"Taking some precautions in case the storm hits us." He centered the wood over a back window and nailed it in place. "This should keep Nadine from blowing the windows out."

"Do you really think she'll hit here?" Faith scanned the cloudless sky for signs of disturbance.

"You know, I'm not usually an alarmist." He descended the ladder to grab another sheet of plywood from the stack on the ground. "But they say this one's going to be the big one. I keep telling Maeve she should prepare, even if it is still a few days out. And your mother, too, if she's going to be here."

"Oh, no. She won't be stay—"

At that, the back porch screen door slapped open. "Don't pay any attention to Bruce." Maeve strode toward them, with Connie following. "Those forecasters got us all riled up last time with Irene. Made every last soul evacuate. And for nothing."

"Maybe around here, but it didn't turn out to be nothing for all those New Englanders when their homes slid off a mountain." Bruce ascended the ladder again, plywood balanced on his shoulder. "I counted, Maeve. We'll need six more sheets for the front windows. I'll stop by the lumberyard today, before they sell out. Is your credit card in the usual spot?"

"All right, Bruce. Whatever you say. And yes, it is." Her back turned, the innkeeper rolled her eyes.

"You'll thank me in a few days." Bruce resumed his hammering on the second-story window.

"Maybe you should listen to him," Faith said.

"Bruce is a good man, but a bit of a worrywart. The storm is days away. It'll probably blow out to sea like always. But I'll let him do his thing, as long as he promises to come back and take down every last one of those boards."

"May I ask why the newspaperman is working on your inn?" Connie asked.

And why he knows where to find your credit card? Faith wanted to add, but didn't.

"You know how it is in a small town. We take care of one another. And he says the physical labor helps him think through his stories."

That part, at least, made sense to Faith. Inspiration in the form of new recipes and platings often struck during the most elemental of tasks, as she chopped and diced in her stainless alcove at Piquant.

Maeve scraped at some peeling paint on a windowsill with her thumbnail. "I wish he came around more to putter. There's always something needing doing around here."

That's for sure, Faith thought, taking another look at the roof. Maybe Bruce should consider replacing a few shingles while he was up there.

"And to tell you the truth"—Maeve lowered her voice conspiratorially—"ever since his wife passed a few years ago, I think he likes to keep busy."

"*Does* he?" Tucking her hair behind her ears, Connie glanced coquettishly over her shoulder in Bruce's direction, like a cat sizing up its prey.

Please let's not go down this road again. Faith threw her head back in despair. For as long as she could remember, Connie had chosen men the way she settled on sweepstakes: with reckless abandon, falling fast and hard. She encouraged almost any man who showed her the slightest interest, exposing her daughter to a string of questionable relationships that soured Faith on the idea of romance.

Always, it fell to Faith to point out the obvious flaw, the gigantic, flapping red flag her mother failed to spot: the man's spotty work schedule, his suspicious unavailability most weekends and holidays, a disturbing fondness for alcohol or horses or another troublesome habit.

When each relationship went south, Connie would find herself out a paycheck or Faith's tuition payment or, in one unsettling case, her car. Single again, she would fall into a sulky silence, as though blaming Faith for her serial attraction to the wrong men.

Faith glanced at her watch. If she had any say about it, Bruce Neery would not become her mother's next distraction. "It's getting late,

Mom. We should get on the road. Don't forget I've got work tonight." Assuming her mother would stay with her, Faith had planned to sleep on the couch.

Maeve and Connie exchanged looks.

"Maeve's had the best idea, Faith," Connie said. "She wants me to stay the week. Shadow her and learn the ropes."

Faith could appreciate an apprenticeship; she'd learned her way around a series of New York kitchens under that sort of tutelage before following Xander to Piquant. But what ropes could Connie navigate when there didn't appear to be anyone staying at the inn?

So far, their enthusiastic tour guide had glossed over the reality that The Mermaid's Purse was in fact empty.

"There will be plenty of time for that, Mom. We can always come back in a few days, once the weather settles." If she could only get her mother alone, she could debrief her after their eye-opening visit.

"Don't tell me you drank Bruce's Kool-Aid." Hands on hips, Maeve cocked her head toward the ladder.

"Really, Faith. You can go. We'll be fine." Connie made a shooing gesture Faith found condescending.

Seeing the two women were set on this plan, Faith shrugged. "Okay. But the second the weather changes—"

"We'll send an SOS to Brooklyn," Maeve finished. "Don't fret, dear. I'll take good care of your mother."

With that, they said their good-byes.

Faith scuffed her feet along the brick path. Maybe a few days in a run-down, empty inn *would* be a good thing for her mother, to demonstrate that running the establishment involved more than baking Bundt cakes and serving afternoon tea, that empty guest rooms equaled an empty cash register. Once the novelty wore off, her mother surely would realize the folly of sacrificing her secure future for this uncertain livelihood.

After all, it was Connie's vacation. If her mother chose to spend that time scrubbing toilets and stripping beds, that was her prerogative.

The trip had turned into a bit of a reality check for Faith as well. She'd driven down to the shore today to indulge her mother, fully expecting her to dismiss this bed-and-breakfast fantasy. But now, leaving Connie behind in Wave's End, the idea that she could actually assume the frayed handles of The Mermaid's Purse seemed like a real possibility.

11

Within days of Faith's visit to Wave's End, officials placed the entire East Coast on high alert, notching up precautions as the upgraded Hurricane Nadine gathered force. Faith arrived at Piquant to find dishwashers stacking sandbags around the restaurant's perimeter while a few hardy patrons braved the afternoon chill to sip cocktails on the patio.

"City just delivered them," Xander explained when Faith questioned him. "Let's hope they keep this place from floating away."

As the approaching storm became more than a gleam in forecasters' eyes, everyone took notice. With the restaurant sound system tuned to the weather station nonstop, Piquant summoned its employees to a mandatory emergency briefing.

"Will we really have to evacuate?" a bartender asked.

"We'll know for sure tomorrow," answered Xander. "The city's saying the seaport could get up to eleven feet of water with the storm surge."

Storm surge: a nightmare scenario predicated on a complicated set of models involving wind shear, tides and the moon's cycle. The rampant media prognostication turned the phrase into a hashtag. Faith could feel the staff's collective anxiety building as their boss outlined Piquant's hurricane contingency plan.

"Everything depends on Nadine's path. We have to be prepared. Tomas, I'll need more sandbags out tomorrow afternoon. The rest of you, concentrate on getting everything up off the floor as best you can." The bar- and waitstaff should report to Xander in the dining room; Faith would strategize in the kitchen. Her gut knotted at the thought of the thousands of dollars of kitchen equipment that required securing.

Storm prep would start tonight after dinner ended, Xander said, resuming at seven the following morning.

"But what if there's no trains?" called a server from the back of the room. Xander acknowledged the possibility of the city's precautionary subway system shutdown.

"Bike it, my friend," cracked a dishwasher.

Pockets of heated conversation broke out, and Xander held up his hand for quiet. "I know you're all worried. I'm worried as shit, too. But with any luck, it will be business as usual come Tuesday."

The waitstaff exchanged anxious glances. Faith could easily imagine what they were thinking: Could the restaurant close?

"Let's just get through tomorrow. Keep those phones charged so we can reach you. There's a good chance we'll lose power, as well."

He and Faith had already discussed that likelihood, retooling menus around Piquant's perishable inventory.

Xander clapped his hands. "All right. That's it. First reservations are in thirty minutes. Get out there tonight and do your thing. And remember: best night ever!"

"Best night ever!" Xander's team shouted the restaurant's nightly rallying cry.

Best night ever. As the staff dispersed, Faith met her boss's grave gaze. If the seaport waters crested as predicted, the restaurant had a great deal more to lose than a freezer full of spoiled meat.

Piquant's best night ever might also be its last.

12

"How 'bout we go by this rule: anything that looks stupid, *is* stupid." Gripping both sides of his podium, the New Jersey governor glared straight into the camera.

In line at her neighborhood bodega before work the next day, Faith watched the coverage of the garrulous official chiding residents in at-risk areas who had any thought of remaining in their homes. He ordered a mandatory evacuation of all barrier islands, then declared a state of emergency for his entire constituency, as his equals in New York and four neighboring states had done the previous day.

"If you think you're being overly clever but you know it looks really stupid, don't do it. That's a good general New Jersey rule." Coverage then returned to live storm tracking, with footage of palm trees in Jamaica, Cuba and Haiti bent sideways by hundred-mile-an-hour winds.

Faith gulped. Would those weather conditions replicate themselves in Wave's End?

Juggling the items she had dashed out to purchase—the market's last bunch of bananas and a dented clamshell of salad—Faith dug for her phone and called her mother and related what she had just seen.

"The governor's talking to *you*, Mom. Why are you and Maeve still there?"

"We're not on a barrier island. There's no reason to leave. Even the mayor said we could stay."

Technically, her mother was right. The inn lay just outside the seaside town's mandatory evacuation area, a redlined region initially limited to two beachfront blocks from north to south. However, each revised forecast swelled the evacuation zone a bit more, so that it now encompassed the eastern half of Wave's End.

"But there's no reason to put yourself in danger when The Mermaid's Purse is empty. Why don't you both hop on the train and come stay with me for a couple of days?" Faith's apartment barely contained room for Connie, let alone Maeve, but they would make it work somehow.

"We'll be fine," her mother replied. "We'll fill the bathtubs tomorrow, and we have enough bottled water to last us until kingdom come, thanks to Bruce."

At least Maeve finally had come to her senses at the eleventh hour, permitting Bruce to board up the remaining windows and remove her awnings. Recalling the inn's neglected roof, Faith shuddered at how that might fare under the predicted high winds.

"Don't worry, Faith. Everything's under control. Maeve's been through this before."

But Nadine might not be like previous storms, Faith thought as she hung up. After all, sixty people had already perished. Setting her intended purchases aside, she left the store. As she walked home, a prescient breeze stirred the remaining leaves on the trees, the scent of imminent rain weighting the air. Under even the most conservative estimates, this weather disturbance could shape up to be the big one, the hundred-year storm, the tempest that would go down in history.

And if her mother was so caught up in her innkeeper fantasy she didn't have sense enough to get out of Nadine's way, there remained only one thing for Faith to do.

13

Faith planned to head directly to Wave's End following that day's abbreviated shift. Since Xander planned to close early that evening, and had preemptively shut Piquant for Tuesday and Wednesday, she figured she could get down to Wave's End Monday night, see her mother and Maeve through the storm, and still be back at work by Thursday—that is, assuming the restaurant survived the hurricane.

She wouldn't think about that remote possibility right now, Faith decided, cramming last-minute toiletries into her bag.

"What are you doing?" The sight of petite, fair-haired Ellie leaning on the door frame made Faith smile. Her roommate's softly rounded belly strained the waist of the clingy, drop-seated onesie Faith had bought them both as gags last Christmas, to the point where Ellie resembled a somewhat pregnant toddler.

"Getting ready to babysit my mother, who insists on going down with the ship. I'm afraid the place is going to tumble down around her ears."

"But you can't leave me here alone," protested Ellie.

Faith looked up from zipping her bag. "You won't be alone. You've got Dennis."

"I called him, but he's not answering." The wobble in Ellie's voice hinted at the waterworks that occurred with more frequency as her pregnancy progressed.

"I'm sure he'll call back soon. How about trying your parents?"

"They're out in the Hamptons. They're worried about the yacht." Ellie trailed Faith into their front hall. "When will you be back?"

"I don't know. In a few days, at most?" Halting at the front door, Faith closed her eyes, wishing she could clone herself to support both her friend and her family. It truly pained her to leave her pregnant friend by herself. On the other hand, with Dennis only a phone call and three subway stops away, Ellie would be fine.

Faith turned and threw her arms around Ellie. "Listen. You're my best friend, and I love you. *And* that future baby of yours. I hate leaving you both alone, but you have loads of other people who love you to call on. Where with my mother, I'm the only one she's got, and she needs me. So I have to go. Be safe, little mama."

With that, Faith grabbed her bag and slung it over her shoulder. After planting a final, resounding kiss on Ellie's cheek, Faith released her and headed for the hall, pausing to smile at her friend one last time before closing the apartment door behind her.

PART 2: IMPACT

14

Faith ducked out of her cab after work, peering up at the prematurely darkening sky over Seventh Avenue as rain pelted her face. On the sidewalk, scurrying pedestrians fought escalating winds for control of umbrellas. Bisecting the crowds, Faith dashed down the escalator into Penn Station and straight to the wall monitor to determine the next train to Wave's End, stopping short to read the message displayed there in bold red letters:

TRAVEL ADVISORY: ALL NEW JERSEY TRANSIT RAIL SERVICES SUSPENDED UNTIL FURTHER NOTICE.

How could she not have known this? She stood stock-still as the equivalent of a rush-hour crowd surged around her. Of course, Xander had mentioned the possible New York shutdown, but in Faith's mind that meant New York subways only. Frantic, she ran down the marbled ramp to the wall of ticket windows.

"How can there be no more trains to New Jersey?" she implored the transit officer behind the glass. "It's only seven o'clock. The storm's not supposed to hit until late tonight or tomorrow."

"You think we can shut down an entire system on a dime?" He jabbed his pencil over her head. "Now, move aside, please. These folks don't look too happy with you." Turning, Faith flushed crimson at the sea of angry faces in the queue she had unwittingly cut.

"I'm so sorry. But I have to get down there. What am I supposed to do?" she asked.

He shrugged. "Rent a car?"

Faith hesitated. Renting the Zipcar to go to the airport had been one thing, but should she become stranded in Wave's End, a rental could turn into an expensive proposition. "Yeah. I can't do that. Any other ideas?"

"Try Port Authority. If you hurry, you might catch the last bus."

"Thank you. And sorry. *Sorry.*" Apologizing to the disgruntled passengers as she raced by them, she then took the Eighth Avenue escalator two steps at a time. Once outside, she sprinted the entire eight blocks to the bus depot, her bag bumping pedestrians as she wove through the masses. By the time she reached it, her wet clothes clung like a second skin and blisters threatened inside her rubber work clogs. Limping into the depot, Faith spotted a sanitation worker spearing trash from the floor and approached him.

"Bus to the Jersey shore?" She leaned against a column to catch her breath while the man withdrew a crumpled map from a back pocket. "That would be University Lines. Fourth level."

"Thanks." As Faith took off for the escalator, the man called to her.

"That'll get you as far south as Ashcroft. *And* you need a ticket." He pointed his map at a bank of ticket windows.

"Right. Of course." Wherever Ashcroft was, at least she was headed in the right direction. Getting herself partway to The Mermaid's Purse would be better than nothing. At the ticket window, Faith joined the queue of customers, watching the clock and shifting her weight from one foot to the other until her turn came.

"Lucky. You made the last bus out. Leaves in five minutes," the clerk said, handing her the ticket.

"From where?"

"Gate three-oh-two. Upstairs." With that, the clerk slammed his window shut.

After racing up yet another escalator, Faith stepped onto the fourth level and trotted around the perimeter of the cavernous depot until she spotted the illuminated gate number in the distance. With dismay, she saw the final passengers disappear through a door in the glossy brick wall.

"Wait! Please stop!" Faith ran to the gate and through the door, where she watched the last rider board the bus and the door slide shut. "Please! Don't leave!" Faith flailed her arms, entreating the passengers staring like zombies as the bus's hydraulic wheeze reverberated in the concrete depot. Just when she was ready to turn away in defeat, the driver slammed on the brakes and opened the door.

"Good way to get run over," he grunted. "Standing room only tonight."

"That's fine. I don't mind." Further soaked with sweat from the exertion, Faith took her place in the aisle, shivering in the air-conditioning. As the coach began its circuitous descent, she gripped the side of the nearest seat for support, apologizing to its occupant, a middle-aged woman wearing distinctive persimmon eyeglasses and clenching her hands in her lap. Getting to her mother in Wave's End was proving a greater challenge than she had bargained for, Faith thought, eyes downcast as the bus slid into the Lincoln Tunnel.

"Lucky we caught the last one, huh?"

Startled, Faith glanced up to see the female passenger speaking to her. "What? Oh, yes. I guess we are."

"Where are you headed?"

"Wave's End. You?"

"Bayport." At Faith's perplexed frown, she added, "Just north of you."

"Sorry. I don't know the area. Do you live there?"

"No, but my aunt does. In her eighties and still on her own."

"We should be so lucky."

"Maybe not so lucky. She's on the beachfront. Moved there as a bride, and refuses to evacuate. Even after the police came by and told her she's writing her own death sentence if she stays."

"So you're going to talk her into leaving? My name's Faith, by the way."

"Tanya. Tanya Lloyd. I'm going to do my best. I didn't have much luck on the phone. I'm an attorney. I argue for a living. But do you think I could convince an eighty-seven-year-old widow to get to safety?" She shook her head ruefully. "My aunt is a stubborn lady."

"It's nice of you to go and check on her."

"I couldn't *not* go. She took such good care of me growing up. Like a second mother. I'm pretty much all she has."

"Me, too. For *my* mother, I mean. She's only in Wave's End temporarily, I hope. Not close to the beach like your aunt, but close enough." That reminded Faith she had no idea how she would make her way to Wave's End once off the bus. "Have you figured out how you're getting from Ashcroft to your aunt's?"

"A cab's meeting me at the park-and-ride. You're welcome to share it. I had a hard enough time reserving this one."

Faith leaned against the seat in relief. "Thank you. I hadn't quite worked out that leg of my trip."

"Your timing is impeccable. They're shutting the parkway tonight from Ashcroft south, but the cab can use back roads."

Warnings about high winds and bridge closures flashed on turnpike overpasses, and gusts bullied the bus and flexed overhead road signs. Eyeing Faith, Tanya bent over and pulled a sweater from a canvas tote at her feet. "Put this on. You look chilled to the bone."

Faith slipped off her soaked jacket, the only outerwear she'd brought, and put on the cardigan. "Thank you. I didn't exactly come prepared."

"And this is only the beginning. I bet your mother will be relieved to see you."

"I hope so. She doesn't exactly know I'm coming."

15

Faith had tried unsuccessfully to reach her mother from work and tried again several times during the ride down. Connie could be frustratingly casual about her phone when she chose.

Meanwhile, travel conditions deteriorated so dramatically during their bus ride to Ashcroft that the driver pulled over several times to sit out torrential downpours that dangerously hampered visibility. Faith and Tanya exchanged nervous glances as merciless winds bore down on the idling bus, which shuddered on the parkway shoulder, blankets of rain rolling across its broad windshield.

"They don't pay me enough for this," the driver said to no one in particular, balancing an unlit cigarette between his lips as he crept back onto the highway.

It might be better Connie *didn't* know she was coming. Her mother would probably fight Faith as surely as she had fought her on almost everything else related to The Mermaid's Purse. Certainly Connie wouldn't be going anywhere on a night this miserable, she thought, staring out the window. The coach limped through a string of coastal towns, around pockets of emergency vehicles and beneath traffic lights undulating like jeweled pendants in the wind, before returning to the parkway.

In Ashcroft, its final destination, the bus emptied of passengers, who raced through ankle-deep waters to cars, leaving only Faith and Tanya in the park-and-ride.

"Is it me, or does it feel like we're the last two people on earth?" Faith said, watching the menacing night swallow the departing coach.

As the two women leaned against the locked ticket office, beside vending machines that rattled and swayed menacingly, Faith wondered if coming to Wave's End had been the right decision. Not that she could turn back now, she reminded herself, yanking down the sleeves of her borrowed sweater.

It took well over an hour and several calls to the dispatcher before the taxi arrived, its driver bursting with complaints about blocked roads and the storm's wrath. "Atlantic City's already underwater," he said. "Those casino folks should have gotten out when the governor told them to. Now they're sunk."

His grievances continued all the way to Bayport, where he turned to Tanya, her aunt's address highlighted on his GPS. "Not sure how close I can get you, ma'am. They're barricading the beach."

Tanya leaned toward the driver's seat. "But my elderly aunt's up there."

"Sorry." He slowed to a crawl. "If I don't follow the rules, I'll lose my license." They were passing a marina now, where abandoned skiffs bobbed atop whitecaps like targets in an arcade shooting gallery, while massive waves hammered the empty slips. Faith watched in alarm as the tin roof of a service shed peeled off like an orange skin, skimmed the surface of the water and whirled into the black sky, a metallic meteor.

Beside her, a tight-lipped Tanya stared at the boats, the boarded-up windows of evacuated coastal homes, the hypnotic whirl of police lights punctuating the approach to Bayport, the paved road now gravel so close to the beach.

"I don't know what my aunt was thinking." Tanya shook her head.

"This is like the end of the world." The driver pulled up to a make-shift checkpoint manned by rain-soaked emergency workers, their hooded citrus slickers glistening like hard candy. "End of the line for me." He threw the cab into park.

"Fine. I'll get out here, then." After grabbing her tote, Tanya handed him a fistful of bills.

"But it's not safe," Faith protested. "Look at those trees." Outside the car, thick-trunked oaks twenty yards away succumbed to the gale's muscle, surrendering limbs and writhing in the manner of the Caribbean palms she had watched on the bodega television.

Tanya stared at the trees a second, then got out of the car. "I've got to find my aunt. Faith, I hope your mother's okay. Safe travels, you guys."

Out of the darkness, an emergency worker in waist-high waders twirled his flashlight, motioning for the cab to leave.

"Please be careful," Faith pleaded. Tanya clung to the wooden barricade as she talked to the workers, wind whipping her hair in every direction.

As the cab pulled away, leaving Tanya negotiating for access, a Jet Ski manned by a wetsuited driver roared by.

The road had become an extension of the ocean.

"Think they'll let her up there?" the driver asked.

"Who knows?" answered Faith. "And who knows what she'll find once she gets there?" Settling back in the taxi, she pictured Tanya's tenacious aunt trapped in her home, threatened by churning seas, while her worried niece risked life and limb to get to her.

With difficulty, they eventually rejoined the inland access road linking the shore towns and continued south. Faith tightened her seat belt as the taxi wove around fallen debris, and realized she still wore Tanya's sweater. Turning around now to return the item was unthinkable. There were few cars on the road besides those of first responders, and her driver's terse, monosyllabic responses to attempts at conversation reflected his intense concentration.

Now nearly dry, Faith removed the borrowed cardigan and folded it in her lap, wishing she had thought to give it back to the generous stranger. She closed her eyes, her thoughts turning to Connie and Maeve and their level of storm preparation. Had Bruce equipped the two women for the duration as her mother expected? More likely, his journalistic responsibilities of covering the disaster would take precedence over tending to the two women.

Faith pulled out her phone to try her mother again. Wondering how close they were, she tapped the driver as they stopped at a light. The question faded in her throat, however, at the sight of the towering fir tree to their left. The fir rocked and lurched violently, the lawn surrounding it rippling and undulating as though a legion of demons below the surface were hell-bent on uprooting it.

Paralyzed, Faith could only stare in horror at the evergreen working its way out of the earth in slow motion, and she ducked instinctively as the tree headed straight for them.

"Holy *sh-i-i-i-t*, lady. Hang on!" The driver floored the cab through the red light, throwing Faith against the back seat as the taxi hydroplaned through the intersection.

16

The crack of timber on macadam slammed through Faith like a gunshot. Curled fetus-like in the back seat, she pressed her hand to her pounding heart.

"Shit. That was *close*." Having expertly maneuvered them out of harm's way a split second before the tree crashed across the road behind them, the cab driver wiped his forehead with his forearm. "Somebody must be watching over you."

Faith slowly raised her head, making herself look out the back window, where the massive tree bisected the road, simultaneously grateful and incredulous that its trajectory had spared them. "And you, too, apparently."

"I'll tell you, I can't wait to park this baby tonight. Go home and kiss my kid." The driver caught Faith's eye in his mirror. "Give me a second here for my heart rate to return to normal, and I'll get us out of here."

With no desire to spend another minute in the cab, Faith felt around the floor for her bag. "It's okay. I'll get out here. My stop's just over there." As they sat catching their breath, Faith had spotted the inn up ahead on the corner. "And thank you. For reacting so quickly." Adding a twenty to her fare, Faith handed him the bills over the seat with a shaking hand.

"Think I'll go buy me some lottery tickets right now." Grinning, he slipped the money into his shirt pocket and patted it.

"You do that. And get home safe," she said as she climbed out of the cab. An onlooker spotted Faith exiting the taxi and headed toward her. Raising a hand to deflect any assistance, Faith bent her head and ran toward the inn, feeling like Dorothy heading home before the tornado as she bucked the gusts to swing open the inn gate and scurry up the front steps. On the darkened porch, she paused, listening to the curious black shell on the mailbox rattle against the house, relieved that, for better or worse, she had made it to Wave's End.

Faith leaned hard on the doorbell of The Mermaid's Purse. When no one answered, she pressed the bell again, peering through the glass pane beside the front door. Had Maeve and her mother decided to evacuate after all? Wishing Connie would have told her, Faith pounded on the door.

A few more seconds passed. Why weren't they answering? She ran down the steps to check the side driveway, finding an ancient station wagon parked there, but unsure if the vehicle belonged to Maeve. And with the memory of the downed tree fresh in her mind, she had little desire to remain outside and investigate.

Back on the porch, she tried the front door, found it open and let herself in, battling a determined gust to shut it behind her. A clamshell nightlight beneath the stairs offered the only illumination.

"Mom? Are you here?" Faith felt her way to a hall light and switched it on. "Maeve? Where are you?"

No response came, not even a hiss from the petulant Pixie. Calling out again, Faith frantically toured the downstairs. As she headed from the salon to the kitchen, the wind escalated, and something struck an outside wall with an earsplitting crack. The house felt like a tomb, and Faith suddenly realized why: Bruce's boards covered every window, creating blackout conditions.

She continued through the house, flipping lights on as she went, calling for her mother and Maeve. Upstairs, she found Connie's things in one room, and the rest of the guest rooms empty.

There had to be a simple reason for the women's absence, she told herself once back in the kitchen. Someone, possibly Bruce, had picked them up earlier and taken them somewhere safe to ride out Nadine. If only her mother would pick up her phone and confirm she was safe!

One ring, two rings; why couldn't Connie keep her phone close in an emergency? Three rings turned to four, and still Faith's mother didn't pick up. It was premature to contact the police, and based on the chaos in Bayport and the cacophony of sirens outside, the authorities were no doubt overwhelmed.

Faith found a glass in a cupboard and began to fill it at the sink, when a door behind her creaked—not the back door but one inside the kitchen. Still reeling from her near miss with the tree, Faith froze. At that moment, the wind wailed and the house went dark. A flashlight's ghostly beam shined over Faith's shoulder, illuminating her own shocked reflection in the boarded-up window over the sink.

17

Faith made herself turn around. "Who's there?" she asked, shielding her eyes from the flashlight's glare.

"My goodness. Is that you, Faith?" The beam dropped. Faith recognized Maeve's voice and sagged against the sink.

"Yes, it's me. I've been trying to call my mother. I've been so worried. Why didn't you answer the door?"

"We didn't hear it. We've been hunkered down in the basement since this afternoon. Thought that would be the safest place. There's some big, old trees near the property, in case you haven't noticed," she added.

"Oh, I've noticed. A huge one just came down across the street."

Just then, the lights came back on. "Thank goodness," said Maeve. "They've been flickering like that all night. Come with me. Your mother will be overjoyed to see you."

As Faith followed Maeve down the rickety stairs, Connie's voice floated up from the cellar.

"Who's that, Maeve? Has Bruce come back?"

"Not yet," Maeve answered.

How much time was the man spending at the inn?

Connie's mouth dropped open as she spotted her daughter. "Faith! What are you doing here? Did you come to Wave's End to check up on me?"

"Of course not." Taking in the cozily lit cinder-block basement, Faith groped for words. "I just . . . Xander decided to close the restaurant, and I thought I should come down and help."

"That's very thoughtful, but you didn't have to. We're snug as bugs here, and Bruce laid in all our supplies in case the power goes out for good." Connie led Faith around, pointing out cases of bottled water, flashlights and fresh batteries, an exhumed television set on an old trunk and tuned to the storm coverage.

"And look what Bruce brought for *me*!" Connie displayed a bottle of her preferred port. "My favorite. Said he went out of his way to find it."

"Very nice." How did Bruce know her mother's taste in wine? Had they gone on a date? How recently had the man's wife passed, anyway? Bruce might only be seeking a little companionship, but Faith couldn't help feeling a little suspicious of his largesse. She had her mother's succession of suitors to thank for showing her that guys who hung around doing favors for nothing usually demanded something in return.

It was an inescapable truth: in life, love and contests, you never got something without having to give.

Faith glanced at two air mattresses made up with quilts.

"As you can see, we're prepared to sleep down here if necessary. I'm sure I've got another mattress upstairs I can make up for you," offered Maeve.

"It's okay. I'll make do with the couch." Impressed by how well the women were coping, Faith began to feel foolish about her rash journey to Wave's End. Cocooned as they were in Maeve's cellar, you wouldn't even know a hurricane raged outside, except for a flickering lamp that reminded them they could lose power at any moment.

"We were just about to eat," said Connie. "There's plenty extra, if you don't mind eating down here."

"Not at all." As the shock from the tree run-in began to wear off, Faith realized how famished she felt. Accepting a plate of pork chops, mashed potatoes and green beans from Maeve, she sat down on the cellar steps to eat.

"So tell us: How did you ever make it out of the city?" Connie asked.

"We've been watching the news all day, and the situation in New York is quite disastrous," added Maeve.

The two women sat side by side in lawn chairs, eating from snack tables.

"It wasn't easy." Faith had just started to describe the horrific scene in Bayport when a distinctive voice on the television caught her attention, and she paused to listen to the mayor of New York City.

"The time to evacuate is over," he intoned.

Fork frozen in midair, Faith stared at live shots from lower Manhattan: torrential waters pouring into Ground Zero, the Brooklyn-Battery Tunnel, a financial district parking deck. Swells of up to four-teen feet pounded Battery Park; some city skyscrapers swayed dizzily in the seventy-mile-an-hour winds.

"Oh, my. Those poor people." Connie tsk-tsked at the spectacle of waterlogged vehicles floating along Wall Street like bumper cars, the pounding deluge of storm water rendering the southern tip of Manhattan without power as they watched, as though someone had flipped a switch.

Faith felt queasy. How had Xander possibly believed sandbags would protect Piquant? She had to call him. Surely he had found some added means of safeguarding the restaurant. She fumbled for her phone, then gasped at the screen: a selfie from Xander, waist-deep in swirling waters, captioned:

We're screwed.

As Faith stared at the image, coverage switched back to the New Jersey governor. "The storm is moving twice as fast as when I spoke to you last time. It is no longer possible to evacuate, and we are no longer able to rescue people. And if you're in one of the affected areas, and you can still hear me," the governor continued, "we need you to hunker down and—"

With that, the power cut out again, swallowing the governor in a pinprick of light and plunging the basement of The Mermaid's Purse into darkness.

18

"I'm sure it will pop back on any minute." Maeve lit several candles, including a dusty pine-infused Santa, then set a battery-operated transistor radio on top of the television and tuned it.

But as the three sat in the candlelight, minutes stretched to a half hour, then to an hour. An upstairs grandfather clock chimed a faraway ten and eventually eleven strikes, and still they remained in the dark, along with hundreds of thousands on the East Coast, according to the crackly radio transmission.

"I suppose there's nothing to do but go to sleep," Maeve said.

"With any luck, we'll wake up to the lights blazing," added Connie.

Saying her good-nights, Faith picked up a flashlight and headed upstairs.

"There's an afghan by the fireplace," Maeve called after her.

In contrast to the basement bunker, the wide-open layout of the inn's main floor amplified the storm's din. In the salon, Faith picked up the throw and sat on the sofa, pondering the resolute residents near the water like Tanya's aunt, who naively refused to evacuate, as well as those who had left their homes as instructed, wondering if, in the end, their decisions would make a difference.

Because, so far, this storm hadn't rewarded the obedient or the prepared. On the contrary: as Nadine savaged the East Coast, she marked her territory, unilaterally claiming whatever stood in her way.

Stretched out on the sofa, Faith burrowed under the blanket, trying to block out the wind's plaintive wail, unable to dismiss the image of Xander struggling at the seaport. Despite the grand lead-up to the storm, she had never truly envisioned Piquant ending up underwater any more than she could have imagined winds mighty enough to fell massive trees in her path.

These were forces to reckon with.

In the dark, she bit her lip, nauseated by the notion of saltwater saturating the restaurant's Brazilian hardwood flooring and seeping into its imported cabinetry. Xander had painstakingly installed both over stolen nights and weekends prior to their opening less than a year ago. Up until now, the place had still smelled new.

No one knew better than Faith the cost of this night: a fortune for repairs, disastrous ruin for a business owner already dangerously tapped out. Xander's bare-bones, high-deductible insurance policy would not begin to cover the damage. For Faith, the destruction meant she would not soon see the funds she had foolishly lent him, swayed by his promise of a swift return on her investment.

She hadn't even asked him what the money was for before entrusting him with her savings.

Now she likely had no job, no financial cushion to fall back on and soon no place to live.

We're screwed, Xander had typed.

Yes, Xander, we are.

Sitting up, she wrapped the afghan around her shoulders, straining for the sound of the wind. Though the scraping of branches against the inn's exterior had all but ceased, she wasn't fooled. The forecasters warned that Nadine would wax and wane overnight. In the uneasy quiet, she considered the irony of coming all this way to ensure her mother's safety, only to find the two women coping quite capably, while things appeared much, much worse in New York.

Faith lay back down and fell into a listless sleep, only to be roused by the wind's scream and branches clawing the plywood on the windows, the sheets creaking in protest against the escalating gales. Spooked by the inky darkness, Faith grabbed the flashlight and tucked a couch cushion under each arm. With the afghan trailing behind her, she shuffled to the kitchen and down to the basement, throwing the cushions onto the floor a few feet from her mother and curling up on them.

19

Faith woke to the skunky odor of gas. She sprang off the couch cushions and upstairs to the candlelit kitchen, where Maeve huddled over the stovetop with a match.

"Advantage of gas," the innkeeper said as a burner sprang to life. "Now I can start some coffee."

"So there's still no power?"

"None. And no sign of anybody working on it, either." On the counter sat an old-style stovetop percolator with a glass-bubbled lid. "Something told me to hang on to that thing," Maeve continued. "How did you sleep?"

"Not very well." As the night wore on and the storm had escalated, even the thick basement walls could not mute every howling gust, every thud of a tree limb on the roof, every emergency siren.

Yawning, Faith dropped onto a stool, watching Maeve fill the round stainless filter with ground coffee. As coffee began to bubble in the pot's transparent top, Faith inhaled the strong aroma, suddenly acutely aware of the quiet. For the first time since she had left Piquant the previous day, heavy, uncomfortable silence surrounded her.

"I've been outside already," said Maeve. "I've walked the entire property. We've lost so many shingles we'll have to patch the roof before the snow comes, or we'll be in trouble. And branches are down every-where. But overall, this place is livable. Something to be said for being a ways from the beach, wouldn't you say, Faith? I can only imagine those poor people up there . . ." Maeve shook her head.

At that, someone rapped on the back door. "Everybody present and accounted for?" a man called.

Without looking, Faith knew it had to be Bruce.

"You look like you've been through the war," Maeve observed as she let Bruce in.

Faith had to agree. In his sand-caked boots, waders and oilcloth slicker, his ever-present camera slung around his neck, Bruce did appear beaten, his eyes bloodshot and his chin sporting several days' growth.

"This town certainly has," he said hoarsely. "I had a front-row seat all night, and Nadine's the clear victor, hands down."

Bruce sat down at Maeve's kitchen table and quietly sipped the coffee she set in front of him. "I just never thought I'd see what I saw last night," he said after a while. "Armageddon . . . my own town. Wind, sand, water . . ." Bruce shook his head. "I tell you: I've never seen people work so hard in my life. There were literally surfers riding people to safety on their surfboards. Can you imagine? All heroes, in my book."

Faith nodded, recounting the Bayport Jet Ski rescue she had witnessed.

"And times that by every seacoast town," added Bruce. Wave's End officials had done a rough estimate, identifying more than three hundred homes rendered unlivable. "And they're not done counting." Families were beginning to gather at a church in town, he said.

"Let's go up to the beach and help," Connie said as she entered the kitchen. She smiled brightly and tossed her hair as she sat beside Bruce. Preoccupied, the reporter appeared oblivious to her mother's behavior, to Faith's relief.

"You can't," replied Bruce. "It's a war zone up there. They're not letting anybody back until the National Guard arrives to secure the area."

"But what about these displaced homeowners? Where will they go?" Maeve asked.

"That's the million-dollar question. And actually, that's another reason I stopped by. The town council held an emergency meeting this morning and voted to set up a contingency fund to temporarily shelter displaced residents. They'll issue vouchers to eligible applicants and make a list of places where these residents might live."

Bruce cleared his throat and got to his feet. "I know you're kind of in transition here, Maeve, what with Connie about to take over. But given this emergency, would you consider housing a family or two?"

Maeve answered without hesitation. "Of course we will. I've lived and worked in Wave's End most of my life. We're blessed that this inn has been spared. Tell that mayor to put The Mermaid's Purse on the list."

"Thank you, Maeve," said Bruce, tipping his imaginary cap.

"How soon should we expect them?" asked Connie.

"That's the thing," he said. "They left their homes with the clothes on their backs, just about. Most of them have nowhere to go. Would tomorrow be too soon?"

20

Galvanized by the twenty-four-hour deadline, Maeve and Connie sprang into action. The innkeeper dictated a list of tasks to Faith's mother, giving Connie a crash course in hospitality in the process. Faith admired Connie's willingness to pitch in but worried how this turn of events might impact her mother's long-term plans.

Meanwhile, Bruce promised to drop off a spare generator from the paper to provide limited electricity and hot water until the power returned.

"Did the council know when that might be?" Maeve asked.

"Out of their hands. With eight million customers up and down the coast without power, we may be in it for the long haul."

Eight million? How high the numbers had climbed overnight, Faith thought.

After pocketing the foil-wrapped scone Maeve pressed on him, Bruce swallowed the rest of his coffee and prepared to head out. Faith followed him to his car.

"Excuse me, but since you seem to have the inside track, could you tell me the best way to get back to the city?"

Bruce smiled thinly, his lips white from fatigue. "Wings, maybe? You *were* listening to me in there, weren't you?"

Why was he patronizing her? "Yes, of course. But the weather's calm now, and I don't see how damage up at the beach—"

"It's not just the beach. There's downed power lines and fallen trees everywhere. Most roads are impassible, and traffic lights are out. And if I heard right, I believe the city's tunnels and bridges are still shut as well. If you want my advice, you should wait a day or two. Let the crews get a handle on the situation and start to clear the debris."

"But I can't wait. I've got to get back to the city." She pulled out her phone and displayed Xander's message. "This is the place I work. *Worked*, I should probably say. My boss needs me."

Bruce peered at the picture. "I'm sure he does. But I expect that area will be restricted, just like our beachfront. One day won't matter, Faith. And if you're talking about need, there's plenty right here."

"I'm sure there is, but I only came down here to check on my mom. And seeing that she's fine, and about to be very busy, I really need to—"

"Hold on a second. You're a chef, right?"

"Yes, but—"

"Grab your coat and come with me."

PART 3: HEROIC

21

Faith read the church billboard as Bruce pulled up:

COME IN TO RECHARGE AND RECOVER.
ALL WELCOME.

"Why are we stopping here?" she asked.

"You'll see soon enough. Go on in. Straight through there." Bruce pointed at a red door.

"But when will you be back?"

"Before too long," he said, before driving away.

Really? You're just going to leave me here stranded? Faith stared after him, dumbfounded. Overhead, the stark black cross on the church spire bisected a cloud. She rubbed her arms, still shaken from the short but sobering ride from The Mermaid's Purse that tendered a glimpse of Nadine's wrath. Not even a block from the inn, Bruce had swerved to avoid a wayward boat teetering on a curb.

"How did that get there?" wide-eyed Faith asked.

"Tip of the iceberg."

Squaring her shoulders, Faith entered the church. She found herself on a landing, a humid wave of caffeinated air washing over her. Below her, dozens of people milled about, a handful energetically, but most standing and talking quietly, their faces strained.

Downstairs, someone had arranged a makeshift buffet on one wall, but few were availing themselves of the chafing dishes. Of the dozen or so tables arranged café-style, only one had occupants: a mother bent over a sleepy child, encouraging her to eat.

Faith felt a tap on her back. "Welcome! If you need housing, we've started a list there." Beside her, a smiling middle-aged brunette pointed to a board half covered with index cards.

"Thank you, but I don't." Faith noticed the woman's name tag read *Alicia*. "Is there anything I can do? I'm a chef."

Alicia grabbed her arm. "Perfect. I've got just the job for you." Pausing at a welcome table to scribble a name tag for Faith, Alicia then pulled her through the knots of people, where snippets of conversation floated by: ". . . lost everything"; ". . . roof fell in"; ". . . never thought I'd ever see a boat on Main Street."

Once in the church kitchen, Alicia patted a mountain of plastic-sleeved loaves of bread. "First order of business is sandwiches. Lots of them. First responders up at the beach have been working all night. All we've got right now is peanut butter and jelly, but that'll have to do."

Faith nodded. "Okay. Easy enough."

"As soon as you're done, someone will run you up to the beach to hand them out."

Faith frowned. "I'm not sure how long I can stay."

Just then, a man called into the kitchen for Alicia.

"Yikes. That's the pastor. I'm needed." Alicia patted Faith's arm. "Whatever you can do. Good luck. Holler if you need help."

And with that, Faith found herself alone in the kitchen. Rummaging through drawers, she located knives, sandwich bags, wax paper to cover the counters. She set up rows of bread and got to work spreading, slicing and wrapping sandwiches. By the time someone shouted into the kitchen for the beach food, she had stacked dozens of sandwiches in disposable aluminum pans.

"It's all set," Faith called.

"Great. Meet us out back. And the guys requested plenty of coffee."

Shortly after, Faith climbed into a public-works truck, its bed crammed with urns of hot coffee, bottles of water, shovels, brooms, trash bags, disposable masks, cans of spray paint. She piled the pans of sandwiches in her lap and on the floor.

"Why spray paint?" Faith asked the driver, Craig.

"To mark the condemned houses."

Faith fell silent as Craig started the truck. They rolled up Main Street, giving Faith her first glimpse of the Wave's End downtown, where storefronts were dark but relatively unscathed. A few blocks farther, dejected customers returned to their cars after finding the supermarket shuttered.

"It doesn't look *that* bad," Faith said hopefully.

"Wait."

Advancing a few more streets, he slowed the truck as the road began to disappear beneath a layer of sand. Looking to her right, Faith started at the sight of a peach bi-level split in half by an ancient oak, a grim admonition of how close she'd come to disaster the previous evening.

"Empty, thank God," Craig said, anticipating her question. As they moved forward, the devastation mounted with each block: buckled roads, toppled cars buried up to their doors in sand. And the boats—boats on lawns and curbs and helter-skelter in the road, as if their captains had been racing merrily through the streets of Wave's End in a nautical free-for-all, then abruptly abandoned ship.

Worst off were the homes. In a catastrophic game of hopscotch, Nadine had gobbled some houses whole, gnawed immense holes in others and spit out the remains, and bizarrely, randomly, turned up her nose at the rest. There appeared to be no reason or sense to Mother Nature's destruction.

Speechless, Faith stared at Craig.

"Like a bomb went off, right?" He pulled over to park the truck. "Okay. This is us."

Faith looked around at the abandoned street. "But there's nobody here. Who are we going to feed?"

"You'll see. We go on foot from here. Slight traffic jam." He jutted his chin at a schooner sprawled across the drawbridge in front of them, its battered masts flattened like the wings of a wounded bird. Faith's breath caught, awed by the force capable of ripping a craft from its moorings and pitching it onto a bridge.

"We'll come back for the cleaning supplies." After grabbing a coffee urn, he trudged toward the span. Faith followed, juggling sandwiches and a sleeve of cups and wondering how much worse things would be on the other side.

22

As she and Craig dispensed sandwiches and coffee block by beachfront block, Faith realized their meager inventory would soon be depleted. In addition to the first responders they had been dispatched to feed, dozens of anxious homeowners swarmed the streets, ignoring the crime tape and violating the town's order to stay away until the area could be secured.

That process might take weeks. Homes tipped and lurched precariously, garages, dormers and porches severed from main residences. Not that this deterred their owners; Faith watched as a man scaled a half-buried truck to enter a house whose sheared-off roof rested in the driveway, until a firefighter convinced him to return to the street.

Sand had found its way everywhere, blanketing streets, saddling houses, penetrating first floors—as though the entire beach had been rolled up like a carpet and fanned over the coastal town.

"You know what's scary about the sand?" Craig asked.

"How hard it will be to remove it?" Faith guessed.

"That, and the fact it acts like a filter. If there's a gas leak, which is fairly common in situations like this, the sand absorbs the gas odor. A house could be about to blow, and you might never even smell it."

"You mean, like right now?" Faith glanced around nervously.

"I'm just saying we'll be better off once the utility trucks get to work up here."

As the two shuffled through the streets, Faith's strides kicked up random items: a child's plastic shovel, a basketball trophy, a woman's bedroom slipper. Photos floated in puddles. Faith retrieved an image of two small blondes in matching plaid sitting on the lap of a shopping mall Santa, their features and the date on the plaque at their feet rubbed off by the sand bath.

Who owned this misplaced memory? she wondered, tracing the photo's pebbled surface. Thinking someone at the church might know, she tucked the photo in her pocket.

As she and Craig walked, residents approached them, wanting to tell their stories about the height floodwaters had attained in their kitchen or the distance their car or bike or swing set had floated from their home, as if in the telling, they might begin to process the tragedy. Long after the sandwiches were gone, Faith stayed and listened, feeling like an intruder yet unable to abandon the shell-shocked Wave's End residents as they came to terms with their losses.

She observed how some homeowners sprang into action right away, carting debris to the curb and phoning insurers. Others could only circle their properties, speechless with shock. When she spotted a middle-aged couple clinging to each other on the sidewalk, Faith had to turn away, going to sit on a far curb while Craig finished his conversation with a police officer. As she waited, Faith overheard a woman's consoling voice behind her.

"Just give it time. He'll turn up. He's smart."

Faith turned to listen, afraid someone had gone missing until she spotted the teenage boy swinging a heavy chain leash and realized they were referring to a lost dog. She had not considered the storm's toll on animals; if the hurricane could flatline a community, what were a dog's chances of survival?

"But Tucker's a puppy, Mom." The boy ran his fingers along the lacquered spikes atop his head. "He doesn't know his way home. And what if he's hurt?"

"Someone will take care of him. I know it. Now come and help me move some of this sand so we can get inside."

Out of the corner of her eye, Faith watched the boy take the shovel his mother offered then angrily attack the wall of sand blocking the front door. After a few attempts, however, he gave up, planting the shovel in a dune and dropping onto the concrete steps. "I'm done," he said. "All you care about is this stupid house in this stupid town you dragged me to. Admit it: you don't give a shit about Tucker because *Dad* gave him to me."

Ouch. Clearly, this family's pain extended beyond miseries inflicted by the storm. Frozen on the sidewalk, Faith didn't dare move. She snuck a look at the mother, who held her cheek as though she'd been struck, and hoped she'd never been that cruel to Connie as a teenager.

23

When Faith and Craig returned to the church in midafternoon, she spotted Bruce at a table having coffee with a middle-aged couple.

"The *Beacon*'s putting out a special storm edition," Alicia said after greeting Faith and Craig. "Hopefully, getting some of the survivors' stories out there will generate some assistance."

"Won't hurt the paper, either," said Craig, as he and Faith moved to the buffet and helped themselves to coffee.

"What do you mean?" Faith asked.

"The *Beacon*'s in trouble. Has been for a while. Everybody wants to read the news on their phones. Anyway, this ought to help their cash flow for a while." Craig waved his cup to encompass the disaster relief effort.

Interesting, Faith thought. When Bruce finished his interview, she sat with him and recounted what she had seen at the beachfront.

"So, did it convince you?" Bruce asked.

"Convince me of what?"

"That you should stay in Wave's End awhile. There will be plenty to do in the coming weeks."

"I'm sure there will be. I feel for everyone who's been affected. I . . . I'm haunted by what I saw today. But my boss is in trouble, too."

"I see."

Faith set down her cup. "With all due respect, Mr. Neery—"

"Please. Call me Bruce."

"Right, Bruce then. With all due respect, Bruce, I don't think you do see. You don't even know me—*or* my mother," she added pointedly. "I'm not a selfish person. I came down to check on my mother, remember? And she's fine. She and Maeve will be occupied with the new people. It doesn't mean I won't come back to Wave's End. But my livelihood is in New York. That has to count for something."

"All right, then." Bruce got to his feet. "You seem pretty set on this. I did ask around. It seems buses to the city will run on a limited basis starting tomorrow morning. But you'll have to get yourself back up to Ashcroft. And you better get there early. With the trains out, there's bound to be a crowd."

Faith clapped her hands. "Thank you. I will. And I'll find a ride."

Relieved her transportation dilemma had been solved, Faith spent the rest of the afternoon at the church, where many more families had sought refuge since her departure. A hardwired generator provided plentiful power.

Also during Faith's absence, donations had begun to arrive: mountains of clothing, food, and cleaning supplies that newly recruited volunteers now sorted. In the kitchen, someone had dropped off a crate of tomatoes and several bags of canned goods. Spotting Alicia, Faith offered to put together some soup.

"Bless you," replied the de facto shelter manager.

By the time Craig stuck his head in to offer a ride back to The Mermaid's Purse, Faith had a makeshift *pasta e fagioli* simmering for the crowd's dinner. She found day-old Italian bread that she buttered and seasoned for garlic bread.

Back at the inn, her mother and Maeve had put in a solid day's work as well, cleaning and freshening rooms as best they could in the cold, dark house. Bruce had been too busy to come by and remove the plywood from the windows or drop off the promised generator.

"I hope Bruce doesn't forget about us." Maeve wrung her hands. "It's going to be so darn gloomy in here without any light."

"He said he wouldn't," said Faith. "He's going to be pretty busy covering the storm's aftermath. I doubt you'll be able to count on him as much right now."

"He always takes care of me," said Maeve.

"Anyway, after all the guests have been through, they'll be happy to have a bed and a roof over their heads," said Faith. By the time she left the church, Alicia's "Housing Wanted" board had been plastered with index cards. Faith had mentioned the inn's availability, and hoped others would come forward to offer shelter.

"So how's this going to work, anyway?" Faith asked. "Will you simply offer the guests breakfast, as usual?"

Maeve shook her head. "Under these circumstances, we'll have to be more 'full service.' Three meals a day—simple ones, but they'll be counting on us for that. As for linens, laundry, housekeeping, we'll play it by ear. See what they need."

"Maybe Faith our chef here would like to work a little magic tomorrow night and whip up a fancy welcome dinner for our new guests?" Winking, Connie nudged her daughter.

"Ordinarily, I'd love to, but I'm heading back to the city tomorrow." Craig's friend drove a cab; Faith had booked him for six o'clock the following morning.

Although they tried to convince her to stay, Faith remained resolute.

"I'm sorry, but I've got to check on Xander and the restaurant. Besides, Mom, Maeve's a pro at this. And now you'll really get to see what it's like to be an innkeeper."

Given the inn's sudden reinvention as a storm haven, Faith decided to table her concerns about Connie becoming a permanent fixture at The Mermaid's Purse. They still had nearly two weeks before her mother was due back at work.

As the three finished leftovers by candlelight, fatigue overtook Faith. Though even a slow night at Piquant could be far more physically taxing than her work today, the last eight hours had depleted her emotionally. She could only imagine how she would feel tomorrow, faced with her ruined restaurant.

Excusing herself, she gathered her belongings and placed them by the couch so she could depart quickly in the morning. She then lay down and closed her eyes, certain she'd fall asleep immediately, except that the recollection of the desolate couple up at the beach kept interfering. Why hadn't she approached them and mentioned the inn's availability? Faith crossed her fingers that word of openings at The Mermaid's Purse had reached them.

Faith sighed and turned over, eventually edging toward slumber, only to be jolted awake by a crash outside the salon window.

24

Once off the couch, Faith could see the nearly full moon through the salon window—odd because she had lain down in the inky darkness imposed by Bruce's storm-proofing. She tried to open the window, but its ancient sash wouldn't budge. She could see nothing in the side yard, but the cries outside sounded like someone suffering excruciating pain.

"Mom. *Mom!*" Faith grabbed a flashlight from the coffee table. "Somebody's outside. I think they're hurt."

"I'm right here." Connie met Faith in the front hall, tightening the belt of her bathrobe.

"We should call the police. Where's Maeve?"

"I assume bed. She said good night."

"Stay here. I'll check." Faith bounded into the kitchen to check Maeve's adjacent living quarters, which were empty, then reported back to her mother. "Where could she have gone?"

"I remember her complaining earlier about the house being too dark for the guests." Connie's eyes widened. "You don't suppose . . ."

Without waiting for her mother, Faith yanked open the front door. She hurried down the steps and around the side of the inn, waving her flashlight and illuminating a splintered sheet of plywood hanging by a corner. Lowering the beam to the ground, Faith dropped to her knees in the damp grass, where Maeve lay crumpled and whimpering next to a fallen ladder, her right leg twisted unnaturally beneath her and a hammer just beyond her reach.

"Mom. Call nine-one-one. Use my phone. It's charged," Faith ordered as her mother caught up to her.

"But how bad—"

"Never mind. Just call."

As Connie fled to summon the EMTs, Maeve reached up in protest. "Just give me a minute, dear, and I'll be fine." She attempted to raise her head, but grimaced and fell back onto the damp lawn. "Oh, my. I think I've really done it."

"You've got to stay still, Maeve." From the ladder's angle and the height of the window, Faith knew Maeve had fallen hard. "Help will be here in a little bit."

"One more yank and I would have had it," Maeve cried softly. "I used to be able to do all these things myself. I hate having to depend on someone else."

"They're on their way." Returning from summoning the authorities, Connie knelt on Maeve's other side and covered her with a blanket. "It's all right. We'll get you to the hospital, and you'll be good as new." But as she met her daughter's gaze over Maeve's chest, Connie's eyes revealed her fear. "This is *bad*," she mouthed.

Lips pressed together, Faith nodded imperceptibly.

After a few minutes, Connie got to her feet, motioning for Faith to follow her a few yards away from Maeve. "I'm going to get dressed," she whispered.

"You're going with her?" Faith asked.

"Who else is there?"

"You might end up at the hospital all night." Faith glanced back at Maeve, who moaned softly.

"Maybe so, but Maeve has no one. We can't let her go alone. And with you leaving at the crack of dawn . . ."

"What about the guests coming tomorrow?"

Connie glanced back at the inn. "I suppose I could leave a note on the door and tell them to make themselves comfortable. Or try to get hold of Bruce."

That man is not everybody's salvation, Faith thought, frustrated.

Faith walked back to where Maeve lay and crouched again to comfort her with a squeeze of her hand. She thought of her packed bag beside the couch, her early-morning cab, the restaurant recovery operation awaiting her in New York. As much as she yearned to hop into that taxi in a few hours and head back to the city, it was clear her mother could not manage both Maeve's medical crisis and the boarders' imminent arrival. Alone in Wave's End, Connie had only Faith to turn to, whereas Xander could at least count on some of the bar- and waitstaff to bail him out—literally, in this case, given the seawaters that surged through Piquant.

Bruce had even said so that morning: another day wouldn't matter.

As the siren's wail announced the ambulance's arrival, Maeve moaned again.

Faith got to her feet, brushing dirt from her sweatpants. "You stay here, Mom. I'll go to the hospital with Maeve."

"But how can you? What about your boss? Piquant?"

"Xander will understand. Stay here at The Mermaid's Purse. That way, when your first boarders arrive tomorrow, you'll be ready to greet them."

25

"You can at least save the wine, can't you?" Faith asked Xander, rubbing her eyes at the predawn light splintering through the hospital blinds. She had been curled up in the waiting room chair for more than an hour now while Maeve had her scans, benefiting from a rare live outlet to charge her phone, while the person next to her eyed her, phone in hand. It had been only two days, but the scarcity of power had already brought out the worst in some people, Faith noticed.

Fortunately, the facility agreed to treat Maeve. Most of the coastal hospitals had been running on generators after evacuating several hundred non-acute patients to inland hospitals the previous day, according to the exhausted nurse who assessed Maeve in the crowded emergency room.

Following that evaluation, Faith sat beside Maeve's stretcher for close to four hours before a technician came and took the woman for her MRI and CAT scans. It might be a long wait, the technician warned her as he wheeled Maeve away. Faith used that opportunity to call her boss.

"The wine is unsalvageable," replied Xander. "I can't risk serving bad wine to customers."

"Oh, Xander. I can't even . . . I'm just so, so sorry." How Xander had prized his carefully curated wine cellar.

"Not that I'm likely to have customers anytime soon. Piquant is done, for now."

Leaning her head against the wall, Faith winced as Xander described how little he had salvaged from the inundated interior, how propping the entrance open the entire first day had done nothing to dissipate the mildewed stench inside. Already, a spongy emerald waterline had sprouted on the dining room walls about four feet from the floor, he said, marking the water's torrential passage through the restaurant.

"What about upstairs?" she asked.

The glass high-rise overhead had the feel of a ghost town, he said, its wealthy owners having evacuated.

Faith massaged her throbbing temples. "Have you thought about what you're going to do?"

"Stick around and get a timeline on the utility repairs to the neighborhood. Then there's the remediation, new wiring, new floors . . ." Xander's voice trailed off, husky with worry.

"Don't worry. I'll help. I'll be back in a couple of days at most." She got up and peered down the hospital hall for any sign of Maeve or the X-ray technician.

"I appreciate that. But Piquant's going to be out of commission for months, at least. I can't afford to pay you."

Or repay you. The words hung between them.

"It doesn't matter." *Why did I say that? It does matter. If only he didn't sound so damned desolate.* "We'll figure something out, Xander. I have a stake in the place, too."

"About that. You have no idea how shitty I feel about the loan. My timing sucked. But there's no point in coming back here right now. There's nothing left."

"Don't say that. *You're* there." Woozy from exhaustion, she fought tears. In Piquant, Faith had finally found the restaurant where she belonged and a boss she respected, even if money management wasn't his finest suit. Back when she began working as a chef in the restaurant

Xander managed, he noticed Faith's potential, encouraging her and connecting her to the top kitchens in the city, finally rewarding her with a spot in his own. She knew the Piquant staff thought there was something romantic between them. And there had been, fleetingly, back when they initially met. But outside the heat of the kitchen, the attraction simmering between them fizzled.

Fortunately, they salvaged their friendship, which remained strong. And now Nadine would wrest all of that from her.

"You're a fantastic chef," Xander continued. "Any restaurant would be lucky to have you."

"Don't say that. I don't want another restaurant." Faith flushed at the rare praise from her boss.

"I know some folks uptown. You might have to go back on the line for a bit, until you show them what you're made of." He paused, exhaling, and Faith pictured him spewing a stream of smoke at Piquant's awnings the way he did on their mutual breaks. Those awnings were probably shredded by now.

"Say the word, and I'll make some calls," Xander prompted.

"No. No calls. Not yet." They'd opened Piquant together, and it would kill her to leave. And even as Xander watched his business wash away, he still looked out for her. "I'll let you know." Faith hung up before he could hear her crying.

26

Once Maeve was admitted, Bruce picked up Faith from the hospital. On the drive back to Wave's End, she outlined Maeve's condition: the scans had ruled out head trauma or internal bleeding, but her X-rays indicated a badly fractured hip. Surgery to place a pin within the joint had to wait until the swelling around it subsided.

"So Maeve's looking at an extended hospital stay," Faith said. "Followed by several weeks of inpatient physical therapy."

Bruce tapped the steering wheel with his thumb. "Well, it's unfortunate, but it could have been far, far worse. Thank you for going with Maeve. For staying with her. I know you had other plans."

Faith stared out the window. "Those plans appear to be on hold at the moment." On the sidewalk, she spotted a very determined Superwoman, whose satin cape rippled as she wrangled a bumblebee on a leash while herding a pint-sized pirate, a witch and a zombie. It was Halloween, Faith realized; she had completely lost track of the days.

"In any event, I'm grateful," Bruce continued. "I'd say your mother taking over the reins of The Mermaid's Purse couldn't have happened at a more opportune time."

Opportune for whom? Faith wanted to ask. "It *is* lucky my mother's there," she said instead. "But she hasn't exactly taken the reins—at least not legally, anyway."

"Is that your understanding?"

Her guard up, Faith eyed him, but Bruce stared resolutely at the road. He seemed like he knew something. Had Connie already taken him into her confidence? *Please, no, Mom.* Bruce seemed like an okay guy, despite being somewhat condescending. She sighed, her neck hot with anxiety, hoping her instincts were wrong and Bruce's inquiry was innocent. "Yes. My mother has some decisions to make. Why do you ask?"

"No reason." Sniffing, he rubbed his nose. "I must have misunderstood."

"Misunderstood what?"

"Nothing. You should have this conversation with your mother. Now, did I mention I hooked up the generator this morning?" Bruce launched into a series of instructions about the inn's temporary power source. "You can have a hot shower when you get home."

When they eventually pulled into the driveway of The Mermaid's Purse, Faith frowned at the earsplitting rumble.

"Generator. You'll get used to it." Bruce hoisted a gas can out of the trunk. "I'm going to go feed the beast. You should head on in. Your mother's anxious to hear how Maeve is."

And I've got a few questions for her. She let herself in through the unlocked back entrance, turning to pull shut the stubborn screen door. As Faith fiddled with it, something hard nailed her squarely in the back. She turned.

"Crap. Sorry. My bad." A tall young man in jeans and a black T-shirt loped across the kitchen to scoop up a Frisbee from the floor, the length of chain around his neck scraping the tile as he did so. "You okay?" he asked.

"Yeah, fine. It's cool." Faith blinked in the stark white kitchen. Something about the teen seemed familiar. "Are you a friend of Maeve's?"

"Maeve? No. I just moved here with my mom. We, like, lost our place."

"I'm Faith. Nice to meet you. And I'm sorry about your house." Why was her mother allowing the inn guests access to the kitchen, a space normally reserved for staff?

"Whatever. It's not like it was totally ours. We were renters. You homeless, too?"

"No. I'm here to help my mother, Mrs. Sterling."

"You mean the owner? Connie seems cool."

Owner? Had her mother represented herself that way to the boarders?

Faith watched him spin the Frisbee toward the tin ceiling, flinching at the ting of plastic on metal. "Gage Castro. What is wrong with you? Apologize right now." The raspy demand came from a tall, slight woman in the kitchen doorway—the boy's mother, Faith presumed. Her long wet hair had left damp patches on her oversized Metallica sweatshirt.

That voice. Faith recognized it from the beach yesterday: the mother and her surly son arguing over the missing dog. Embarrassed to have been eavesdropping, she was relieved that neither guest appeared to recognize her.

"Chill, Mom. I did already." Gage rolled his eyes. "I'm out of here."

"Nervous energy. Sorry if he was bothering you," she said once her son had bounded out the back door. "It's been a long couple of days. I'm Roxanne." She extended a thin hand, ringless save for a thick silver ankh thumb band. "Mother of Gage, obviously. So, what brings you here? Sand damage? Trees? Six feet of water in your basement?"

"Actually, my place in Brooklyn didn't even lose power. I'm Faith, Connie's daughter. I'm here helping, sort of."

"That's nice of you. Everybody's been so kind." Her eyes filled. "Damn. Sorry." She tore a paper towel from a roll by the sink and dabbed her eyes. "I thought I had finished crying. Guess I haven't. You must think I'm nuts."

"I don't. You've been through a lot."

"It's just . . . I thought I'd finally gotten us settled once and for all after my husband and I separated. I had this crazy idea it would be an adventure for Gage and me to take a winter rental near the water." She wiped her nose with the towel. "Then the damn storm hit. Some adventure."

"Did you lose a lot?" Faith thought of the mountains of discarded belongings beginning to accumulate at the beach.

She shook her head. "Not that much, compared to others. We left our last place in kind of a rush. That part's complicated. But the things I brought there have a lot of sentimental value. We also lost—misplaced, I hope—the one thing that means anything to Gage: the new puppy from his dad."

No wonder Gage had been so angry up at their beach house.

"That night, I told him to keep Tucker on the leash. But did he listen? Now my son's wearing that leash like a necklace. He even sleeps with it. Like that's going to bring that dog back."

"Try to think positively. Maybe somebody found him."

"I'd like to think so. Friends have taken Gage to check the shelters in the area, but so far, nothing. There's still so much confusion." Roxanne shook her head. "I feel so guilty. Stupidly, we didn't elevate the furniture or . . . No one thought the water would come up that high. And now I have to uproot my kid again." She blew her nose. "I know what you're thinking. I'm a terrible mother."

"No, you're not," Faith murmured. Speaking of mothers, where might hers be? Boarders or no boarders, the two needed to talk. "Can I make you a cup of tea or something?"

"Nope, I'm good." Roxanne coiled her wet hair over one shoulder. "I know I sound ungrateful. I'm not. This place is a gift. Your mom gave us the two upstairs singles. But I just want to get us back into our own place as soon as possible. Our lives back to normal, whatever that will be. But I can barely find the energy to—" With a sigh, Roxanne glanced up at the kitchen clock. "Yikes. It's late. I need to get back up to the beach. The town said everything has to be out by the curb by tomorrow. Before the bulldozers come. Thank God friends are coming to help, or I might never get through it." Roxanne sniffed, then wiped her eyes with her sleeve. "Anyway, thanks for listening. I better find Gage now."

Watching Roxanne through the window over the sink (Bruce had taken care of the plywood removal as well), it struck Faith that she had learned more about the inn's new boarders Roxanne and Gage in those few minutes than she had ever discovered about even her most faithful Piquant customer. Had Roxanne simply overshared, her emotions raw from the storm's trauma, or were guests at the inn always this open?

Faith leaned on the sink. Before even boiling water at The Mermaid's Purse, she felt the weight of the boarders' concerns. This was going to be different from life at Piquant, that much was clear.

Squaring her shoulders, she went in search of her mother.

27

Faith found Connie in the salon folding towels and raised her eyebrows at the startling transformation. Her mother had abandoned her habitual flowing skirts for tailored slacks and a long-sleeved cotton shirt. She had knotted a white canvas butcher's apron at her waist and pulled her silver hair into a bun.

In short, her mother seemed to have channeled Maeve's style to greet the new boarders.

"Faith!" Connie exclaimed, getting up from the couch. "I've been so worried about Maeve. I couldn't get through to the hospital. Tell me everything."

Anxious as she was to get to the bottom of Bruce's evasiveness, Faith set those concerns aside to fill her mother in about Maeve.

"That poor woman," Connie said when Faith finished. "She's lucky we were here."

"Right. About us being here. We need to talk, Mom."

"All right, but I only have a minute. Some guests have already arrived."

"I know. I met Roxanne and Gage. And I think it's wonderful you want to help them. And any others that might come. But things are different now."

"What are you talking about?"

"Maeve's going to be out of commission for quite a while. I think we need a better plan."

"If you're talking about running this place, these guests aren't expecting the Ritz. I expect things will be pretty relaxed."

"Of course. I get that. Between the two of us, we can manage things for the time being. But what happens in a couple of weeks, when you have to go back to work? This started out as a trial run, remember?"

"Tell that to Nadine."

"I'm just saying that maybe you should go back to Maeve. Ask her to contact the contest's runner-up."

"And give this place up before I've even given it a try?"

Faith moistened her lips. "You'll have your turn for a bit, and then there could be . . . a transition period between you two. You have a lot to lose here by being impulsive, Mom."

Connie sat down again and took another towel from the pile to fold. "I'm very aware of that," she said, shaking the towel.

"Good. Because we've been here before. Let me see." Faith tapped her chin, mentally riffling through her mother's exploits. "Remember when you jumped into that work-at-home assembly job?" When Faith was in high school, her mother impulsively signed on to purchase thousands of dollars in poorly made craft materials, only to have her employer reject most of her assembly work.

"This is completely different. You can't compare yarn to people's lives. And by the way, thank you for reminding me of my failures."

Here we go: Teflon Connie. "That wasn't a failure, but it *was* rash. I'm suggesting you see these boarders through the next few weeks. Then, maybe one day, after you retire, you can come back—"

"Out of the question." Her mother's voice tightened. "If you won't help me, I'll find another way to make this work."

"I never said I wouldn't help. I just want you to see the big picture. You know, nothing's been right about this from the start. Maybe Maeve's accident is a sign you should just walk away from The Mermaid's Purse."

"I love this place already. And anyway, I can't walk away."

Fear flushed Faith's neck again. "Why not?"

"Because I signed the transfer-of-ownership papers. The day after you dropped me off."

This was what Bruce had hesitated to say: her mother had rushed headlong into full ownership.

"Did Bruce talk you into doing that?"

Eyes on the laundry, Connie grabbed another towel without finishing the previous one. "Of course he didn't. Why would you think that?"

"Because he seemed to know about it."

"Well, I might have mentioned . . ." Connie smoothed the newly folded towel repeatedly. "I know you told me not to commit, but just once, I wanted something all my own."

"But the day I drove you down here, we decided you would wait."

"No, Faith. *You* decided. *You* wanted me to wait. But why should I hold out when I won this place fair and square?"

"So all that talk about just taking some vacation time?"

"That *was* true. At the time."

Faith crossed her arms. "Please tell me you didn't quit the factory."

Connie looked away, silently fiddling with her apron strings.

"Please *tell* me you didn't give up your apartment. Throw away your entire future."

"The apartment was a rental. And I don't view this as throwing away my future. The Mermaid's Purse will be my security. Coastal real estate is a good investment, isn't it?"

Faith stared. "Usually, unless a hundred-year storm rips through it. Have you given a thought to taxes? Utilities? Maintenance? Staff salaries?" Faith could go on and on, but what was the point? The damage was done. "Can I at least look at the papers?"

"They're with Mr. Walker, Maeve's accountant. And anyway, it's too late to change anything. The Mermaid's Purse is mine fair and square, for better or worse. And these families coming need our help." Connie got up and walked over to the fireplace where Faith now stood. "So it's up to you: are you staying in Wave's End, or not?"

28

Quivering with indignation, Faith stormed outside, where Bruce had just loaded the empty gas tank into his trunk.

"You knew about those ownership papers, didn't you?" Faith said. "That's what you wouldn't tell me in the car earlier."

"I don't like to get in the middle of things."

"Why do I have the feeling you already have?"

"I'm not sure what you're implying, Faith, but your mother's a grown woman. She can make her own decisions."

Barely two weeks in and this guy was already going to bat for her mother? This level of loyalty was fast, even for Connie. Tempted to give Bruce an earful about some of her mother's more memorable choices, Faith kept herself in check. "You don't know her very well. She can be . . . impulsive." Faith paced in the driveway. "There's got to be a loophole. Aren't there review periods or something for these things?"

"In some cases, but I believe that window has closed." Bruce crossed his arms and leaned on his car. "Why exactly are you so riled up?"

"Because . . . because I know how this works. At some point, I'll have to clean up this mess."

"Of course I don't know the history between you two—"

"No, you don't."

"And it may not be my concern, but there might be another way to look at this situation."

"Really? And how is that?"

"Maybe you're meant to see that your mother got to Wave's End in the nick of time. That you should cut her some slack while she gets those poor families settled. They've been through hell over the last few days." After a final, deliberate look at Faith, Bruce climbed into his truck and started the engine.

You're right: it's not your concern. Mind your own damn business, Faith thought as Bruce departed. How dare he question her compassion for the storm survivors after she spent the previous day assisting them? And didn't Xander fit in the same category?

Going to sit on the back steps, Faith felt drained from the hours at the hospital with Maeve, and from her depressing conversation with Xander that had essentially left her unemployed. She just didn't have it in her at the moment to fight Connie on this one, not after her mother's latest disclosure.

A month ago, Faith had slept soundly with the knowledge that, thanks to Connie's food-processing job, her mother would soon be solvent enough to never worry about food, shelter, medical care. And in spite of Connie's trip east, Faith had convinced herself her mother would never jeopardize that security. But then her mother had done that very thing, by virtue of signing those papers and tying herself inextricably to the inn.

Faith could see no way out of this one. And hell, maybe Bruce was right. Her mother was a grown-up. If Connie Sterling wanted to be an innkeeper, then she *should* damn well be an innkeeper, come hell or high water—the latter being something of a liability in Wave's End. And as her mother said, the inn was now legally Connie's; she could always sell the property if necessary.

Inside, Connie was back on the couch, flanked by piles of folded towels.

"You know what, Mom?" Faith said, hands on hips. "This inn is yours now. And since it looks like I'm out of a job, I'll stay for a bit and help. At least until you figure out another plan."

Shoulders slumping in relief, Connie rose and hugged her daughter. "I can't tell you how happy this makes me, honey."

"So I guess that means I'm working for you." Faith attempted a smile.

"Great. Because I've actually thought of a few things that need doing." Connie rummaged for a paper in her apron pocket. "For starters, a restaurant up at the beach has offered to donate some food, as long as someone could come and collect it. I'd go myself, except I still need to get ready for an older couple arriving this afternoon."

"No problem. Just point me in the right direction." Faith spotted her bag beside the couch. "But may I at least throw my things upstairs before you put me to work? I mean, I *do* merit a bed now that I'm working here, don't I?"

"Of course you do." Connie tapped her chin. "Let's see: second floor, first door on the right."

Upstairs, Faith recognized the room from Maeve's tour and dropped her bag beside the wrought-iron trundle bed.

"Find it okay?" Connie poked her head in.

"Yes, thanks. Oh, wait a second. You forgot something." From a brass hook Faith grabbed the paisley skirt Connie wore the day at the airport and tossed it to her mother.

"No, I didn't." Catching the skirt, Connie then folded it and slid it into a drawer.

"Why are you putting it in there?"

"Because that's where the rest of my things are."

"But . . . but you just said this was *my* room."

"It is. You're bunking with me, honey. Make yourself comfortable. We're going to be roommates."

PART 4: HONEYMOON

29

As she drove to the beach in the old wood-paneled wagon that turned out to be Maeve's, Faith told herself she'd be fine on the trundle bed alongside her mother in the cramped bedroom, although the thought of sleeping so near to Connie did make her a little uncomfortable. The closest they had come had been sharing a set of bunk beds long ago, an experience so far in Faith's past she could barely recall it. Maybe as a child she had been afraid to sleep alone, and her mother kept her company. She'd have to remember to ask Connie about it when she got back.

But as for the current arrangements, as her mother had just explained, it made sense to make the inn's remaining rooms available for additional families; also, doubling up would save electricity, relieving the burden on the overtaxed generator.

Besides, she'd stay in Wave's End only long enough to settle her mother into her innkeeping routine. During that interim, the two likely would be so exhausted from running The Mermaid's Purse all day they'd fall asleep the second their heads hit the pillows.

A block ahead, the beachfront loomed. The town had reinforced the barricade since yesterday; today, uniformed guards patrolled the line of hazard-orange sawhorses stretched across the road. Faith pulled over and called the number for David Huntington that her mother had given her.

"Tell them you're here for me," the restaurant owner instructed. "The Blue Osprey. I put you on the list."

Sure enough, after Faith mentioned David's name, the officer waved her through. As she followed the beach road in a direction she hadn't gone the day before, her mouth fell open at lifeguard stands splintered like matchsticks, stretches of boardwalk peeled back like the chocolate shavings she used to garnish Piquant desserts, concrete benches corralled in a vacant lot after detaching from their boardwalk stations.

A few blocks beyond, the road veered sharply right at a sparkling expanse of water. Faith spotted the top half of a sign—THE BLUE—its bottom buried in a sand dune. A tanned, wiry, thirtyish man in a long-sleeved T-shirt and baseball cap worn backward over his ponytail shoveled furiously, working to free the sign.

Faith rolled down her window. "I'm looking for David? I'm from The Mermaid's Purse." Behind him, the restaurant's aluminum roof buckled under the sand's weight.

The man pulled off his sunglasses and squinted at her. "Right. The food. Park as best you can." He pointed his glasses at the debris-filled street and disappeared inside a screen door. After finding a spot to leave the car, Faith followed, taken aback at the sand blanketing the dining room floor. Despite the barrage of beach that had forced its way inside, some tables had survived the onslaught, remaining upright, frozen in time, still set expectantly with white tablecloths and mismatched chairs, fall mums wilting in bud vases, awaiting patrons who might stroll in at any moment.

The rest of the tables had been piled against a back wall.

Faith found David inside the narrow, well-equipped galley kitchen. A large cutout serving window offered a view of the entire dining room, as well as the waters beyond, thanks to floor-to-ceiling windows.

"This is a beautiful setting," Faith said.

"Yeah, it is. *Was*." He cleared his throat. "Anyway, I've got bread, produce and some semi-defrosted pumpkin–sweet potato bisque if you're interested. The soup will be fine if you serve it in the next day or two." He pulled stainless pots from the fridge and set them on the counter. After accepting a ladle, Faith began to transfer the soup into plastic lidded buckets he set in front of her.

"Mamouna's. Yummy Brooklyn sorbet," she said, recognizing the containers. "I love their lychee cilantro."

"One of our best sellers here in the summer."

"We sold it, too. Until the storm." Faith detailed the pummeling Piquant suffered at Nadine's hand, and her reasons for coming to the inn's aid in Wave's End.

"Lottery, huh? I heard something about that. After the last few days, I bet your mother's feeling like she won the booby prize."

"Quite the opposite, actually. I'm not sure she totally understands what she's gotten herself into."

"Did any of us?" David clapped the lid on the last bucket. "I guess this little place doesn't exactly measure up to your fancy city restaurant."

"I wouldn't say that." Faith surveyed the menu taped above David's prep station: grilled watermelon and conch salad, shrimp and grits, prosciutto-and-arugula-topped pizzettes—all from locally sourced ingredients. "Looks like you know what you're doing. Where did you train?"

"Self-taught, mostly. Picked up a few things in the Caribbean. I worked in a bunch of restaurants there to support my surfing habit. Dream of mine forever to open a restaurant." David hopped up onto the counter. "We opened last Memorial Day. To pretty good reviews, I must say."

"That's always a good start."

Piquant's stressful opening wasn't so far in Faith's past that she couldn't recall those anxious early days, wringing her hands beside Xander on the restaurant's patio, willing passersby to come in.

"I was counting on the momentum carrying us through fall," David said. "Especially after adding the liquor license. But then, this happened." As he jerked his head toward the water, an armored jeep hurtled around the bend.

"But if you can get through the next few months until the area is cleaned up, you can get back on your feet."

"Yeah, except that I'm about to load my entire summer's profits into your car."

"Really? You weren't able to put anything away?" If Faith ever had her own restaurant, she'd make sure she had a ton in savings before opening her doors.

"Nope. No contingency fund. The liquor license ate up everything I had. I even gave up my apartment in town."

Faith raised an eyebrow, thinking there must be plenty of women willing to rescue a good-looking, personable chef.

"Don't believe me?" he said. "Come check out my crib."

Inside a closet-like space, a desk and a single bed were piled high with restaurant supplies. On the file cabinet beside the bed, Faith spotted several empty beer bottles, a greasy paper sack and a telltale tomato-red cardboard container. "I see we share the same gourmet taste," she joked.

"I won't tell if you won't." David swept the trash into a garbage bin under the desk. "Like I said, this place left me no budget for fine dining."

"You don't have a business partner?"

"Me, myself and I. I put my heart and soul into this place." He turned away, grabbed a plastic milk crate and began to fill it with bags of dinner rolls and sliced bread for Faith to take back to the inn.

Faith's heart ached for the entrepreneur; another dream crushed by the hurricane. She was about to ask him his plans for work when the screen door slapped open.

"Anybody home?"

Faith frowned at the disconcertingly familiar male voice. To her surprise, Bruce Neery strolled into the kitchen a second later. Was the man the town busybody, or what?

"I see you've made some progress with the sand," Bruce said. "Oh, hello, Faith. What are you doing here?"

"I was about to ask you the same thing."

"I think he's looking for me," David said. "Faith Sterling, meet my dad."

30

Back at The Mermaid's Purse, Faith lugged David's donations into the kitchen, thinking the expedition had all the markings of one of her mother's matchups. David's different last name ("Huntington's my mother's side," was all the chef offered as explanation) had thrown Faith off.

"Hey, Mom," she called. "If you were trying to fix me up with Bruce's son—"

"We're out here, Faith." Connie's soft, measured response from the front of the house sounded like a mother trying not to disturb a sleeping baby. Faith headed toward the salon, where her mother sat on the couch beside an elderly man.

"Faith, this is Fred. He's come to stay with us for a while."

"Nice to meet you, Fred." Faith took in the man's shock of white hair, his fleece zipped over a thick ski sweater, his white socks pulled up over the bottoms of his jeans. Shaking his hand, Faith found the man's rough in hers, his fingers wrapped in places with surgical tape. "Welcome to The Mermaid's Purse. I only just got here myself, but we'll do our best to make you comfortable."

"Thank you. We were doing okay on our own for a while, neighbors running over with firewood and food from the church and whatnot."

"You're lucky to have good neighbors," said Connie.

"That I am. But then we ran out of wood. And I started to worry about my wife. Mona, say hello to Faith here."

Faith turned. Fred's wife, Mona, a fine-boned woman unaccountably dressed in a high-necked ruffled white nightgown, sat in the brocade armchair next to the fireplace, her translucent skin like porcelain china.

"Mona?" Fred repeated.

Mona didn't respond, her gaze fixed on the fire.

"I must apologize," Fred said. "My wife doesn't always feel like chatting these days."

"That's perfectly fine." Connie unfolded a crocheted afghan and tucked it around Mona. The woman didn't acknowledge the gesture nor grab the blanket when it slipped off her shoulder.

"Her mind wanders off sometimes, too. Some days farther than others."

Faith sat down next to the man. "That's all right, Fred. I'm going to heat up some soup in a minute. How does that sound?"

"Soup sounds wonderful," Fred said. "I may need to help Mona a bit with it."

"It's from that restaurant," she clarified to her mother. "And remind me. I have a question about that place."

∽

A short while later, Fred and Mona sat kitty-corner at a table in the Mermaid's Purse dining room. Faith watched from the kitchen doorway as Fred patiently spooned soup into his wife's mouth, pausing occasionally to wipe her face with the napkin he tucked into the neck of her nightgown. After each spoonful, Mona closed her eyes and swallowed, like a baby bird taking sustenance from its mother, while Fred waited with the next portion.

"Mom," Faith whispered. "Come look at this."

Holding her own bowl of soup and a round of David's warmed bread, Connie paused behind her daughter. "He's a saint," she said. "We should be so lucky."

"Do they have any children?"

"They had one. A son. Fred told me he passed of a heart attack a few years ago. Their church recommended them for the town's temporary housing program."

"No other family?"

"Only a brother of Fred's, but he's all the way out in Iowa, with health problems of his own."

"Do you think Mona will be okay here?" Faith asked.

"Of course. Why do you ask?"

"I'm a little worried about her. She seems to require a lot of care."

"Fred appears to be very good at that."

"But he's fragile, too." Although alert and sharp, Fred had moved slowly as he helped his wife to the dining room.

"They're still better off here than they were in their house, all alone. When I think of the two of them there without power . . ." Connie shuddered.

"Of course they're better off. I'm just trying to be practical and think about the support they'll need. And about you."

"Wasn't that the point of *your* staying? To help out? Honestly, Faith. We just had this conversation. You haven't even unpacked and already you're trying to run things. As far as I'm concerned, Fred and Mona are our guests. And they can stay as long as they like. So if you're through giving me advice, I think I'll go and sit." She started toward the dining room with her bowl.

"Mom, wait. Where are you going?"

Connie turned in surprise. "To eat with Fred and Mona, of course."

"But you're the innkeeper. The guests don't expect you to eat with them. We—the staff—usually eat in here. Even bed-and-breakfast staff."

Connie discounted Faith's comments with a wave of her bread. "That's the most ridiculous thing I've ever heard. The next thing I know, you'll be showing up in that chef's coat and beanie of yours."

"Come on, Mom. I would never . . ."

"Maeve and I talked about it. After the trauma of the storm, we want these people to feel very much at home, for as long as they're here. That means we bend the rules some. Now, if you prefer to eat alone in the kitchen like a servant, be my guest. I'll be taking my meals in the dining room. *With* my guests." With that, Connie went and settled herself at Fred and Mona's table.

Frustrated, Faith filled a bowl for herself and dragged a lone stool up to the counter. She hadn't given much thought to the inn's operation under these emergency conditions, but now that her mother had clarified things, she would try to adjust. Unfortunately, in her professional experience, things could get awkward when boundaries were crossed, like Faith's awkwardness with Piquant's penthouse customer.

Faith swirled a piece of bread in David's soup, finding them both unexpectedly tasty. Yes, she thought, there were fewer surprises when guests and staff knew their place.

31

Though Faith had set places for them in the dining room, Roxanne and Gage didn't return for dinner. After the meal, Connie settled Fred and Mona in Maeve's hastily cleared first-floor quarters while Faith spent the evening prepping the coffee urn and assembling a breakfast strata from odds and ends of cheese and vegetables that she found in Maeve's crisper.

When mother and son still had not returned by the time Faith slid the breakfast casserole into the fridge, she began to wonder if the pair were stuck up at the beach, or if something had happened to them. Three-quarters of the town remained in darkness, a hardship that led the town to impose an eight o'clock curfew.

Shutting the refrigerator, Faith thought she heard a car door slam and slipped out back to investigate. From the dark driveway, she followed the path around front, where a police cruiser had pulled over a Suburban packed with teenagers.

"Didn't your folks tell you about the curfew?" The officer twirled his flashlight inside the car. "Until everybody has power again, everybody's inside by eight." For good measure, he ordered all of the passengers out of the car. Faith squinted, but the darkness made it difficult to make out any of their features. Certainly they were about Gage's age, but she couldn't determine if he was among them. The officer then put the driver through the paces of a sobriety test. Faith covered a smile as the burly boy in a hoodie gamely touched his nose and tightrope-walked the stretch of road illuminated by the officer's flashlight while his friends giggled on the sidewalk. Satisfied, the policeman allowed everyone back into the vehicle.

"Go home now. I'll give you thirty seconds before I start taking names and calling parents. And don't forget: you're allowed only one other passenger besides the driver. Next time, I'll ticket you for that."

Faith watched the two sets of taillights recede into the night, then decided to go to bed. She was upstairs brushing her teeth when she heard the front door open. After stepping out to the darkened second-floor hallway, Faith saw Roxanne slip inside alone, shut the door soundlessly behind her, then lean against it, eyes closed, her chest convulsing with sobs.

Roxanne remained there a few moments. Eventually, she appeared to compose herself. She ran up the stairs to her room, passing right by Faith, who had hidden in an alcove.

"Did you put the trash out like I asked? It's an early pickup tomorrow." Connie whispered once Faith slid into bed.

"Crap. I forgot. I'll take care of it right now."

Faith did a quick tour of the inn, bundling the refuse from unoccupied rooms. She grabbed a flashlight and carried the trash outside to a pair of plastic receptacles. As she was about to stuff the garbage inside the first one, something at the bottom caught her eye.

Setting the trash down, Faith aimed her flashlight at what was clearly a photo album. The large gold-rimmed oval cutout on its cover framed a pair of newlyweds. Faith recognized the bride instantly: Roxanne, in a body-hugging mermaid gown, a pearl tiara nestled in coils of permed hair, smiling dreamily at her new husband.

Roxanne had thrown out her wedding album.

Faith glanced over her shoulder, as though the woman might materialize and accuse her of snooping, then quickly picked up the trash and dropped it on top of the album. As she walked back inside, Faith wondered why Roxanne hadn't just discarded the album up at the beach with all her other ruined belongings. Had she intended to save the wedding memento, then had second thoughts?

She couldn't blame any of the storm survivors for those doubts. It must be torturous to make those decisions under such pressure, forced in the heat of the moment to choose what to keep, and what to abandon.

32

When Faith came down just before six the next morning, she found Roxanne at the kitchen farm table, freshly showered and nursing a cup of coffee.

"Hope you don't mind. I helped myself." Roxanne lifted her cup, her eyes red-rimmed and puffy—from crying, Faith assumed as she preheated the oven.

"I just wish I'd beaten you down here." Faith poured herself a mug. "They won't keep me around here very long if the guests wake up before the cook."

"Your mom's the boss. I think your job is safe."

"I'm putting everything out in the dining room shortly." Faith stacked butter and jam on a tray, hoping Roxanne would take the hint. After yesterday's conversation with her mother, Faith was all for communal dining, but did that mean everyone would have full run of the kitchen, too? She and Connie hadn't really defined that boundary.

"Join me." Roxanne patted the place next to hers.

"Would love to, but I'm on duty. We missed you at dinner." Faith slid the strata into the oven.

"I'm so sorry. I should have called, I guess. It's just . . . We were almost done, everything packed and ready to go, and then Mitch showed up."

At the man's name, Roxanne's voice caught. Faith turned to see her gripping her mug, lips pressed together fiercely.

"Mitch?" Faith asked.

"My ex. Gage's dad. He's being really difficult about custody, in spite of . . . Anyway, he showed up last night, and ended up taking Gage. Not 'taking' taking," she clarified, at Faith's look of alarm. "He took Gage to his place. He stays with him a lot. It's part of our arrangement. For now, anyway. I only wanted to make sure the girlfriend wouldn't be there before I let Gage leave. That set Mitch off."

"But isn't that a normal thing to ask in these situations?" Some of Faith's friends who dated single fathers had told Faith how protective the ex-wives were about their kids.

"You would think." Roxanne shook her head. "But not according to Mitch. He made this huge scene in front of all the volunteers. *And* Gage."

"I'm sorry," Faith said awkwardly, surprised at how much personal information Roxanne had shared.

"Don't be. Mitch's a jerk. Especially when he's angry. The main reason I left him." Roxanne got up from the table. "But he's Gage's father, so I have to act like he's human. And try to be civil. That's what my divorced girlfriends say, anyway."

"What does your lawyer say?"

Roxanne sighed. "We haven't gotten that far yet. Things happened . . . fast. He's still fighting me on the separation. Says he can't understand how I could split up our family."

As Roxanne elaborated on her estranged husband's behavior, Faith began to see why she had ditched her wedding album.

"And I suppose this storm thing will drag things out even further. I know I should be doing something, but I can't even find the energy. I feel like I'm paralyzed."

"Anyway." Roxanne attempted a smile. "Enough about me. Whatever you've made smells heavenly. Tarragon, right?"

"Exactly. Good nose. You like to cook?"

"I dabble. Nothing fancier than bar food, usually. It's the only job where I could work my hours around Gage. Mitch would watch him at night. Until he started getting jealous of some of my customers, and I'd have to move to another bar. But that's the extent of my cooking experience. Maybe I can help out here at some point. *If* I ever get my own act together. But for now . . ." She grabbed a granola bar from the basket Faith was filling. "I've got to get back to my house before my friend's truck gets there. She managed to reserve the last remaining storage locker in the county for me yesterday. Our entire life at the moment fits into a ten-by-ten-foot cubbyhole. How depressing is that?"

Very depressing. Faith could relate to the limited belongings. She and her mother had traveled pretty lightly when she was growing up, whittling down their possessions over a number of moves. But if nothing else, the experience had taught Faith how to prioritize. She was shifting the strata to the other oven rack to cook it evenly when the doorbell's shrill rasp pierced the heart of the inn.

At the same time, Fred wandered into the kitchen, wearing his exact layers from the night before. "Good morning. Could I bother you for a cup of tea for Mona? I like to let it cool a bit before she drinks it."

"Of course. Give me one second. I've got to get the door. And breakfast is nearly ready." The front buzzer jangled again, more insistently this time. Where was her mother to run interference? Fingers of panic pinched Faith's gut, which struck her as ridiculous, given the fact that she routinely turned out a hundred or more multicourse meals every night at Piquant.

This is going to take some getting used to. Heading to the door, she longed for the buffer that had insulated her from restaurant clientele. Here at the inn, Faith felt ill equipped to help the boarders cope with their problems.

Faith cut off the buzzer's third blip by opening the door. Two middle-aged women stood on the inn's porch: an athletic brunette with a ponytail clutching a suitcase, and a shorter female leaning on a metal cane, her hair tucked under a fuchsia baseball cap. The pair regarded Faith with similar hazel gazes over matching freckled noses. Sisters, Faith decided. It would have been nice if Connie had given her a heads-up about their newest boarders, but her mother had yet to make an appearance that morning.

"Come on in." Faith smiled to hide her annoyance. "We're so happy the mayor sent you our way."

The brunette frowned. "Nobody sent us. We found you online."

Had someone advertised the inn's offer to host storm survivors? Faith raised her eyebrows. "You know, it doesn't matter how you got here. We're happy to help anyone impacted by the hurricane." They would figure out the finances later, she thought.

"We weren't impacted at all," said the woman in the baseball cap. "I'm Grace Abbott, and this is my sister, Merrill. We've come to Wave's End to volunteer, and we're looking for a place to stay."

Merrill offered Faith her phone. "This came up when we searched for inns in the area."

Faith took the phone and stared. There, in full color on the *Beacon's* website, under the headline "New Innkeeper Claims Her Prize," were Maeve, Connie and Faith in the photo Bruce had taken on this very porch, accompanied by a lengthy article that Faith didn't bother to read. When had her mother sat for an interview? Well, of *course* Connie would make herself available if it involved spending time with Bruce Neery.

"I told you we should have phoned," said Grace, watching Faith's reaction.

Merrill took her phone back. "With so much lovely publicity, I'm not surprised you're filled up."

"We've come all the way from Lancaster, Pennsylvania. Can you recommend someplace else to stay?" Grace asked, leaning on her cane. Faith hesitated only a second before reaching out to take Merrill's suitcase.

"Don't be silly. Of course you'll stay here. We've got plenty of room." With that, she opened the door to her mother's first official paying guests— the only ones who wouldn't rely on the town's emergency vouchers.

"Welcome to The Mermaid's Purse, ladies. You're just in time for breakfast."

33

"Coming here was Grace's idea," explained Merrill, the taller sister and older by three years, digging into the slice of strata Faith set in front of her. Merrill had overruled an antsy Grace, insisting they wait and eat a hot breakfast before volunteering.

Sickened by the storm's devastation chronicled on television, Grace had compelled them to travel the nearly one hundred and fifty miles from their Pennsylvania homes.

"The birds were the last straw." Grace leaned her cane against the table. "It's bad enough these families have to endure the destruction," she said, her hand trembling as she brought a bite of the egg dish to her mouth. "But when they talked on television about how the local birds had left the shore area . . . Well, when Mother Nature drives even the native birds away, that's when you know things are tough. We had to come and do something."

Watching the woman struggle to eat, Faith wondered how much she could physically contribute to the relief effort.

"Okay, you're all set," announced Connie, who had met the sisters earlier as Faith was seating them in the dining room. "I've arranged a room for the two of you on the second floor. That is, if you're sure the stairs won't be too much for you." She eyed Grace's cane.

"Not at all, thank you. In fact, I'll go with you now and have a look."

With Grace out of sight, Faith leaned over, unsure how to pose her question. "Will your sister be okay here?" she asked.

Merrill set down her fork. "Grace is quite the independent one. And tougher than she looks. Although if her oncologist had any idea she were here, she'd probably shoot the both of us. As it is, we skipped out on a doctor's visit today."

"Should you have done that?"

"My sister's doing very well. She's tired, but her treatments are done, and the doctors are optimistic. She's supposed to be home resting, though, not running up and down the East Coast volunteering." Merrill leaned over confidingly. "But just try to keep that woman down. When you've been a midwife as long as she has, delivering babies at all hours, it's kind of hard to just relax."

"She's a midwife? That's so cool, helping mothers give birth at home."

"Actually, most of the women deliver at a hospital. But if you want my advice, don't even get into that hospital-versus-home-birth debate with my sister. She'll win every time. Grace has some hospital stories that'll curl your hair."

"Not mine! It's poker straight after the chemo," laughed Grace, rejoining them.

"I was just telling Faith about your journey," explained Merrill.

Grace grimaced. "Journey *schmourney*. Please just say cancer, will you? It came down to me needing a break from my cancer, Faith, and my sister here offering to drive my getaway car."

"We're a regular Thelma and Louise," Merrill said with a grin.

Grace grabbed her cane. "Come on, Thelma. Let's go figure out how we can help these poor folks, since they're the reason we came all this way."

34

With their newest guests off to serve the Wave's End community by volunteering at the church, as suggested by Faith, and with Fred and Mona comfortable in the salon, Fred reading to his wife from *National Geographic*, Connie decided to go food shopping.

"I might be a while," she said after she and Faith made the food list. "There's still only one supermarket with power."

Enjoying the solitude of the kitchen after the hectic morning, Faith unearthed a pair of well-used cookie sheets from a drawer under the oven and set about oiling them. While dinner preparations would have to wait until her mother's return, she could at least get a jump start on a roasted vegetable soup that would use up the produce in Maeve's fridge. Soup and a spiral ham, she decided, the leftover meat going for sandwiches. She could already see that with the comings and goings of guests, mealtimes at The Mermaid's Purse needed to be flexible; things like soups and salads would be handy "grab-and-go" options.

In quick succession, Faith peeled and sliced sweet potatoes, then cored and chopped red peppers, piling all onto the sheets before topping them with onion rounds, a drizzle of olive oil, and generous handfuls of dried oregano and parsley plus a sprinkle of red pepper flakes.

It might take a little while, she thought, sliding the sheets into the heated oven, but she would find her rhythm in this Spartan kitchen. Sometimes cooking could be about keeping things simple, reducing the art to the most common denominator—like toasting rounds of leftover Blue Osprey bread under the broiler and topping them with melted cheese to serve with the soup.

Just the act of organizing the meal in the solitude of the kitchen relaxed Faith; she hummed softly as the vegetables began to meld together and give off a strong, savory aroma. In the kitchen, she was in control—the way a certain hotel chef had commanded his station many years ago, on a seminal night that had changed Faith's life.

It had happened during one of her mother's tedious time-share weekends, the third or fourth she dragged Faith to in as many months. After sitting through hours of confusing presentations on ownership, exchanges and vacation club points, her mother accepted the salesman's invitation for a drink. She set up Faith alongside her with a Shirley Temple and a crossword puzzle book, but the bored ten-year-old managed to slip away. Faith explored the hotel and ended up in the darkened, deserted dining room. From here she could observe the imposing chef in the open kitchen at the far end; his tall, pleated hat quivered as he labored beneath white-hot stainless lamps. His hands flew as he diced, scraped and stacked with precision, oblivious to the wide-eyed young girl inching toward him.

Mesmerized, Faith imagined herself performing the same culinary sleight of hand under the lights one day, wielding knives like surgical instruments.

Eventually, the chef sensed her presence and looked up, raising his knife in salutation. He pointed to a table, inviting her to come closer.

This acknowledgment was all it took. By the time her panicked mother located her a few minutes later, Faith had decided to become a chef.

From that point on, she never looked back, and she worked in any restaurant that would hire her, in any capacity. She hostessed, bused, waitressed, and washed dishes, absorbing both dining room and kitchen operations even after moving east to attend culinary school.

The rest was history, she thought, checking the tenderness of the roasting vegetables. Now she needed a pot large enough to hold soup for ten; certainly Maeve would have a stockpot or lobster pot somewhere. As she began to rummage through the cabinets, a howl like a caged animal's came from the direction of the salon.

Pixie. Annoyed, Faith set the stockpot on the counter and hurried out.

But the scene she encountered in the salon had nothing to do with the recalcitrant pet. Instead, it was Mona, come to life, up on her feet and growling and clawing at her sweet husband like an out-of-control alley cat.

35

"It's all right," Fred told Faith. "Stay back. She gets like this sometimes." He held his hands in front of his face, shielding himself from his wife's flailing.

"What should I do?" Faith asked, panicked. "Call nine-one-one?"

"No. Please don't. She'll calm down in a minute."

Faith inched closer, keeping outside the range of Mona's blows, some of which were landing dangerously close to Fred's ears. "Tell me what to do," she whispered.

Instead of answering, Fred cooed at his wife. "Mona, sweetie. It's me, Fred. Everything's okay. You're safe. I'm here." He kept up a steady stream of reassurances like mantras until Mona began to calm down, her fists unclenching as the agitation visibly drained from her body. The pair stared at each other for a few long moments, Fred's eyes warm and loving and Mona's like a trapped animal's, until Mona eventually dropped her arms in surrender and licked her lips thirstily.

Once he was certain the episode had ended, Fred, whose gaze never left his wife's face, tentatively reached for Mona's hand. As though someone were adjusting an interior dimmer, Mona's vacant eyes gradually brightened in recognition. She stepped toward her husband and dropped her face onto Fred's shoulder, soaking his shirt with her sweat.

Mona allowed Fred to lead her back to the sofa, where she crumpled into the corner. Fred leaned over and brushed a lock of damp hair from her eyes.

Faith perched on the sofa arm beside them. "Does this happen often?"

Fred hesitated. "From time to time. She doesn't know this place. I imagine it's scary for her. Disorienting."

"Of course it is, especially after the comfort of your home. Are you okay? Did she scratch you?"

"Don't worry about me, dear."

Faith put a hand on his shoulder. "Somebody needs to."

His shoulders slumped under her touch. "You mustn't say a word. Your mother promised she wouldn't tell."

"My mother knows about these . . . episodes?"

"She saw Mona have a little spell last night."

Faith sighed. "These are more than spells, Fred."

"Please. Don't tell anyone." Fred's bandaged fingers gripped Faith's. "They'll take my Mona away from me. I don't know what will happen to her if they do. And I . . . I would die without her."

36

Faith put the kettle on for Fred and Mona, then slipped outside and dropped onto the back steps. She should be angry with Connie for her complicity, but she understood her reluctance to tear apart such a devoted couple. Clearly, Fred would be lost without his wife.

Perhaps Fred was right. Maybe in a day or two, when Mona felt more at home at The Mermaid's Purse, her "spells," as Fred quaintly referred to them, would taper off. If they didn't, Faith and her mother would have to find another solution.

"Early in the day for a break, isn't it?"

Faith looked up with a start to find David standing on the sidewalk holding a red gas tank.

"Relax. I come in peace. With diesel and wood." He set the gas tank on the top step. "Dad's tied up at the paper. He asked me to swing by with reinforcements."

At the mention of Bruce, Faith realized she had never quizzed her mother about the men's connection.

"What's wrong?" he asked, leaning on the banister.

Faith pressed her hands on her knees. "One of our new boarders became a little . . . out of sorts, is all."

He mounted the steps, then peered through the window into the kitchen. "My father said you would be housing some locals. How's it going so far?"

"All right, I guess. It's barely been a couple of days. There's a mother and son who lost their rental, a couple of sisters from Pennsylvania who came to volunteer and an older couple. I think my mother said they lived over on Vine Street."

David turned. "You mean Fred and Mona?"

"You know them?"

"Yeah. I volunteer at the senior center sometimes. I lead some tai chi and relaxation classes. Mind if I go in and say hello?"

"I guess it's okay. But don't startle them. Mona's a little—" Before Faith could find the right word, David had opened the back door, releasing the smoky essence of Faith's roasted vegetables.

"Damn. The vegetables. I totally forgot about them." Faith scrambled up the steps.

"Rookie," David cracked.

"Don't even go there. You have no idea what's been going on around here this afternoon."

"I'm kidding." He held the door for her. "You rescue the veggies. I'll see about your guests."

Thankfully, the vegetables needed only a stir and a few more minutes. She set the timer for good measure, then wandered into the living room, where she found David sitting knee to knee with Mona, his hands cupping her ears and his forehead touching hers as he murmured words only Mona could hear.

"Something I picked up down in the islands," David said, releasing Mona, whose eyes remained closed. "Transference. Mona likes it, don't you, Mona?"

Mona's brows lifted slightly, her eyes darting beneath her lids like a baby's in slumber. A reflex, Faith decided, heading back to the kitchen. The earlier episode had already worn Mona out; David's voice simply had lulled her to a calmer place.

David followed her. "Skeptical, huh? You should try it."

"Why? Do you think I need calming?"

"It's very centering. I can show you. I'm not trying to make a move here, I swear."

"I wasn't worried about that. Thanks, but maybe another time. You know, the whole thing reminds me of my mother and her crystals," Faith said, opening and closing drawers under the pretext of searching for a utensil. In truth, she had turned away to hide her flushed cheeks, the consequence of imagining the not unpleasant sensation of David's head pressed to hers.

"What's the matter? You don't believe in that stuff, either?" he asked.

"Let's just say one too many quartzes for positivity is what landed her in this situation." Having scraped the roasted vegetables into the stockpot, she dropped a handful of bouillon cubes into a mixing bowl and diluted them with warm water before pouring that liquid into the stockpot. *Breathe,* she told herself.

"Bouillon *cubes?*" Swooning, David laid the back of his hand against his forehead in mock horror. "*Quelle horreur!* What would Bocuse say?"

Faith turned from the stove, impressed with his knowledge of Paul Bocuse, the Lyonnais chef who revolutionized French cooking in the sixties. "He would say that in a state of emergency, *vous improvisez.* You improvise." Using Maeve's hand mixer, Faith transformed the mixture into semi-smoothness as best she could. She set a low flame under the pot, then seasoned the soup with salt and pepper. *Ahh.* Her breathing had returned to normal.

"May I?" David plucked a wooden spoon from a drawer.

"Be my guest." Stepping aside, she watched him dip the spoon into the soup, then scrape a sample with his finger and taste it. "Mmm. Almost perfect. Except for one thing." He pulled a crumpled brown paper bag from his pocket and shook some of its contents onto his palm. Getting a look at the small, brown, crescent-shaped seeds, Faith grinned.

"Knew it. You one of those stoner cooks who throws pot seeds into everything?"

"Ha. Wrong. It's *kala jeera*. An Indian buddy of mine in the Caribbean introduced me to it."

"You always travel with your spices?"

"Not always. I grabbed it from the Osprey's kitchen earlier." He waved his palm near her face. "Smell. It's got a nutty-grassy thing going on."

"Nutty-grassy. Appetizing." Faith wrinkled her nose at its bitter odor. "I think I'll pass."

"Come on. Just a pinch. It'll complement the red pepper. I promise. Chefs are supposed to be open-minded."

"I am. I just know what I like."

"How can you be so sure if you haven't tried it?" David's tone bordered on flirtatious.

"All right. But just a smidge."

After crumbling some seeds into the soup, David stirred the mixture with a clean spoon and offered the utensil to Faith. Her tongue tingled as she rolled the flavors around in her mouth; the *kala jeera* elevated her soup from excellent to exotic. She could envision the zing his spice would add to rice or meat dishes.

"So? What do you think?" he pressed.

Faith set the spoon down. "It's kicky."

"I *told* you," he said, smacking the counter.

"Kind of like . . . a reggae band in my mouth," she cracked.

David's grin emphasized the tanned creases around his eyes. "So the fancy New York chef has a sense of humor."

"I have my moments. Sorry I doubted you."

"Apology accepted." Rubbing his hands together in anticipation, David glanced around the kitchen. "So, now that I've wowed you, what else can we cook up around here?"

"Sorry, my friend. This was a one-time collaboration. I run a pretty tight operation."

"Come on. You have to let me earn my keep."

Faith frowned. "What 'keep' is that?"

"Didn't your mother tell you? She invited me to stay here. As of this afternoon, I'm officially a boarder at The Mermaid's Purse."

37

Sure enough, the voucher David presented to Faith authorized the same short-term housing stipend from the town council as the other boarders'. Because Wave's End had condemned The Blue Osprey, David couldn't legally spend another night in his restaurant's cramped office/bedroom. That qualified the chef for emergency funding.

Reading the shock on Faith's face, David shoved his hands in his pockets. "Listen: if you have a problem with me staying here, I can try one of the other inns. No big deal."

"I didn't say that." Faith returned the voucher to him. "Besides, it's not my decision."

"Good, because rumor has it the others are full up. No room at the inn, as they say."

"Can't you stay with your father?"

"Ever since he downsized last year, he doesn't have much more space than I had at the restaurant."

"Why did he downsize?"

"Said he was trying to simplify things. Cut costs."

"Really?" Was Bruce's scaling back a result of his troubles at the paper?

"My mother really loved that house," David continued. "She'd be sad to know he sold it. Anyway, staying with him in that confined space would be . . . counterproductive. Bruce and me, we're like oil and water."

"Come on. My mother and I aren't exactly BFFs, and we're managing. Given the circumstances, couldn't you try to make it work?"

"It's complicated, Faith. When my mother died, I lost my ally. She always got me, so much more so than he did. Maybe because she and I were more left-brain, 'different drummer' kind of people. Where with my father, things always came very easily. For example, one day he decided this town needed a newspaper and built the *Beacon* from nothing."

"Don't sell yourself short. You built a business, too."

"I did, eventually. But back when I first told him my plan to go and work in the islands, he wasn't thrilled. He hated seeing me give up college. Chasing a pipe dream, I believe were his words."

"What did you do?"

"I left anyway, without even saying good-bye." He sniffed. "Not my proudest moment."

"But you came back."

David held up his hand. "I did. Prodigal son. Today, we're a work in progress, and I'd rather not rock that boat. He did offer his couch, but if it's all the same to you, I'd rather stay here. I *do* qualify, you know." David waved his voucher at her again.

"Yes, you do. I guess if it's okay with my mother, it's okay with me." Privately, Faith wasn't so sure this kitchen would be big enough for both of them. But David's presence might allow her to explore Bruce's motives for insinuating himself into the inn's—and therefore her mother's—business. Before she could frame her first question, the slam of a car door scuttled her plan. "And there's my mother now."

The two went outside to help Connie unload the car.

"Would you believe the supermarket generator blew right after I paid?" Connie asked once she was inside, setting the last of the groceries on the counter. "The entire place went dark. All the shoppers behind me were out of luck."

"I'm not surprised," said David. "They've been running that generator nonstop. They're the only game in town until the power is restored."

"I don't know where we'd be without your dad's generator, David. On my way back, I saw a guy on the highway selling generators out of a trailer. He had a line of customers a mile long." She left the room with an armload of paper products, leaving Faith and David alone in the kitchen.

"Desperate times, huh, Faith?"

Faith produced a net bundle from a grocery bag and dangled it in front of him. "What I *desperately* need is to have these onions chopped."

"I'm on it."

Despite her shock at David's new living arrangements, Faith had to admit she enjoyed collaborating with him on the evening meal. His unorthodox training aside, the man clearly knew his way around a kitchen, chopping the vegetables for Faith's chicken curry with the dexterity of a classically trained chef, then cleaning up in his own wake, methodically washing, wiping and storing utensils as soon as he finished with them.

"Do you mind?" he asked, a hand on the transistor radio. When Faith shook her head, David switched from the news station it had been tuned to since her arrival to a Spanish music station. Humming as he washed the last of the cookware, David then salsaed out to the living room to invite Fred and Mona to join them for a cup of tea. Dish towel draped over his arm, he fussed over the couple's table, speaking in an exaggerated Italian accent, his antics reviving the subdued Fred.

Indeed, once David departed for some pre-dusk surfing, Faith realized that her time with him in the kitchen had been the first occasion she had truly laughed since Nadine made landfall. The ponytailed chef with the surfboards in his jeep brought considerably more to the table than a paper sack of *kala jeera*.

His absence afforded Faith a chance to discuss Mona's earlier episode with her mother. "You should have told me when it happened," she said, as she and Connie put out plates and silverware for dinner.

"I know." Her mother shook her head. "It broke my heart to watch her. I wanted to talk to you about it. It's one thing to be a bit forgetful, but if Mona's a danger to herself or Fred, we might need to make a change."

"It's lucky David knows Fred and Mona. He helped to calm her."

"Yes. I'd say he's helped quite a bit." Connie's eyebrow arched as she set down a stack of plates with a clatter.

Faith resolutely tightened her ponytail. "Anyway, you're right. We need to do something. Let me give it some thought." She busied herself slicing some Italian bread Connie had bought home, refusing to take her mother's bait. Transference or no transference, Faith's stay at The Mermaid's Purse had an expiration date, even if her mother's departure seemed uncertain.

She had no intention of becoming too attached to the inn *or* to its newest boarder, no matter how much his presence seasoned the atmosphere.

38

With only the night's dessert left to prepare—bananas baked with a splash of orange juice and sprinklings of brown sugar, nutmeg and cinnamon—Faith opted for a nap upstairs, far from the generator's rumble, the inn's life support reduced to a distant hum. On her back on the trundle bed, however, her thoughts meandered back to David: whether he had a girlfriend, what type of woman might attract him. Chic hippie, she decided, rolling over and punching her pillow. He probably wooed her with beach picnics, homemade wine and puka beads—which *still* would be a damn sight better than any of her recent dates.

Faith's social life of late had been limited to texted banter with matches from her online dating profile that Ellie had set up as a joke. Faith found the matchmaking site a safe space from which to appraise the dating landscape without actually having to dive in—the way she observed her diners without ever leaving her kitchen.

At Ellie's urging, she'd gone on a few dates recently, none memorable. Many wrongly assumed Faith's presence on the site signaled a readiness to leap into their beds. She wasn't a prude, but it took more than a swipe to hold her interest. There was plenty of action around the kitchen if that's all she wanted.

One or two of the least terrible dates kept in touch, but, if anything, the experience sent Faith scurrying back to the safe haven of her kitchen, with its well-defined boundaries—well-defined, that is, until David appeared on the scene with his Caribbean *woo-woo*. Contrary to his earlier claim, he probably used that transference act as a pickup line.

At least the presence of another young man at the inn might be good for Gage. Faith felt for him: a teenager in a strange school in a strange town, a fish out of water while his parents navigated the tumultuous waters of divorce. Faith had suffered similarly through multiple moves, the threat of new partners in her mother's life, wondering how they would take to her, how much of her mother they would take from her.

Faith propped up her head on her elbow. Was Gage still with the dad and his girlfriend? She had no clue what parenting a teenage boy entailed, let alone one whose parents had recently split. She knew only that Roxanne, by her own admission, appeared overwhelmed. Merrill and Grace might be good company for the single mother, she thought, looking forward to the residents meeting one another at dinner.

Rolling over, she thought about the sisters at the church and hoped the ailing Grace wasn't overdoing it. Faith had only to look at Fred to see the consequences of that.

On her back again, she rubbed her face. Though her body yearned for rest, her overactive mind wouldn't cooperate. Finally, Faith sat up, a nap now out of the question. She decided to use the time to organize her things, which remained a jumbled mess in her suitcase. It took all of ten minutes to refold her belongings, place them in the bureau drawers Connie had assigned her, and slide her empty bag back into the closet alongside her mother's three boxes from the airport. What prized possessions had made the journey with her mother to Wave's End? Faith wondered, sitting down in front of the closet.

The first box rattled suspiciously when she picked it up: Connie's crystals. Of course they made the trip. She set that box aside.

Faith pulled back a flap of the second carton and caught a vivid splash of serape: the fringed blankets that had draped her mother's sofa and walls back in Albuquerque. Connie should spread them around The

Mermaid's Purse, she thought, visualizing the contrast of the brilliant Aztec designs against Maeve's sedate calicos and making a mental note to suggest this.

The final carton marked *Files and Contests* had sides as soft as flannel from frequent handling during their many moves. Faith could predict the files it held, having managed her mother's bank accounts and tax statements from the time she could wield a calculator.

Not that there'd ever been much to manage. Life with Connie had been a 1040A, with no schedules attached. Curious about her mother's state of affairs without her, Faith tugged that carton open, riffling through familiar folders labeled *Taxes, Rent, Utilities, Court* (an unfortunate incident when, after one mojito too many, Connie had been moved to join a street protest; mercifully, the judge let her off with community service). As for the *Contests* folder, Connie had no doubt already filed her winning Mermaid's Purse essay. Someday Faith would ask her to share it so she could find out what had so endeared her mother to Maeve.

About to close the box, she spotted one last folder at the back, its cardstock tab crudely lettered with a single name: *AUDREY*.

Faith frowned. She hadn't seen this folder before, and yet the name seemed familiar. Curious, she flipped open the file, which contained a single document: a yellowed birth certificate, the embossed notary's seal at the top corner rough under her finger.

This is a true certification of name and birth facts recorded in this office.

The certificate had been issued by a Dr. Robinson, an OB-GYN her mother saw for years, even after they had moved many miles from his practice. His office had an endless supply of lollipops, the fancy kind with chocolate centers, Faith recalled.

Though the field for the father's name had been left blank, the mother's name was filled in: *Rita Hennessey*.

Any agreement or difference between the child's surname and the surname of its father does not imply legitimacy or illegitimacy.

Below this statement, someone had neatly printed the child's full name: *Audrey Hennessey*.

Once again, the name stirred something in Faith, though nothing concrete came to mind. She couldn't even determine the child's age, since both the date of birth and the certificate's issue date had been blacked out with thick marker. Frustrated, she took the paper to the window, holding it up to the light to try to decipher the blocked-out fields. Why would someone alter a birth certificate, and why had her mother saved this one?

Unable to make out either date, Faith was turning the certificate over to try to interpret it from that angle when the bedroom door opened.

"Thought you might be ready to—" Connie halted, her sweeping gaze registering first the folder on the floor, then her daughter holding a paper up to the window.

"Faith Sterling! Who gave you permission to snoop through my things?"

39

Connie strode toward the window and snatched the certificate from Faith, who dropped onto the bed indignantly.

"I wasn't snooping. I used to take care of all that stuff, remember? And who's Audrey, anyway?"

Connie scooped the folder from the floor and tucked the certificate inside, hugging it to her chest. "Someone I knew a long time ago."

"Why do *you* have her birth certificate? Shouldn't her parents have it?"

"For . . . safekeeping."

Faith sat up suddenly. "Oh, my God. They're dead, right? Did they perish in some horrible accident?"

"Oh, my goodness, Faith. Of course they didn't."

"Well, that's a relief. So how old is Audrey now? The dates are blocked out."

"What is this, an interrogation?" Connie forced a chuckle, her hand on the doorknob. "It all happened years ago. It really doesn't matter."

Faith leaned back on her elbows. "Wait a minute. Was this, like, some scandalous unwed mother back in the day?" she teased. "Because that's not a big deal anymore."

"Of course not. Some things are just . . . private. I promised a friend a long time ago I'd hold on to it for safekeeping. That's all." The finality of her tone indicated the subject of the mysterious Audrey was closed.

Faith frowned. "Come on, Mom. What's the big mystery? You've never once mentioned a friend named Rita. We're both adults here. Can't you just be straight with me?"

Connie stared at her a moment, then slowly walked to the bed. She sat down next to Faith and opened the folder. "Actually, maybe it's time I was." With a trembling hand, she passed the certificate to her daughter. "It's time I told you about Audrey, Faith. Because Audrey is *you*."

40

Her blood pounding in her ears, Faith stared in confusion at the child's name—*her* birth name—on the certificate she now gripped. For a split second, while her mother struggled to explain, she expected to learn she'd been adopted. What other explanation could there be?

But no. That's not what Connie was saying at all. She wasn't talking about adoption. Instead, she repeated these words: "Faith Sterling *was* Audrey Hennessey. And Connie Sterling *was* Rita Hennessey."

Finally, after they'd gone around and around, Faith began to understand. In a quiet yet life-changing moment more than twenty years ago, a sympathetic sheriff had helped a distraught Rita Hennessey change her name and that of her child to the ones they answered to today: Connie and Faith Sterling.

"But why?" Faith's fingers left damp prints on the brittle certificate.

"To protect us," said Connie simply. When she attempted to take Faith's hand, her daughter pulled it away.

"Protect us from what?"

"From your father's temper. From everything." Drawing a long, tremulous breath, her mother got up and gazed out the window. "I was desperate. This one night. You were barely four. Your father and I had a terrible argument." She glanced back at Faith. "Do you remember us fighting a lot?"

"Fighting? I don't think so. I barely remember *him*."

"We fought all the time. I always tried to shield you as best I could. Anyway, that night, I couldn't. He came home, completely out of his mind drunk, after losing a lot of money in a card game. He went crazy: cursing, throwing things, even putting his fist through a wall."

"Where was I?"

Connie massaged her face, her back still turned. "You were . . . sleeping. In your room. Anyway, that night was the last straw. The next day, I left you with a neighbor and went to the police. And after what the sheriff said . . ."

"What did he say? Mom, please look at me."

"He said . . ." Connie turned, her arms crossed across her chest, the strain of reliving the memory reflected in her trembling voice. "That the smartest thing to do would be to move the both of us far away."

"And did you?"

"Oh, I certainly did. I got us a ride from the shelter one night, in a friend's pickup truck."

"Wait, we stayed at a shelter?" Having volunteered often in New York's shelters and soup kitchens, it rattled Faith to learn she and her mother once needed those services themselves.

"Just for a short while. Anyway, on that bitterly cold night, I picked you up out of your bunk and—"

"*That's* where the bunk beds were," Faith said softly.

"What?" Connie looked over at Faith, bewildered.

"I was thinking about those bunk beds the other day. I couldn't remember where they were, except that you tucked me into the top one."

"I did. There was a woman, Alice, in the next bed. She cried all the time." Connie rubbed her nose. "Anyway, I wrapped you tight in a blanket and held you in my arms the entire way."

Faith massaged her neck, trying to picture the scenario. "Where did we go?"

"That night? To another shelter about a hundred miles away."

"How did you decide where to go?"

"Decide? I don't know, Faith. I may have tossed a coin, for all I know. You used to like that game. I only knew we had to put as many miles as possible between that man and us. The main thing was we made it out of there."

Faith sat a moment, digesting her mother's words.

"And what happened after that?"

"We stayed at the shelter for almost a month. I got some piecework at a factory and saved up enough to move us again, to a small apartment near the train tracks."

Reclining on the bed again, Faith stared at the ceiling. "This is surreal. Why don't I remember any of this?"

"I'm grateful you don't recall that nightmare time."

"Did you ever talk to him . . . my father . . . after that?"

"No."

"Did he ever come looking for us?"

"Not that I know of. But remember: the Internet didn't exist back then. There was no Google to look up people and places. Besides, our new names made it that much harder for him to find us."

It was as though her mother had signed them both into the witness protection program.

No wonder the name Audrey had felt familiar; her parents had addressed her that way for the first few years of her life—until the night she and her mother escaped her father's wrath by jumping into the back of a pickup and speeding away on a New Mexico highway.

A pickup truck, a midnight getaway, an assumed name. Her mother's story had all the makings of a Lifetime movie—except that until now, a pivotal scene, the big reveal, hadn't made it into the final cut.

"I'm sorry." Her mother's apology broke the long silence. "I should have told you. But as time went by, that moment in our lives seemed like a bad dream. I couldn't think of an easy way to explain the name change."

"So instead, you allowed me to live a lie all these years."

"It's not a lie. This is our truth, Faith."

"Maybe it's *your* truth, but I've barely had ten minutes to live with it." Faith got to her feet.

"Please don't be mad." Connie picked up the forgotten folder and offered it to her. "Here. It's yours now. No more secrets."

Faith got up and backed away, holding up her hands. "I'm not mad, exactly. Truthfully, I don't know how I feel. And I don't want that certificate. She . . . Audrey . . . doesn't exist."

"I understand you're upset, but—"

"*Do* you understand, Mom? I'm not so sure." Faith trembled as years of pent-up resentment resurfaced over her mother's blindsiding: her contests, her men, her fake vacations, her assuming ownership of this broken-down inn.

And now this revelation. It was too much.

"I understand you did this to protect me—us—and I appreciate that. I really do. But I need some time to process it." Faith studied her hands. "Maybe it would be better if I went back to New York."

"But you can't do that. The boarders are counting on you. You promised."

"You want to talk about promises? Your *moon and stars* and all that? Seriously, Mom. At the moment, your word is worth about as much as that stupid locket."

After Connie left her alone as she had requested, Faith lay on her back, shaken by the confrontation, the shock of hearing the first chapter of her life rewritten. From the time she had been small, *moon and stars* had been her mother's mantra, a postscript softening every wrenching announcement: that they were moving house once again because Connie couldn't make rent, or that she would have to eat cereal for dinner because that's all her mother's paycheck could cover. *You'll make lots of friends in the new town. Moon and stars.* Or *We'll have steak for your next birthday. Moon and stars.*

The expression became her mother's way of saying, "Cross my heart"—her pledge to do everything in her power to make good on those promises.

As a kid, Faith had been both reassured and enchanted by this declaration, due to its association with the antique gold locket nestled against the emerald satin lining of her mother's jewelry box. During the rare times Connie allowed her to take out the necklace, Faith would run her fingers over the diamond-encrusted crescent moon and orbit of stars on its front.

Connie would ease open the medallion with a fingernail, and Faith would make up stories about the young girl with the outsized hair bow on the left (Connie at age four), and the squinting boy on the right—Faith's uncle, seven years old and sporting a crew cut. Faith imagined her grandmother pressing the pictures into the miniature frames to hold son and daughter close to her heart.

This fantasy persisted into Faith's adolescence, until the day she confided her dream of wearing the locket on her wedding day, and her mother revealed the truth about the gold-plated necklace: that it had been an unwanted gift to her mother, Edna, Faith's grandmother. Its glittering stones weren't diamonds but cut glass, and though the images inside *were* of Connie and Connie's brother Lionel, they had been placed there by Connie's aunt, who fashioned the sentimental piece in the hopes of luring her sister, Edna, back to her husband and children.

Upon hearing that her grandmother had rejected the locket and sent it back from Las Vegas without a note, the piece lost all promise for Faith, as did the moon and stars mantra—although until now, she had tolerated the latter.

Connie hadn't hesitated to tell Faith the truth about her grand-mother that day. Why couldn't she have found a moment to divulge this other family secret?

But she hadn't. And now, all these years later, *moon and stars* left only a bitter taste in Faith's mouth, the legend of the locket and all it stood for as phony as the names on her birth certificate.

41

She didn't even *look* like an Audrey, Faith decided later, catching sight of herself in the china cabinet glass as she poured water into the dining room steam trays. An Audrey would have blond ringlets and a red bike and a father who showed up for birthdays and graduations and restaurant openings.

As Faith turned this way and that, a reproachful voice within chastised her for her heated words to her mother, reminding her that Connie's actions stemmed from a desperate but well-intentioned place. Still, Faith couldn't help feeling off-kilter after the revelation. Had her mother acted impetuously in whisking Faith away that night? Her parents' fighting sounded awful, but perhaps if they had seen a marriage counselor she wouldn't be standing here today with a different name.

Who are you? Faith demanded of her reflection. Was there a whole other life she might have lived as Audrey Hennessey?

Don't be ridiculous. A name's just a label, words on paper that don't define someone, she repeated to herself as she went about on autopilot, lighting chargers and toting pans of food between kitchen and dining room.

Once the evening meal was ready to serve, she slipped out onto the front porch to escape. Faith had set two goals for the evening: survive the dinner service and avoid her mother until she felt calm enough to discuss things.

Settled in a rocker, Faith mined her subconscious for memories of the long-ago desert night Connie had just described. Her mother must have cushioned her well from her father's misbehavior, because she recalled none of it. For better or worse, she remembered little of the man at all.

And to be swaddled and whisked away in the dead of night! Surely that adventure would have made an impression, bumping along in a pickup under the stars. She leaned her head on her hand, conjuring nothing. At least it explained the bunk beds, she thought as a tap-tapping in the dusk caused her to look up.

"Anybody home?" The tapping belonged to Grace, half of the Abbott sisters returning from their long day of volunteering. "Merrill let me out in front. Less walking."

Faith jumped up and helped her to the porch, where Grace waved her cane at the rockers. "May I join you?"

Reluctantly, Faith agreed, forcing herself to make conversation. "How was your afternoon at the church?"

"There's so much to do. It's overwhelming for these poor people. They are literally shell-shocked. One minute they're going about their business, and the next day their lives are turned upside down. Can you imagine such a thing?"

"Maybe," Faith said softly. "You're very kind to come here and help."

"It's not kindness. It's pure selfishness. Like I told Merrill when I asked her to bring me here, I'm playing the cancer card."

"*This* is your idea of a winning hand? A visit to Armageddon?" Faith's broad wave encompassed The Mermaid's Purse and beyond. "Why not take a dream vacation to Hawaii? Or Bali?"

Grace chuckled. "I've traveled plenty. I don't begrudge anyone who celebrates the end of treatment with something like that. It's unfair to judge; you never know what motivates people."

"That's for damn sure."

"Though I do feel a bit insignificant working in the church kitchen," Grace mused. "I'd love to be up there at the beach, shoveling sand

and tearing down Sheetrock; doing something tangible to start them on their rebuilding process. But clearly I'm not ready for *that*." Grace tapped her cane for emphasis.

"But they have to eat," Faith said. "You're fulfilling a basic human need while they cope with everything else. You're taking that one extra thing off their plate, so to speak."

"You're right, Faith. I hadn't thought of it quite like that. But of course *you* would. You're a chef." Aiming her cane at the mailbox, Grace tapped the ebony casing that swung beneath it. "Do you know what this is?"

"A mermaid's purse. This place is named for them, apparently."

"An apt choice, I'd say." Grace got to her feet and lifted the black casing from the mailbox rack, balancing it on her lap as she sat back down. "Mermaids' purses are egg sacs. They safeguard the fertilized eggs of certain types of fish. Skate, ray, dogfish. Even some sharks."

"Sharks?" Faith glanced up in surprise. "How in the world do you know that?"

The midwife grinned. "You're looking at an amateur conchologist. Merrill and I grew up on the coast of Maine. Picked up a few tidbits about sea life." Grace knocked on the mermaid's purse. "Anyway, these hard black shells remain after the eggs safely hatch. So you can see how vital the mermaid's purse's contribution is, nurturing those bodies within."

"Yes, of course." Faith's thoughts wandered back to the conflict with Connie.

"Not unlike what you and your mother are doing here at The Mermaid's Purse. Providing temporary shelter to the displaced in their time of need. I'm sure you didn't expect to find yourself in this position, but these people will remember your kindness long after they leave." Grace carefully rehung the egg case on the mailbox, then rapped it twice. "Long after The Mermaid's Purse is empty."

42

Faith holed up in the kitchen for most of dinner, studiously ignoring her mother as Connie came and went with bins of dirty dishes. After the meal was over, Merrill came looking for her.

"Sorry to bother you, but we made a mountain of garlic bread at the church today, and I reek of it," said Merrill. "Any ideas for getting this god-awful smell off my hands?"

"In my business, garlic's practically my perfume. Rubbing a little salt and lemon juice on them will do it." Faith found a lemon in the crisper and gave it to Merrill.

"Thank you. And great dinner, by the way. Your mother's lucky to have you here."

I'm not sure for how much longer. "And you're blessed to have such a fantastic sister. I just had a chat with her outside."

"You mean the Energizer bunny?" Merrill laughed. "I don't know how Grace does it. I felt exhausted by four o'clock."

"Seriously, the hours you two put in today would kill a—" Horrified at her own thoughtlessness, Faith clapped her hand to her mouth. "God, I'm so sorry. I just meant—"

Merrill waved away the apology. "No harm done. I think the work is the best medicine for Grace right now. Now as for me . . ." She glanced around the kitchen. "You wouldn't by chance have any wine around, would you? Not many places open with the power still out, or I would have stopped."

Although unsure the bed-and-breakfast could legally serve alcohol to guests, after her own roller coaster of a day, Faith decided the idea of unwinding with a drink was worth flouting a law or two. It provided the excuse she needed to avoid both her mother and her own thoughts.

"You're in luck," Faith replied. "I happen to know The Mermaid's Purse has quite the stash."

Maeve certainly would not deny her temporary staff a glass of wine or two, Faith thought, unearthing a dusty cabernet from beneath the cellar stairs. Glasses in hand, Faith and Merrill settled in front of the fireplace in the salon. They had the room to themselves: Fred and Mona retired right after dinner, there had been no sign of David since he left to go surfing earlier, Grace had long since said her good-nights, and Connie soon followed with a thin smile and a wave.

Only Roxanne, solo again while Gage spent another evening at his father's, briefly considered Faith's invitation to join them.

"Maybe another time," she said finally. "I'm not really good company right now. Besides, I've got some paperwork from the insurance company. I can't bear to look at it, but I've got to make myself do it."

"*Salut.*" Merrill touched her glass to Faith's as Roxanne headed up to her room.

"I'd say we've earned this." Sipping her wine, Faith thought back over the last ten hours, lingering first on Mona's disturbing attack on Fred, then on her mother's unsettling revelation.

"Grace will be upset to learn she missed out."

"What? Oh, well. Maybe another night." Setting her glass down, Faith focused on her guest. "Speaking of Grace, it must be so exciting to be a midwife."

"A lot of lost sleep, that's for sure." Merrill sipped her wine. "But she loves it. I'm sure she could tell you the exact number of babies she's brought into the world."

Reminded of Ellie, Faith proceeded to tell the story of how, when her roommate first revealed her pregnancy, she talked about wanting to experience a natural, drug-free delivery. She persuaded Faith to watch an episode of *Call the Midwife* with her, but switched it off in horror halfway through.

"Midwifery is quite a bit more modern these days," Merrill laughed.

How *was* Ellie making out without her? Faith wondered. "Did you ever want kids yourself?"

"I did. Problem was, my husband didn't. Thus ended that fairy-tale marriage," she said wryly. "After that, it never seemed to be the right time. Or the right guy." Merrill's work as a technology consultant offered a flexible schedule, which accommodated this trip to Wave's End, Faith learned as they chatted.

"Yes, the guy thing. Why is that part always so hard?" Faith sipped her wine. "Does Grace keep in touch with the moms after?"

"Are you kidding? They're devoted to her. It's like a cult. Some even name their babies for her."

Baby names. Faith couldn't escape the subject if she tried. Why had her mother christened her Audrey, and how had Connie come up with their new names? "What a lovely tribute." Faith groped for another subject. "So what about the rest of your family?"

"Well, we have a brother who's an attorney in San Francisco, and another—"

"Hold on a second." Faith cocked her head, distracted by a thud on the front porch. "Did you hear that?"

"Hear what?"

At a subsequent thump, Merrill nodded. "What do you think it is?"

"It's probably just David, another resident who arrived this afternoon. Maybe he's bringing his stuff back. I'll go see."

"What if it's not?" Merrill asked worriedly.

"Then I'll scare them off. I live in New York, remember? I've slapped away a pickpocket or two in my time," Faith joked.

But at another loud bump from outside, the sound of a rocker hitting the house, Faith felt a twinge of anxiety. She started toward the entrance, only to halt as the door swung open, bringing her face-to-face with the hooded figure lurching into the Mermaid's Purse's front hall.

43

"Jesus, Gage!" Faith sagged against the hallway wall. "What the hell are you doing? You scared me."

"Sorry. Trying to be quiet," Gage mumbled. The teen swayed slightly and reeked of smoke, as though he'd spent the evening around a campfire—a campfire with cocktail service, Faith judged from his heavy breath and slurred speech.

"Well, you didn't exactly nail that. It's okay. I know him," Faith said as a wide-eyed Merrill joined them. "This is Gage, Roxanne's son. You met her earlier? Gage, Merrill's staying here with her sister. They've come to Wave's End to volunteer."

"Cool." Blinking, Gage did his best to focus on them. When he swayed again, each woman grabbed an arm and guided the boy to sit on the couch, where he promptly flopped forward like a rag doll.

"You okay?" Faith squatted in front of the boy.

"Yes. No. Leave me alone." Gage swatted the air.

"I'll get your mom, then."

Gage's head jerked up. "No. Def do *not* do that. She'll be super pissed." In his inebriated state, *super* came out like *shuper*.

Faith agreed with the boy's prediction, imagining the hard-talking Roxanne's reaction to her son's current condition.

Gage rubbed his face just then, his hand coming away bloody.

"What happened?" Looking closer, Faith noticed Gage's bruised cheek. "Did you get into a fight?"

"No. It's cool. We were just messing around."

"That's a pretty nasty cut for just messing around."

"I could wake Grace to come and take a look at it," Merrill offered.

"I think we'll let Roxanne deal with this," Faith responded. "But maybe you could get some ice for him while I wake her up?"

As Faith headed upstairs, a siren pierced the night. Such sounds were practically white noise in her Brooklyn neighborhood, but in the foreign landscape of Wave's End, she couldn't always decipher the sounds of the seaside in crisis. Like the mournful bleat of a foghorn this morning, which Fred helpfully explained had nothing to do with encroaching mist but instead alerted residents to an imminent high tide and threat of local flooding.

This siren sounded dire. As she reached the second floor on her way to Roxanne's room, a fresh wave of alarms whined, followed by another, each louder and more insistent, layers of distress responses from surrounding towns. Faith let herself onto the balcony that ran the length of the second story and faced the Atlantic Ocean.

Outside in the fall night, the sirens grew deafening and ominous. Overhead, spotlights crisscrossed the eastern sky with metronome precision, dissecting billowing clouds of smoke like lasers. The acrid aroma of smoke saturating the crisp air stung Faith's nostrils—the same caustic odor clinging to the inebriated thirteen-year-old snoring noisily on Maeve's couch downstairs.

Please don't let Gage have anything to do with this, she willed as the emergency sirens reached fever pitch east of The Mermaid's Purse. With any luck, Gage had spent the evening at a friend's home, absorbing the smoky essence of a backyard fire pit.

"Hey, Faith. Where's all that smoke coming from?"

Startled, Faith turned to find Roxanne behind her in a slip of a nightgown, hugging herself against the crisp night that hinted at winter.

"The beach, I think."

"As if everyone up there hasn't been through enough already."

"Come inside. You'll freeze. We'll find out soon enough what's going on." Back in the second-floor hallway, Faith chose her words carefully. "Listen: I think we might have a situation with Gage. I need to show you something."

Mystified, Roxanne followed Faith to the railing.

"There." Faith pointed down at the couch where the teen now sprawled, snoring noisily. Hearing them, a kneeling Merrill held an ice pack up at them in greeting.

"What the . . . ?" Roxanne dashed downstairs to the sofa, where she stared at her son. "I don't get it. He was supposed to be at his dad's," she said when Faith caught up.

"Looks like you have this covered." Merrill handed Faith the ice, then slipped upstairs.

Meanwhile, Roxanne had spotted the gash on her son's cheek, and bent over for a closer look. "If that rat bastard laid a hand on him, I'll kill him. First thing tomorrow, I'm calling a lawyer. If Mitch thinks he can do this, then he can just forget about shared cus—"

"You might want to talk to Gage first."

"Why?" Roxanne's wary eyes narrowed.

"Because I saw Gage when he got home. And he seemed a little . . . messed up."

"I can see that. He might even need stitches. Why didn't you wake me up?"

"I was on my way to do that. But by messed up, I mean he was pretty—"

Just then, Gage made his presence known with a strangled cough. Faith dove for the couch, yanking a throw rug out of harm's way seconds before the boy rolled over and vomited mightily all over Maeve's hardwood floor.

44

With the mortified Roxanne refusing all assistance, Faith finally left her and the dry-heaving Gage around one thirty and slipped into bed, leaving her door ajar in case Roxanne needed her.

Not completely at ease beside her mother, it took Faith a while to fall asleep. When she did, she slept fitfully, caught up in a disturbing dream in which she found herself crammed in the back of a pickup truck with a pack of pregnant women, each in the throes of labor and tended to by Faith's mother. As each woman delivered, Faith would ask the baby's name, but the newborn's cries drowned out their response. Agitated and desperate to escape, Faith pounded on the window of the cab to get the driver's attention, but he ignored her banging. She woke up disoriented as dawn's first diluted light streamed through the blinds and squinted at the clock: 5:40 a.m. Permitting herself five more minutes, she lay back down, crossing her arms beneath her head and replaying Gage's dramatic homecoming, which ended with the boy as sick as a dog.

Dog. Faith sat up, remembering a detail from the previous night. She'd only known Gage a few days, but in that brief time, he'd never been without that length of chain, his link to the missing Tucker. Even Roxanne had half joked she'd have to wean her son from the dog leash when school reopened, like separating a toddler from a security blanket.

Last night, however, when the smoky and slurring Gage stumbled in, there had been no sign of Tucker's leash. Maybe it was still at his father's, or misplaced in the night's confusion. Either way, Faith imagined that once the boy sobered up, the leash's absence would upset him.

Faith dressed quietly, then slipped downstairs before anyone else had stirred at the inn. In the kitchen, she set about frenetically peeling and slicing apples and pears for a breakfast compote. While the fruit simmered in a nutmeg and cinnamon bath, its scent a rejuvenating aromatherapy, Faith searched the fridge for last night's leftover ham in preparation for breakfast fajitas. Oddly, the diced meat, along with some tomatoes she had chopped and the deli cheddar Connie had purchased the day before, had disappeared.

David. He must have gotten in late and made himself a feast. Sure enough, she found broken eggshells, toast crusts and greasy napkins in the trash. Thanks to his thoughtlessness, everyone would have a little less to eat this morning, she thought, slamming the fridge shut.

After pouring herself a second cup of coffee, she sat at the table, massaging the spot between her eyebrows where a headache threatened. David wasn't the only self-centered person at the inn, she realized. Yes, her mother's bombshell the previous day had unsettled her, but Faith had severely overreacted—especially with her ridiculous threat to return to New York. It would be impulsive and selfish for her to walk away. And to what? Piquant was no more; Faith had no maddening dinner rush in which to lose herself.

She still needed some income in the meantime, however; maybe Ellie would consider subletting her room so she'd be off the hook for rent. Faith grabbed her phone and shot Ellie a text: Good morning, mama!!!!

She hadn't expected a response at this hour, but Ellie fired off an answer immediately: Miss you!!!!!!! punctuated by a chorus line of kiss-blowing emojis.

Heartened, Faith hit speed dial, and Ellie answered on the first ring.

"Hey, girl." After her cheery text, Ellie's voice sounded oddly flat, but Faith chalked it up to the early hour.

"Hey! What's going on? I miss you!"

"Miss you, too."

There could be no mistaking her leaden tone. "Are you okay? Is the baby okay?"

"The baby's fine. I'm feeling as big as a house; nothing fits. But otherwise, the pregnancy's going super great."

"Then what's wrong?"

After a few seconds, she answered. "It's Dennis and me. We're having some issues."

With a little probing, Faith determined that Ellie had decided a few unanswered calls and some questionable behavior on her fiancé's part added up to Dennis seeing someone on the side.

"Dennis can't possibly be cheating on you. He adores you."

"Then why won't he answer when I call him at work?" Ellie asked. "This baby and I should be the most important thing in the world to him right now."

"And you are." Faith paced around Maeve's heirloom table. Ellie had been hard on boyfriends in the past, but pregnancy elevated her relationship insecurities to a whole new level.

"And what about *this*: when I asked him to bring me Chinese food the other night, he said he couldn't. He was probably out with *her*."

Faith could practically see Ellie's lower lip jutting out. "Now you're being silly. The poor guy has work in the morning. Unlike you, who can show up at your dad's office *whenever*."

"That's what Dennis said. He told me I'm selfish. As if I can control the crazy cravings his baby gives me."

Overhead, Faith heard the sounds of boarders stirring for breakfast: the flush of toilets, the tap-tap of Grace's cane. She bit her lip, half agreeing with Dennis's assessment and wishing she'd never reached out to Ellie. "You guys will work it out. Things are getting busy here, so I better go."

"But I need help with this."

"Ellie, right now I can't even . . . You know, I called you this morning because *I* needed a shoulder for once. I've lost my job, I'm down here in this godforsaken town and yesterday my mother freaked me out so badly . . ." As she carried the carafe to the dining room, Faith spotted Grace making her way down the stairs and turned away so she couldn't hear. "Believe it or not, Ellie, other people have *actual* problems. But don't worry about me. I'll be fine."

In the quiet that ensued on the line, Faith had time to double back to the kitchen, re-season the compote and ice an aluminum pan of yogurts. "Geeze, El, are you even there?" she snapped, wiping condensation from the pan with her apron.

"Oh, I'm here. Thanks a lot, Faith. You make me sound like an unfeeling monster."

"This is so typical: instead of owning this, you turn it back on me. For crying out loud, the guy loves you, Ellie. And if you throw that away now, you're really, really stupid. I'm sorry, El, but I've got to go now."

Faith ended the call and picked up the compote, forcing her lips into a smile before reentering the dining room. There had been no sign yet of Merrill, but Grace waved from her table for two. Huddled at their own table were a tight-lipped Roxanne and a yawning Gage, still in his hooded sweatshirt from the night before. After setting down the fruit, Faith approached their table with coffee. Eyes on her son, Roxanne slid her mug toward Faith.

"How's everybody doing this morning?" Faith attempted her brightest tone.

Gage grunted, then pushed back his chair and bolted out of the dining room.

"Sick all night." Roxanne sipped her coffee. "He's pretty miserable, but I'm not inclined to show much sympathy until he comes clean about last night."

Faith slid into Gage's vacated seat. "Did he tell you where he went?" she asked.

"Nope. Not saying a word. Protecting some people, I'm sure."

"Did you check with his dad?"

"He said Gage changed his mind and wanted to come back here and stay with me. Though why Mitch didn't give me a heads-up . . ." Roxanne rested her chin in her hand. "Anyway, he swears he dropped Gage here around dinnertime."

"I never saw him."

"Of course you didn't. He probably went right back out again." Roxanne wiped her mouth with a napkin, her eyes dark with worry. "The question is, *where* did he go, and who else was with him? And worst of all, could Gage somehow have been involved with *that*?" Roxanne jerked her thumb in the general direction of the beach.

"We don't know that. What kind of crowd is he hanging with?"

"We haven't been here long enough for him to *find* a crowd. But with all the crap he's been through since the storm, and the free time these kids have with school being closed . . ." Roxanne flattened her hands on the glass tabletop, her fingertips leaving faint impressions. "I don't know what to do, Faith. I've got to find something to keep Gage busy. And out of trouble."

Faith patted her arm. "Try not to worry. I'm sure everything's going to be fine."

"I hope so. That's what David said, too."

"David? When did you even meet him?"

"Last night. Or rather, early this morning. He came in after you went to bed. He took one look at Gage and figured out what was what. Helped me get him upstairs."

"That was nice," Faith murmured.

"Very sweet. He even made us omelets after."

"Really? For the two of you?" So David hadn't been so self-serving after all.

"Anyway, he's a cool guy." Roxanne's fleeting smile faded as she stared past Faith in alarm. "But if you and David are right about things turning out okay, what's *he* doing here?"

45

The Wave's End police officer sauntered into the Mermaid's Purse's dining room, a clipboard in one hand and the inn's copy of the *Beacon* in its plastic sleeve dangling from the other.

"Stay here," Faith instructed an ashen Roxanne, who gripped the edges of her table. At the same time, Connie crossed the dining room.

"Can I help you, officer?" Connie asked.

Faith joined them. "Good morning," she said cautiously.

"Sorry. Let myself in." The policeman handed the newspaper to Faith. "I'm just alerting the neighborhood to some news."

"I hope it's good." Faith could feel Roxanne's eyes boring into her back.

"I would say it is, for the folks getting their power back shortly. We've got some out-of-state crews working on the lines around here over the next few days. Since they won't be the usual trucks, we're circulating pictures of their badges so you'll recognize them." He unclipped a sheet from his clipboard and handed it to Connie. "If you see anything funny, let us know right away."

"Funny how?" asked Connie.

"Some scammers have been trying to pull fast ones with homeowners. Fake IDs and so forth, hoping to gain entry into their homes. But in this case, our workers don't have to come inside to complete the repairs."

"Thank you. We'll keep our eyes out." Faith signaled Roxanne with the barest thumbs-up: *the officer wasn't here for Gage.*

The officer riffled through more papers on his clipboard. "Looks like you folks have priority for the work orders. Says here you're part of the program the town is subsidizing to house these families. Nice thing you're doing."

"We're happy to help," Connie said. "We're so lucky we didn't suffer any damage ourselves."

The officer glanced around the inn. "You should be thankful. Especially after that fire last night. Insult to injury, I'd say."

Just then, Merrill came down the stairs, halting at the sight of the officer and widening her eyes at Faith.

"I thought I heard sirens last night," Connie said. "Sounded like the Second Coming."

"Four-alarmer up at the beach," said the officer. "Four houses at once. Went up like matchboxes." He snapped his fingers.

Queasy, Faith leaned against the wall. "What about the people inside?"

"There were none, as far as we know. Places were empty. Good thing the wind had died down, or the fire might have spread. Those houses are crammed together like books on a shelf."

"How did it start?" Merrill asked.

"Don't know yet. We're not ruling anything out. Even arson." He tipped his hat. "Anyway, you folks have a good day."

As Connie walked the officer out the door, Faith unwrapped the newspaper. Images from the fire blanketed the *Beacon*'s front page: flames licking the skyline, huddles of blanket-wrapped neighbors watching firefighters battle the blaze, the charred shells of the burned-out homes. Bruce and his staff must have been working all night.

"Do we know anything?" Merrill murmured.

"Nope. Gage won't talk."

"Is he under suspicion?"

"Not as far as I know. But the investigation is only beginning."

"Oh, boy. Let's just hope . . ." Shaking her head, Merrill glanced back at Roxanne. "Just let me know if you hear anything," she finished, before breaking away to join Grace for breakfast.

Faith was still engrossed in the newspaper when Gage trudged down the stairs in a clean shirt, still looking a little green but freshly showered at least, his hair waxed into its trademark bristle. Focused on his phone, he headed for the front door.

"Hold on there, bud," Roxanne called. "Where do you think you're going?"

"Out. There's no school, remember?"

"Did you forget you're grounded for the next two weeks?" His mother strode toward him.

"You can't ground me in *this* place." Gage glanced around the inn's entrance with disdain. "There's nothing to do."

"Don't you worry about that. I've got a list of things to keep you busy until you decide to tell me the truth about last night."

"I told you everything. Anyway, Dad said I can go." He thrust his phone at his mother, who took the device, her lips white-tight as she scrolled.

"I doubt your father has heard the whole story," she said finally. "I will fill him in. And in the meantime, I'll hold on to *this*." Roxanne pocketed her son's phone.

"You can't take that." Fury blotched Gage's pallid cheeks.

"I just did. You'll get it back in two weeks."

"*Two* weeks? You're ruining my life!"

"You're forgetting you *have* no life for the next fourteen days." Hands on her hips, Roxanne looked her son up and down. "And where's Tucker's chain, by the way?"

So Roxanne *had* noticed, Faith realized.

Scowling, Gage took a step back. "Fine. Keep the phone. I don't need it." Before Roxanne could even respond, he bolted out the front door.

46

In pursuit of her son, a distraught Roxanne brushed past Connie, who had just escorted the officer out.

"What's that all about?" Connie asked Faith.

"I'm not sure, exactly. Roxanne's got her hands full, that's for sure." Setting down the newspaper, Faith addressed her mother for the first time since the birth certificate episode.

"Faith, I don't know what to do—" Connie began.

"Mom, I'm sorry to interrupt you, but I need to say a couple of things." Spotting David helping himself from the breakfast buffet, Faith ushered Connie into the salon for privacy. "First, I want to apologize about . . ." She couldn't bring herself to say the name "Audrey" aloud. "The birth certificate thing. About freaking out. I know that must have been a desperate time for you."

"But you don't—"

Faith held up her hand. "Also, I didn't mean what I said about leaving. Of course I'll stay for a while, the way I promised."

"I need to—"

"Just one more thing, Mom." She cleared her throat. "Can you help me to set some boundaries with the guests?"

"Boundaries?" Connie's forehead wrinkled.

"Yes. Like asking before they take any food. I went to make breakfast this morning and my ingredients were gone."

"But—" Agitated, Connie attempted to break in once again, but Faith plodded on.

"I know these are special circumstances, and we're running things informally. But with a few guidelines, I can take care of the kitchen and keep everyone fed." Faith folded her arms. "So, I guess that's it. Thanks for hearing me out. Now, what did you want to say?"

"Just that . . . I found this outside." From behind her back, Connie produced a saffron sheet of paper and handed it to her daughter. "Someone tacked it by the door. I have no idea what it means."

"A flyer? You heard the officer. It's probably just some scam," Faith scoffed, taking the sheet. But as she read it, her breath caught:

FORECLOSURE NOTICE:

Notice of intent to terminate right of occupancy for nonpayment in 60 days.

PART 5:
DISILLUSIONMENT

47

"'NOTICE OF DEFAULT AND ELECTION TO SELL UNDER DEED OF TRUST.

Unless you take action to protect your property it may be sold at public sale.'"

Maeve could only bear to read aloud the first paragraph of the foreclosure flyer before setting it beside her on the hospital bed. "I give you both my word: I had no idea about any of this."

Maeve's distress *seemed* authentic, Faith thought, eyeing the patient, but how much did they really know about this woman beyond her glossy, misleading magazine spread? Could she have colluded with someone, with Bruce even, in this million-dollar scam? "Is this why you held your contest?" Faith asked softly. "So you'd have money to pay off your debts?"

"Faith! How can you accuse her of that?" Connie went to the head of Maeve's bed in solidarity.

"I'm sorry, Mom, but people have done crazier things."

"Well, Maeve's not one of them." Connie took the innkeeper's hand. "I'm sorry about my daughter. She's not the most trusting of souls."

"Honestly, can you blame me, Mom?" Faith crossed her arms, unable to resist the jab.

"It's all right," Maeve said tearily. "You're just trying to protect your mother. I saw that in you from the first day." She pulled a tissue from a bedside box. "But I told you: I held that contest to find the best person to carry on with The Mermaid's Purse after me."

"But how do you give away a property in *foreclosure*?"

"Because I had no idea. Lenny assured me he had put all my business affairs in order."

"Who's Lenny?" asked Faith.

"Lenny Walker, Maeve's accountant. I told you about him," Connie said.

"Oh, right, the guy in such a hurry for you to sign the transfer of ownership papers," said Faith.

"Lenny's father Harold handled the inn's business for years," said Maeve. "Lenny took over the firm a few years ago. He assured me he deposited all the lottery proceeds. I just had to say the word once I chose the new Mermaid's Purse owner."

"Maybe he missed a mortgage payment," suggested Connie.

"I've always paid my bills on time. And if one had been late, the bank would have contacted me, wouldn't they have?" Maeve looked to each of them for confirmation.

"I'm sure it's just a bookkeeping slipup," offered Connie.

It *could* be a clerical error, Faith thought. But if this Lenny person handled Maeve's financial affairs, he might have rerouted all the woman's bank correspondence directly to his office, which would make it very simple to hide any shady dealings from his client.

Maeve blew her nose noisily. "And what if it's not a bookkeeping mistake? What if Lenny Walker has made an old fool of me?"

And of my mother by association. The inn's foreclosure might place Connie Sterling's rightful ownership of The Mermaid's Purse at risk, which would leave Connie with nothing. Meanwhile, the inn was filled with residents, with Maeve in no shape to tend to them.

What a mess, Faith thought, massaging her lower lip. With weeks of recuperation still ahead of her, Maeve could not be counted on to deal with this crisis—a crisis that threatened her mother's financial security. And based on Connie's reckless choices regarding the inn, Faith didn't trust her mother to see the matter through on her own.

Someone had to address the situation and get to the bottom of what Faith sincerely hoped would turn out to be a gross misunderstanding.

And that someone, Faith reluctantly realized, would have to be her.

48

"There's been a storm, all right. A shit storm, and this guy's smack in the middle of it." Muttering, Faith jotted down the phone number from the sign taped to the locked door of the accountant's office, although she harbored little hope of reaching him.

Per Maeve's instructions, mother and daughter had located the darkened office of Harold Walker and Son on the main street in Wave's End, on the second story of a floor-coverings store.

"Where do you suppose he is?" Connie asked.

"If I had to guess . . ." Faith jumped a couple of times, hoping for a look through the transom window over Walker's door. "I'd say he's probably on a plane to the Cayman Islands. His office looks deserted. Cleaned out, even." Fatigued, Faith leaned against the wall. "You met the guy, Mom. Did he say anything, do anything that might give us any clue where he was headed?"

Connie thought a moment, then shook her head. "No, nothing. Other than rushing me to sign, no."

Downstairs, the carpeting store manager could only shrug. He hadn't seen his tenant since before the storm.

"What do we do now?" Connie asked outside the building.

Faith crossed her arms as she stared up at Walker's second-floor window. "We tell Maeve to find herself a new accountant. *And* a good lawyer."

"We should speak to Bruce," suggested Connie as they pulled into the Mermaid's Purse's driveway.

"Good idea. He might know something."

"What's that supposed to mean?"

"Nothing, Mom. Just that he seems to know an awful lot about what goes on around here."

"He's a journalist, Faith. It's his job to know what's happening." The two were out of the car now, making their way to the back porch.

"Maybe, but don't you think it's a little odd he's always hanging around?"

"No, I don't. I think it's nice. Are you implying he's involved in this somehow? My goodness. First you accused Maeve—"

"I didn't *accuse* her. I simply asked her a question."

"And now Bruce. I had no idea you had such a suspicious nature. As for Bruce, he happens to be a very thoughtful, helpful man. Did you know his mother and Maeve went to school together?"

"No, I didn't. But that doesn't entitle him to her credit card." Faith stopped and grabbed her mother's arm. "Mom, forget about Bruce for a second. You do realize how serious this situation is, don't you? That you may not actually own The Mermaid's Purse?"

"We don't know that for sure."

"Maybe not, but we have to start thinking—"

Before she could finish her thought, the back door opened and Roxanne emerged on the porch. "Oh. It's only you two." Roxanne's shoulders slumped. "I was hoping it might be Gage coming back early."

"So you found him?" asked Faith.

"Yes. He made it to a friend's house and called his father from there. Mitch picked him up. Said he'll bring him back for dinner. Which is just as well, since it gives me time to cool off."

"I'm glad to hear he's safe," Connie said.

"Safe from my wrath, at least. How is Maeve? David told me where you went."

Faith and Connie glanced at each other. Other than a hurried mention to David that they needed to check on Maeve, mother and daughter had tacitly agreed to keep the foreclosure to themselves for now.

"Coming along, but she still has a long way to go," said Faith.

"Oh, my gosh. I totally forgot." Roxanne coiled her hair over one shoulder. "Speaking of a long way, someone's inside to see you, Faith."

"Me? I barely know a soul in Wave's End." Curious, Faith hurried inside.

49

Faith blinked, flabbergasted. Standing in the Mermaid's Purse's front hall, a midsized designer suitcase at her feet, stood an unmistakably pregnant, extremely penitent Ellie, who promptly burst into tears at the sight of her friend.

"You were right," Ellie said, dashing over to throw her arms around Faith. "About everything. I *am* a selfish cow. And yes, feel free to say it. I'm quite literally a cow." She glanced down at her belly, which clearly had popped in the short time since Faith had left Brooklyn.

"You're not. You look beautiful. Glowing." Faith held her at arm's length. "But what are you doing here?"

"My dad's driver brought me. I did a lot of thinking after we hung up this morning. And now I've come to make everything up to you."

"There's nothing to make up. I said some pretty harsh things myself." Twining her fingers in Ellie's, Faith noticed that Ellie's were bare. "Hey, where's your engagement ring?"

"My mother is holding it."

"Why? Are your fingers swelling?" Faith turned over Ellie's hands, examining them.

"My hands are fine." Ellie cleared her throat. "It's Dennis and me. We're just . . . taking a break."

Faith dropped her friend's hand and stared. "But you can't! You just had a big misunderstanding. And you're about to be parents."

"I'm not worried about that. Dennis will be there for the baby. We're just having some trust issues at the moment. I'm sure we'll figure it out." Ellie forced a smile. "Please. I didn't come here to talk about my problems. I want to make up for all my whining this morning. You reached out to me and I should have—"

"Well, look who's here!"

Faith watched her mother and friend embrace in the dining room.

"This is all so cool, Connie." Ellie did a half turn in the hall, her hands in the air. "Is being an innkeeper everything you dreamed of?"

"There've been . . . a few surprises," Connie said, with a sideways glance at Faith. "But look at *you*!" Bustling around Ellie, Connie took the young woman's hand. "All grown up and expecting a baby! How exciting is that? Why, the last time we saw each other, you girls were finishing college."

And what a visit that had been. Connie had met Ellie and her family only once, at a graduation lunch at Le Bernardin, everyone wilted after the hours-long awarding of diplomas on that sweltering May day. The two mothers could not have been more different.

Having asked about Ellie's parents in the inn's dining room now, Connie listened sympathetically as Ellie related her family's storm-related troubles, which involved their second home in the Hamptons. Thankfully, their third residence in Palm Beach was outside of the hurricane's path. "Nadine certainly has stirred up a lot of heartache." Connie shot Faith another meaningful look.

"I know," Ellie said. "Faith made me see that. Which is why I'm ready." Ellie tugged her shirt down over her burgeoning belly.

"Ready for what?" Faith asked.

"Why, to help, silly," Ellie said with smile. "You and Dennis claim I only ever think of myself, so I came down to The Mermaid's Purse to prove you both wrong. I'll do anything. Just put me to work."

50

Excusing herself, Faith fled to the downstairs powder room to think. Since learning about her identity switch the day before, she'd been plotting a path back to New York as soon as feasible. But one event after another, the latest being Ellie's arrival, conspired to tether her to The Mermaid's Purse.

One thing was certain: under no circumstances could Ellie stay. Her roommate had been sweet to come all the way to Wave's End, but as much as Faith appreciated the gesture, Ellie needed to patch things up with Dennis.

Besides, she seriously couldn't think of a single task to assign her—at least nothing that wouldn't require trailing after Ellie to ensure the job was completed correctly. Faith had done enough of that in their Brooklyn apartment; she didn't have the luxury of time to do that in Wave's End, especially with the added burden of investigating the foreclosure.

Please let me be diplomatic, Faith beseeched her image in the tarnished mirror before returning to the dining room.

"Oh, good. You're back." Ellie clapped her hands, a luminous smile lighting up her face. "Connie's just been telling me about all the wonderful people staying here. I can't wait to meet everyone."

"Listen, Ellie. About that. I really don't have—" Staring at the floor, Faith searched for words that wouldn't reduce her friend to a puddle of hormonal tears.

"And who do we have here?" Ellie interrupted, leaning around Faith.

Faith turned to see Fred lead Mona into the living room, Mona's hand resting atop her husband's like a minuet partner's, a shawl-collar cardigan of Fred's over her nightgown. Mona focused on something distant, her vacant stare a hallmark of her detachment from reality.

"Hello. I'm Ellie." She greeted the couple.

Ignoring the young woman's extended hand, Mona tilted her head, her gaze landing on Ellie's bulging belly.

"Yes, dear. She's expecting," Fred said. "Remember how much you love babies?"

Trembling, Mona reached toward Ellie's midsection. With a pang, Faith recalled the couple's loss of their adult son.

"Do you want to feel it?" Ellie asked. "It's okay. Everybody wants to. Even strangers on the subway," she giggled. "They don't even ask first. Here, I'll help you." Ellie took Mona's shaking hand and guided it to her abdomen. "It's something, isn't it?"

Faith shook her hand in front of her mouth, a heads-up that Mona didn't talk, so Ellie wouldn't expect a response. But then, to her amazement, Mona *did* speak.

"A baby." Mona's eyes blazed with joy as she addressed Ellie. "Such a wonderful blessing."

"Yes, it is." Widening her eyes at Faith, Ellie shifted Mona's hand to the other side of her stomach. "You feel this? This is his favorite spot to kick me."

"*His?* Since when did the Teletubby become a 'he'?" Belatedly, Faith realized she had used her private name for Ellie's pregnancy.

"Since another sonogram this week. It's a boy." Ellie spoke softly, her hand still over Mona's as the older woman massaged her stomach. "I didn't have a chance to tell you. Dennis and I got to see his 'equipment.'"

"Hello, baby boy," Mona murmured.

The women's hands moved in tandem. Ellie's eyes were closed, a half smile on her lips, Mona lost in a similar reverie, as though the pair had entered a private universe, with Ellie's baby at the center.

And suddenly, an idea came to Faith. If Ellie really, truly wanted to make herself useful at The Mermaid's Purse, Faith knew a way her friend could contribute.

51

"My job's no problem. I can work from here." Ellie dismissed Faith's worry with a wave of her hand as they kicked around Faith's idea of Ellie becoming Mona's secondary caretaker. Faith wanted to gauge Ellie's willingness before speaking to Fred about the possibility.

Fred's wife reminded Ellie of her nana, who had experienced similar periods of disorientation, Ellie confided on the front porch, where they'd gone to speak privately. "She lived with us while I was in high school. I loved spending time with her. And I was good with her, Faith." Ultimately, Ellie's grandmother moved to a nursing home. "I'll do my best to keep Mona safe. She's lovely."

"And she certainly took to you. But she's a bit unpredictable, too." They would all need to be vigilant, she added, explaining about Mona's spells.

Relieved to have lined up some potential relief for Fred, Faith grabbed Ellie's suitcase and led her friend to the last remaining room on the second floor.

"Sorry, El, but all the en suites are taken. You'll have to share a bath with my mother and me."

"No problem. It'll be like old times in the dorm." Ellie tested the edge of the four-poster bed.

"True." Laughing, Faith impulsively hugged her friend, the unpleasantness of their early-morning exchange evaporating as she realized how much Ellie's unexpected appearance at The Mermaid's Purse cheered her.

Because if Faith had ever needed a friend to confide in, it was now.

◠⌒◡

Due to the way the day unrolled, it was late afternoon before Faith began to throw together a supper of chicken potpies and salad for the evening's nine diners, minus Gage—Fred and Mona, the Abbott sisters, David, Roxanne, Connie, Faith and the newly installed Ellie. While chicken breasts poached in a soak of broth, cream and sherry, Faith peeled, chopped and blanched root vegetables and whipped up a velvety béchamel.

David came through as Faith assembled the piecrust dough on Maeve's worn table. "Let me do that," he said. He took her rolling pin and deftly flattened the dough, then twirled the floury round over his head.

"Is that how they make a Caribbean pizza?" asked Faith, laughing.

"Actually, I've been helping in a friend's pizzeria since The Osprey closed. That's why I got back so late last night."

"Will that be a regular thing?"

"Doubt it. I did talk to a caterer who does a lot of craft service in the city. She needs someone to truck the stuff in there and serve it. It'll be a lot of early mornings, but I need every penny if I'm ever going to open another restaurant."

"That sounds like a good start." Faith took the dough from David and pressed it into a pie tin. "So, I heard you ran into Gage and Roxanne last night."

"Yup. That kid was in rough shape. I felt bad for the mom."

"So bad you had to use up all my breakfast ham and tomatoes?"

"*Your* ham and tomatoes?" David crossed his arms. "Roxanne was a wreck over her kid, Faith. I was just being nice."

"I know, but we have a fair amount of people to feed here, and—"

"Are you seriously giving me shit over some *ham*? I mean, I'll go buy some right now if it's such a big deal."

"No. Don't be silly. It's not a big deal. It's fine." Flustered, Faith turned away in search of a towel to wipe her hands. "I guess I can be a bit of a kitchen Nazi. I just like things to be there when I need them."

"And *I* like to be there when a *human* needs me."

Faith feared he was mocking her, but when she turned around, David's gaze was earnest.

"I'm sorry," she said. "What you did for Roxanne and Gage was sweet. And speaking of Gage, I have an idea. I think you should take him surfing."

David paused mid-roll. "I barely know the kid, outside of practically carrying him upstairs last night."

"You don't have to be his best friend. Just take him out once or twice. Show him the basics, so he'll feel more comfortable here." Faith grabbed David's baseball cap, placed it on her head and twisted it backward. "You know: make him feel like one of the *dudes*."

Now it was David's turn to laugh. "If it'll get you to take off that hat, I'll do it."

❧

Just as Faith was turning out the kitchen light before bed, Gage surprised her by poking his head in the doorway. He had returned toward the end of dinner, sullen and uncommunicative, refusing anything to eat and going straight to his room.

"My mom said I had to apologize. So, like, I'm totally sorry about last night." His words tumbled out in a rehearsed rush.

Faith folded her arms. "We were pretty worried about you."

"Last time. I swear. So, like, are we cool?" Avoiding her eyes, Gage drummed the door frame.

"Yeah. We're cool." Faith smiled at him. She'd been in similar straits at that age a number of times: new town, new school. It could be painful to try and fit in.

Gage ceased his drumming. "Awesome. 'Night."

"Good night, Gage." A forced apology was better than none, Faith thought, heading upstairs. And she gave him a lot of credit for approaching her at all. Maybe with David's help, Gage could find his way in Wave's End, making some new friends and acquiring some new interests.

52

Unbeknownst to Faith, while she had coped with Ellie's arrival, Connie had wasted no time recruiting Bruce to piece together the Mermaid's Purse's financial puzzle. Clearing the breakfast service the following morning, Faith glanced up to see her mother walking the newspaperman into the dining room.

"Bruce is going to help us," said Connie.

"Really? Help how?"

"Well, for starters," Bruce said, "Maeve has granted me power of attorney—"

"Power of attorney?" Mouth agape, Faith dropped into a chair. It was one thing for Maeve to let Bruce stormproof a few windows, but to hand him control of her affairs? Was Faith the only one who found Bruce's involvement extreme?

"Yes. That way, I'm able to find out what the bank knows," explained Bruce. "I've just come from reviewing Maeve's accounts."

"Accounts." Faith drummed her fingers on the table.

"But before we get into that," Bruce continued, "let me just say I've been warning Maeve about Lenny Walker for a while. Walker had a reputation around town as a heavy gambler, some pretty high-stakes stuff."

There had been signs over the last few years, Bruce explained: the accountant's ostentatious three-story home on the inlet, the extravagant yacht docked in front, investment in a waterfront seafood restaurant. "And then right after the storm, it was as though the guy dropped off the face of the earth. His restaurant went dark, and he walked away from everything."

"How do you know all of this?" Faith asked.

"I have my sources. And I did try to alert Maeve, but she refused to listen. Said the Walkers had always taken care of The Mermaid's Purse."

"You mean, had their greedy hands *in* The Mermaid's Purse," said Faith. "Can't you do something? Publish a story about the fraud and expose Walker?"

"And be sued for slander? At this point, it's only hearsay. I can't print a word until charges are filed."

Faith leaned forward. "So there *will* be charges."

"Sorry. I can't say anything more." He tipped his chair back.

"But if charges *are* filed, and Walker's found guilty, what happens to the contract my mother signed?"

"It's too early to determine the actual owner of the inn." Bruce tapped his fingers together. "The short answer is, the bank will repossess this inn unless the total amount in arrears is paid."

"And how do they expect us to do that?" asked Connie.

"They've given us a couple of options for repayment." Bruce cleared his throat as he opened a folder. "The first and simplest option would be for the building owner to grant permission for the bank to sell the inn."

"That will never happen. Maeve won't agree, and neither will I." Connie flattened her palms on the table, ready to do battle.

"That's what I told them," Bruce said. "If you choose the second option, to fight for the property, the bank would grant you a three-month repayment period starting from their initial notice." Bruce riffled through some papers. "Which went to Walker a month ago, according to their records."

"But Maeve never knew about that," Faith protested.

Bruce shrugged. "This is what they've told me. They will allow you to occupy the property during the repayment period, which ends December 31."

"Looks like we have no choice but to go for that one," said Connie.

"But that's crazy," protested Faith. "That's barely enough time for the boarders to find other living arrangements."

"And where do you propose they go, Faith?" Connie asked. "We know there's not enough housing to go around. Aren't I right, Bruce?"

"Unfortunately, yes. Although if the state extends the temporary housing allowance period, they can stay here a while longer."

"*If* our doors stay open," lamented Connie. "Surely the bank could offer some leniency in light of Maeve's thief accountant."

"They might have, had the homeowner let them know they were having difficulty. They did reach out to Maeve several times." As proof, he offered a sheaf of notices on bank letterhead addressed to Maeve.

"Letters Walker obviously intercepted," Faith guessed.

"So at this point, the bank's time frame is firm," Bruce said.

"And if we can't raise the money in two months?" Faith asked.

"Sheriff's sale." Bruce shifted some papers in the folder. "And I'm afraid there's more. Walker opened a credit line against The Mermaid's Purse."

"If Maeve had fallen behind on her payments, why would the bank ever approve a line of credit?" Faith asked, incredulous.

"Because Walker was smart. He opened the credit line before his shenanigans started, when the inn was still in good financial standing. Under the guise of financing renovations."

"Well, that's a joke." Faith thought of the inn's damaged roof, peeling shutters and antiquated fixtures.

The bank had since closed that account, but not before Walker had written upwards of ten thousand dollars in checks against it, Bruce finished.

"But that's fraud! That grubby . . . Hold on a sec." Faith got up and rummaged in a kitchen drawer for a pen and paper. "Okay. We're talking a couple of back mortgage payments, plus the ten-thousand-dollar credit advance," she said, jotting down the figures. "It's a big debt. We can't get around that. But why not just use Maeve's lottery proceeds to pay what she owes?" Triumphant, Faith set the scratch paper on the table for all to see.

Exhaling, Bruce twisted his lips before responding. "Actually, there are two problems with that. First, Maeve received only about half of the fifty-six hundred essay entries she needed."

"Then she should have cancelled the contest. Or extended the deadline," said Faith, recalling the contest rules.

"What? And create more competition for me?" protested Connie.

"I suggested both of those options, but apparently Walker convinced Maeve to cut her losses, that a contest extension would dilute interest in the inn."

"He cut her losses, all right." Faith scribbled a few more numbers. "Even so, half the entries still leave her with several hundred thousand dollars. Why not start with that?"

"We can't." Shaking his head, Bruce closed his folder. "Her lottery proceeds have disappeared."

"But he told Maeve he deposited them," protested Connie.

"He told Maeve a lot of things, Mom. Bruce, what do you think happened to the money?" Faith asked.

"I could imagine any number of scenarios: gambling, secret bank account, Ponzi scheme. We won't know for sure until they find Walker."

❧

There was one small piece of good news, Bruce said after the women had digested the information. Walker hadn't touched Maeve's household checking account. The balance there remained healthy enough to pay for Maeve's incidentals while she recuperated, as well as carry the inn's operating expenses for the two months, providing they budgeted carefully, he said.

"Somehow, we have to drum up business for The Mermaid's Purse." Connie snapped her fingers. "I know! What about a holiday tour? Faith, you and David can cook up some nibbles to serve, and I'll lead the visitors around the inn. We could hire some musicians—"

Faith frowned. "A tour's nice, but David's working all kinds of crazy hours. And there'd be costs for food, decorations, entertainment. Besides that, Thanksgiving's less than three weeks away. Do you think we could pull together an event like that so quickly?" Faith looked to Bruce for feedback.

"Truthfully, no. And while I admire your initiative, thanks to all the media attention about the storm, it's going to be hard enough to entice folks back to Wave's End next summer for a vacation, let alone this Christmas." With a glance at his watch, Bruce pushed his chair back from the table and stood.

"Sorry, ladies, but I'm due at the paper. I think we have to face reality here. Two months isn't enough time to save this place. The Mermaid's Purse has had a long, satisfying run in Wave's End, but come the new year, the inn will have to shut its doors."

And what would happen to Connie if it did?

Standing, Faith met Bruce's gaze. Why had he shot down Connie's idea so quickly? With his allegiance to Maeve, she would have expected him to fight a little harder. "Certainly, you know Maeve and this town better than either of us, Bruce. But I'd like to ask a favor: that we don't say anything to the guests just yet about the foreclosure. I want to give this a little more thought, just to see if there's any way out of this."

53

Once the three agreed Bruce would go back to the bank with their decision, the journalist gathered his documents and prepared to leave.

"Bruce, can I ask you one more thing?" Faith hurried to catch up with him outside.

"I told you everything the bank went over with me."

"I know. It's not about that. Actually, I was wondering if you'd heard anything more about that fire up at the beach." Even though Faith had resolved to steer clear of the Castro family drama, she couldn't help but notice how preoccupied Roxanne had seemed since that night. Gage's mother spent hours napping in her room, and when she did come to meals, she picked at the food on her plate. Faith was anxious for any information that might exonerate Gage, and therefore lighten Roxanne's burden.

"Nothing concrete yet from the fire chief, but these investigations take time." Bruce leaned against his car. "Why the interest?"

"Just curious."

"Is this about the boy?" Bruce angled his head toward the house. "David told me Gage was MIA that night. Still having trouble accounting for his activities, is he?"

"Or maybe he's protecting somebody. Either way, his mother's pretty worried."

"Well, it's no picnic parenting a young man. Especially alone. I can vouch for that. Tell you what: if I hear something, I'll give you a heads-up." With a sympathetic clasp of Faith's shoulder, Bruce was gone.

54

"I'll have to call you Audrey from now on," Ellie said wickedly.

The friends were splayed across Ellie's bed one afternoon a week after her arrival. To Faith's relief, Ellie was doing so well as Mona's companion that Fred practically had to pry his wife from the side of the expectant mother.

Initially, Fred had been too nervous to leave the two women alone. But once he saw how gently but firmly Faith's friend cared for her charge, he relaxed a little, even permitting Ellie to take Mona for brief walks.

Watching the gentle man enjoy a moment to sit and read by himself for the first time since the couple's arrival, Faith had been awash in guilt. How could she have doubted Ellie's parenting ability? If her friend showed half the tenderness toward her newborn that she exhibited with Mona, she'd be a wonderful mother.

There had been another bonus: Mona hadn't had a single spell since Ellie's arrival.

"You know I'm kidding," Ellie continued. "But Audrey might be a good alias if you were thinking of editing your online dating profile."

"I was thinking of deleting it altogether, for all the luck I've had with it. And it's not funny." Faith swatted Ellie's thigh. "How would you feel if your parents suddenly announced you were born with a different name?"

"I'd be upset, of course. But your mother did that to protect you." Lying back, Ellie popped a chocolate-covered caramel into her mouth.

"I get that, but why didn't she tell me sooner? My father's dead; there hasn't been anything or anyone to be afraid of for years. And are those things good for the baby, by the way?" she asked.

"Dark chocolate. Antioxidants," Ellie mumbled, her mouth full. "Listen, when a woman is abused, even psychologically, the way your mother was, the trauma stays with her. Remember Jenna from freshman year? The girl with the jealous stalker boyfriend?"

Faith scratched her head. "I remember. We were all so envious at first, because he paid her so much attention."

"Until the guy freaked out on Jenna so bad she had to drop out of school."

At that moment, David and Roxanne strolled by Ellie's room, their voices low. Faith leaned toward the hall, straining to hear their conversation. Ever since Gage had warily accepted David's invitation to go surfing a few days ago, the boy's mood had improved, to Roxanne's relief.

"Right. Dropout," Faith echoed as Roxanne's door closed. Had David gone inside? she wondered. It didn't matter; she thought she had heard Gage come upstairs earlier, too.

Stop it. There's nothing between them, besides David being a bit of a mentor for Gage.

Faith tossed the empty candy box at Ellie. "All I'm saying is, nothing good ever comes from keeping secrets. I only wish my mother had told me about my name change sooner."

"She probably felt guilty. She didn't want to be *that* mother, who let her child down, whose kid lost out on a dad because she picked the wrong guy." Ellie sat up at the head of the bed, stroking her belly. "This is what you have to ask yourself, Faith Sterling: would your life have been any different, or any better, as Audrey Hennessey?"

It was the same question that had been running through Faith's brain on a nonstop loop ever since she had stumbled on her original birth certificate. "I've been thinking about that, and—"

"Miss Faith? Miss Ellie? Are you in there?"

At Fred's frantic call, Faith slid off the bed. She found him outside the door, white-faced and wringing his bandaged fingers. "When is Miss Ellie going to help Mona get ready for her nap?"

Ellie joined the pair in the hall. "I did, a little while ago. She was sleeping like a baby when I left her."

"Didn't I ask you to tell me when you did that, Ellie? So I could look in on her? You left Mona alone, and now she's gone!"

55

Ellie clutched her belly. "What do you mean, Mona's gone? Maybe she's in the bathroom."

"She's not," Fred said. "I've checked everywhere in the house."

"What are we going to do?" Ellie asked. "I'm so sorry I screwed up, Fred. I'll come with you to look for her, of course."

Faith worked her lower lip. "No. I think it's better if you both stay here. That way, when Mona comes back, the two of you will be here to calm her."

In truth, Faith had no idea if this was the best strategy. Dashing around the inn, she collected Connie, David, Gage and Roxanne and explained what had happened. After dispatching Gage to search The Mermaid's Purse from attic to cellar, she instructed the others to take their phones and fan out into the garden and surrounding neighborhood. If they should spot Mona, they shouldn't shout or otherwise startle her but simply stay with her while getting word to one of the others.

If Mona were frightened, there was no telling what she might do.

Outside, dusk capped the brilliant sunset, striating the horizon pumpkin and violet. Her heart hammering, Faith trudged south, block by block, past the nautical bungalow, wishing she had grabbed a flashlight to illuminate the shrubs and shadows and aiming her phone's light instead.

"Mona," she called softly. Beside her, the rush-hour traffic built, and Faith brushed away the possibility that a confused Mona might decide to step into the street. "Mona. Please. It's Faith. It's time to come home."

After walking for nearly a half hour, she had reached the outskirts of downtown. It was dark now; even in her sweatshirt, Faith felt chilled. No one else from the inn had contacted her with any leads. This was foolish: they were wasting valuable time when the police were much better equipped for these situations. She was about to call 9-1-1 when, peering into the darkness one more time, Faith clutched her chest with relief. Up ahead, on the bench of the glass-walled bus stop, sat the snowy-haired Mona, still clad in her nightgown. Smiling serenely when Faith appeared in front of her, Mona patted the empty place beside her.

"Hello, dear," she said, as casually as if the two had bumped into each other at breakfast. "You going to the city, too? How fun. We'll take the bus together."

"I can't today, Mona. Maybe another time." Sitting down, Faith carefully placed her hand next to Mona's. "Fred's a little worried. He doesn't know where you are."

"Fred?" Mona frowned a moment, then brightened. "Such a dear man. Doesn't he know I can take care of myself?"

Faith's pinkie touched hers. "He does. But here's the thing: Fred's the one who needs taking care of at the moment. Could you come back with me and help him?"

"But my job . . ." Mona got up and gathered the dirt-stained hem of her nightgown around her. Peering down the road, she teetered so close to the curb Faith leaped up to pull her back inside the bus stop. "Where is that darned bus, anyway?" Sounding for all the world like a frustrated commuter, Mona exhaled dramatically and turned to Faith. "Oh, well. I suppose I can always catch the next one. We should go back now."

Arm in arm, the two walked back to the inn together, Mona wondering aloud what her colleagues would think of her calling in sick for the first time. "I don't tolerate weakness in my staff," she said, wagging a finger at Faith. The woman must have been a force in her day, Faith thought, tucking Mona's arm into hers.

Back at The Mermaid's Purse, Ellie huddled by the door watching an agitated Fred hurry down the front steps and embrace his wife.

"You know you can't wander off like that. You scared the bejesus out of me." Fred kissed Mona's forehead tenderly, then led her inside, where he pulled off his sweater and began to dress her in it.

But before Fred could secure the last button, the stoniness Faith had come to recognize fell over Mona's face like a mask. How crushing to witness your beloved spouse disappear—in more ways than one, Faith thought, watching the man walk his wife to their bedroom.

56

"Mona hasn't worked in the city in twenty-five years," Fred told Faith the next morning. As usual, he had been the first to rise, the suspenders he wore over his sweater providing Faith a glimpse of the man as a young boy.

Faith set a cup of tea in front of him, shocked at the toll Mona's disappearance had taken on him overnight. His complexion had grayed, and his hands shook as he set his teacup in its saucer.

"Has Mona done this before?" Faith asked.

"Her meandering? Once or twice." Distracted, he glanced repeatedly toward the bedroom. "I'll put something in front of the door tonight while we're sleeping so she can't get out."

And if, God forbid, there were ever a fire, they might not be able to move it in time, Faith thought, sitting down beside him. "I'm not sure that's the answer," she said softly. "It might be time to do something, Fred. Before something worse happens."

His head dropped. "I promised Mona I'd take care of her."

"And you are. You will. But you have your own health to think about, too. How would Mona feel if something happened to you? She was very worried about you yesterday, on our walk back."

"Was she?" Fred's wistful smile made Faith want to cry. "When Mona was more . . . herself, she always kept after me about my pills and things."

"I bet she did. She loves you, Fred."

"I thought bringing her here to the inn would be good for her. That having other people around would bring back to her old self." He looked up at Faith, his lips quivering. "But I see now it's made everything worse."

~೨

By the time Fred finished a second cup of tea, Faith had secured his permission to reach out to his pastor about the couple's difficulties. Faith felt Fred relax beside her as she contacted the clergyman. *No one should have to shoulder this burden alone,* she thought.

Though consumed by his congregants' problems in Nadine's wake, Pastor Wilkins kindly agreed to help the couple.

With that hurdle cleared, Faith returned to the dilemma at hand. Ever since Bruce had rerouted the Mermaid's Purse's financial statements to the inn, the morning mail delivered a daily reality check. Flipping through the backlog of bills in the empty dining room that afternoon, she was relieved to discover a check from the town covering the boarders' first week. Some money was better than none; barely two weeks remained before Thanksgiving, and the stress of hiding the inn's financial woes from the boarders was wearing on her.

Sighing, Faith sat down and had begun to sort the bills when a glum-looking Ellie wandered in, clutching a mug of tea. Even though Fred assured Ellie repeatedly over breakfast that morning that she wasn't to blame for Mona's wandering off, Faith's friend was clearly finding it difficult to forgive herself.

"What are you doing?" Ellie asked.

"High finances." Faith set aside any bills she thought could wait a month. "I'm dreading having to show these to Maeve." Feeling much stronger now that she had transitioned to a short-term nursing home,

Maeve insisted on an honest appraisal of the inn's finances, although she still permitted Bruce to wage the inn's bigger battles with the bank.

"I'll keep you company," Ellie said, pulling up a chair. "Let me know if I can help."

Faith found Ellie's presence reassuring. In the course of unloading her burdens, Faith had also confided the fate of The Mermaid's Purse, swearing Ellie to secrecy, which Ellie immediately pointed out as being ironic, given Faith's reaction to her mother's birth certificate bombshell.

"I'm almost afraid to ask, Faith, but how bad—" Connie entered the dining room, but stopped short when she spotted Ellie. She tucked the book she carried under her arm and glared at the envelopes spread on the table, then at Faith. "Did you . . . ?" She angled her head ever so slightly in Ellie's direction.

"It's okay, Mrs. Sterling," Ellie said smoothly. "I won't say a word."

Connie sighed. "So you know, too. It's a shame. All poor Maeve has left is her memories." Connie set her book on the table. "I thought I'd take one of these guest books along on our next visit, to try and cushion the blow of the financial statements. Have you seen them, Ellie? There are so many sweet comments from people who've loved staying here."

Ellie picked up the guest book, opened to a random page and began to read: "'My husband and I spent our first wedding anniversary at The Mermaid's Purse twenty-five years ago, returning every year since. Maeve always treats us like honeymooners. I'm pleased to find that inn has retained its romantic charm, old-fashioned hospitality and first-rate service.'

"And here's another one." Ellie turned the page. "'My parents took us to The Mermaid's Purse every summer for twenty years. I'm thrilled to continue this tradition with my family and return with my own children.'

"They are lovely thoughts, but do you think seeing them might depress Maeve even more?" Ellie asked as she closed the book.

"Not necessarily," answered Faith. "May I see that, El?"

Her friend slid the registry across the table, and Faith began to flip through the pages, skimming the entries. "This is amazing: here's a review from Sonoma, California, in 2009. And Montreal. And another from Lincoln, Nebraska. Some of these guests come from quite a distance."

"*Came.*" Connie wiped the tabletop with her apron. "Business hasn't been that brisk in quite a while, from what Bruce tells me."

"But they still came back." Faith closed the guest book, an idea taking shape. "You said there's more of these books, Mom?"

"Yes. A whole shelf by the front door. Why?"

"Humor me. I'll be right back." Faith dashed out of the dining room, returning a moment later with an armload of the guest books. "I can't believe we didn't think of this before."

"Think of what?" asked Connie.

"*This.*" Faith dumped the books onto the table. "*This* is how we're going to save The Mermaid's Purse."

57

Faith strewed the guest registries among the three with the dexterity of a blackjack dealer. "Go ahead. Have a look."

"And what exactly are we looking for?" Ellie asked. "Did somebody slip a million-dollar check between the pages?"

"Funny. But you're on the right track. They *are* worth something." Seated again, Faith chose a guest book and opened it. "It's simple. These books provide the entire history of The Mermaid's Purse's visitors. All we have to do is go through them, identify the most impassioned guests and reach out to them."

"For money?" Connie asked.

"Not directly. We have to think like marketers. Tap into their emotions."

"You mean, appeal to their fond memories of coming to The Mermaid's Purse?" Connie asked hesitantly.

"Exactly. Make them want to invest in the legacy of the place, so future visitors can have the same delightful experience."

"The Mermaid's Purse alumni association," Ellie joked.

"Laugh if you want, but remember when our college wanted to knock down Evander Hall?"

Ellie nodded, recalling the popular campus meeting place. "I loved that old building. It smelled like rubber cement and pine. And it had the most comfortable chairs to curl up in."

"Exactly. And when the school wanted to tear it down, the alumni launched a campaign to save it."

"You think the inn guests might do the same thing to save The Mermaid's Purse?" asked Connie.

"It's worth a shot." Faith flipped through a guest book. "Some of these messages go all the way back to the sixties. They'll be perfect for the campaign."

"What campaign?" Ellie asked.

"I'm not sure of the details yet. I need to give it some thought."

Connie crossed her arms on the table. "Should we be asking Maeve about this? She may not want to be so public."

"Public? The woman raffled off her inn in a national magazine," Faith replied. "If it means her beloved Mermaid's Purse stays in business, I'm pretty sure she'll be on board." She turned to her friend. "Ellie, don't you have some design connections in the city?"

"Well, yes. One of my dad's companies does web design."

"Can you put me in touch with someone so we can brainstorm a bit? You'll have to tell them there's zero budget, though. Do you think your father will go for it?" Faith knew there would be no problem. She had witnessed Ellie sweet-talk her father into plenty of things over the course of their friendship.

"I'll . . . I'll certainly try. I really want to do my part." Ellie perked up, grateful for the responsibility. "I'll go call him right now."

"Perfect. The Mermaid's Purse isn't going down without a fight." Getting up, Faith gathered the registries. "I mean, who knows?" She hugged the books to her chest. "There might be somebody in here with a real soft spot for this place."

58

Faith tapped her foot in line at the supermarket register, before impulsively wheeling her cart out of line and back to frozen foods to pick up a second turkey. The purchase would put their Thanksgiving feast slightly over budget, but the leftovers would offset the cost of future meals, she rationalized, dropping the twenty pounds of netted poultry into her cart. How Xander would sneer at frozen over freshly killed. *Desperate times, boss.*

Just two days remained before the holiday, and Faith had thrown herself into the preparations, even insisting on shopping for the food herself today over her mother's objections. Following the emotional highs and lows of the last three weeks, from the foreclosure bombshell to Mona's disappearance to the handoff of Faith's fundraising ideas to the design team, the errand offered a welcome diversion. Maneuvering among the throng of impatient shoppers, Faith scanned the produce selection with a practiced eye, sniffing and rejecting squash, sweet potatoes, Brussels sprouts and cranberries until satisfied, nostalgic suddenly for her stainless steel Piquant workstation in the now-shuttered city seaport.

Counting her mother, Ellie and all the boarders, Faith initially anticipated ten around the Mermaid's Purse Thanksgiving table. But at the last minute she overheard Connie invite Bruce, which made eleven, and then Grace and Merrill had inquired whether Pastor Wilkins from the church might be included, bringing the holiday diners to an even dozen. And of course Faith would prepare a care package for Maeve, who, despite making good progress, still wasn't strong enough to leave the nursing facility, even for a few hours.

Back in line at the register, Faith was composing mental to-do lists for the next few days when a slight middle-aged blonde got in line behind her, a couple of frozen dinners in her arms, her head down as she flipped through a tabloid.

"Why don't you go in front of me?" Faith offered.

"Thank you. They seem to have closed the express line." Sliding past her, the woman patted Faith's arm without looking at her. "Love that sweater. My favorite color."

Faith glanced down at the cardigan she'd thoughtlessly thrown on for shopping, then up at the woman's face. She hadn't recognized her without her distinctive red eyeglasses, but at the sweater's mention, something clicked.

"This *is* your sweater," Faith exclaimed. "And it's about time I give it back to you!"

59

The customer who took Faith's place in line was Tanya Lloyd, the attorney who had shared both her taxi and her cardigan the night of the women's harrowing exodus from New York. "Contacts," Tanya laughed, pointing to her eyes. "I'm still not used to them. No wonder I didn't recognize you right away."

The two women chatted for so long in the supermarket parking lot that Faith began to worry about the frozen turkeys defrosting in her cart. It turned out that Tanya had spent that first confusing evening in Bayport up at the beachfront. She had assumed her aunt Hilda remained trapped in her bungalow, only to find out Hilda *had* been evacuated hours earlier and moved to a temporary shelter at Bayport High School. The next morning, Tanya had wept with relief at finding her aunt safe from harm and playing cards at a cafeteria table with her fellow evacuees.

The determined Hilda refused to leave her beloved shore town, despite Tanya's insistence, instead accepting a temporary room from a member of her bridge club.

Reluctantly, Tanya had returned to New York, sending money to cover her aunt's care and returning to the shore every week to look in on her.

"But what's going to happen to her bungalow?" Faith asked.

"That's another story," Tanya said grimly. "She took it upon herself to hire a contractor to rebuild the place. Even gave him a hefty deposit, without even a phone call to me."

Given their impulsivity, Tanya's aunt Hilda and Connie would probably get along famously, Faith thought.

"The problem is," Tanya continued, "that house won't be rebuilt anytime soon. The contractor turned out to be a con artist. A fly-by-night who stayed in Bayport long enough to cash my mother's check and quite a few others, then vanished into thin air."

"Oh, no. Your poor aunt."

"If I ever find that guy, I will take him *down*." Tanya leaned against her car. "It's so surreal. I mean, look at you. Did you ever imagine when you jumped on that bus in Port Authority that you'd end up running a bed-and-breakfast? Maybe this will be a new career for you."

Faith laughed drily. "Doubtful."

"Why not? Not enough excitement for you?"

"Oh, there's excitement all right." At Tanya's tilted head, Faith hesitated only a moment. After all, she'd already confided in Ellie, and the boarders would find out about the foreclosure right after Thanksgiving. "What would you say if I told you the bank was about to take possession of the Mermaid's Purse?"

∽

"That's unbelievable," Tanya said when Faith had finished. She wasn't an expert in financial law, but she offered to consult with a colleague who specialized in that area. "I can try to get back to you next week, when I'm back in my office."

"So you're around for Thanksgiving, then?"

"Yes. I'm taking my aunt out to dinner."

"To a restaurant? No way." Faith slammed the station wagon's hatch shut after loading her groceries. Having worked plenty of restaurant

Thanksgivings, she always wondered why some families chose to dine out that day, no matter how elegant the setting. Maybe because she had never experienced a greeting-card type of holiday meal surrounded by loads of family, she always imagined Thanksgiving as more memorable at home. "You and your aunt have to celebrate Thanksgiving with us at The Mermaid's Purse."

Visibly moved, Tanya happily accepted the invitation—and her sweater—before saying good-bye. Faith drove home from the supermarket in the approaching darkness, mentally multiplying holiday place settings and recipes as she swung into a fast food drive-in for an extra-large order of fries and an apple pie to consume as she drove. Some prepping of desserts and side dishes could commence that evening, she decided, turning onto the main road a few miles north of the inn.

This planning so engrossed Faith she found herself driving nearly on autopilot, not even noticing she'd finished the last fry. Focusing again, she gazed at the homes on either side of the road, disturbed to find that she recognized not a single landmark and fearing she had made a wrong turn. But then, with relief, she spotted The Mermaid's Purse up ahead.

Approaching the inn, Faith suddenly realized the reason for her disorientation: the streetlights in Wave's End were back on! After weeks of forced darkness, power had been restored. Lamps shone like beacons in the windows of house after house.

Faith rolled down the car window and delighted in the unaccustomed silence, the generators' hums stilled just in time for the holiday.

Despite her lingering financial woes, Faith allowed herself a moment of optimism, humming as she unloaded groceries from the back of Maeve's wagon. A good omen, the restoration of power relieved a huge burden on an exhausted community strained to its limits. With such blessings to be counted, could there be any harm in hoping Ellie's team could shine some light on the Mermaid's Purse's predicament?

As Faith set the last of the grocery bags on the back porch, she felt her phone thrum in her pocket and sat on the bottom step to answer Bruce's call. "I guess you know the lights are back on. You can come and collect your generator now."

"I'll be doing that shortly. It's a relief the power's back. Superintendent just announced school can open on Monday."

"I'll give Gage the good news his vacation is about to end."

Bruce chuckled. "I'm sure he'll be thrilled. That's not why I'm calling, though. Remember that information you wanted?"

Faith gulped, knowing he meant her question about the fire. "What did you find out?"

"The investigation is still ongoing. However, they did release some preliminary findings in the hopes someone will come forward with more information. The paper's already gone to press, but I wanted to give you a heads-up before you see tomorrow's story."

"A heads-up about what?"

"They found something in one of the houses the owner couldn't identify as his."

Bracing herself, Faith hunched her shoulders and scrunched her eyes shut. "What was it?"

"A length of metal chain. Seemed to think it might be a dog leash."

60

Faith headed inside, torn between telling Roxanne what she had just learned, or simply letting her read it herself in the paper. *It's none of your business,* she reminded herself. But having witnessed Gage drunk and incoherent that evening, she felt a duty to prepare the teen's mother.

And so, the night before the leash's discovery would be made public, Faith knocked on Roxanne's door, and, finding her alone, repeated what Bruce had told her. After their conversation, Faith sat on the steps, straining to listen to the fallout from her disclosure: Roxanne calling her son upstairs and grilling him within an inch of his life.

"I wasn't there. I promise," Gage swore over and over.

"Then how did Tucker's leash end up in that house?"

"How do you know it's Tucker's leash? Was he the only dog in Wave's End? Did it have his *dog* prints on it?"

"Don't be smart with me. I haven't seen that leash since that night. Can you tell me where it is?"

"I told you. I lost it."

"How could you lose it? You never let it out of your sight."

"Well, I guess I did, didn't I?"

Trying another tack, Roxanne softened her voice. "If you tell me the truth, we can go to the police now, before things get out of hand, and explain that it was all a misunderstanding."

"Four houses burned down, Mom. Like they *might* see that as a misunderstanding."

Faith flinched at the one-two slam of upstairs doors as Gage left his mother's bedroom for his.

61

The weather in Wave's End turned cold and blustery almost overnight, glazing the leaf blanket on the back lawn with frost. Faith shivered in sweatpants and an old barn jacket of Maeve's as she slipped outside at sunrise on Thanksgiving morning for a moment to herself.

Despite her covert strategy to rescue The Mermaid's Purse, executed via numerous phone calls and strategy sessions with Ellie's New York–based creative team, guilt still consumed Faith over keeping the inn's fate from their guests. It would require some strong acting today to keep the charade going.

She breathed deeply, savoring the tang of extinguished hearths peppering the air like the lingering aroma of a delicious meal. When the screen door banged behind her, she jumped.

"Happy Thanksgiving," murmured a soft female voice.

As Grace began to make her way outside, Faith hurried to hold the door. "You should be inside. It's chilly."

"I don't care. This is my favorite time of day." Joining Faith at the porch rail, Grace pulled her fleece tight around her. "In my line of work, I'd often just be getting home at this hour. Babies can't tell time, you know."

Faith chuckled. "Neither could some of the diners in my restaurant. They'd sit there into the wee hours, not caring whether we had a life to go home to. Anyway, what a lovely way to start the day, bringing a baby into the world."

"Nothing better. You know, I had an offer once to work nine to five for an OB-GYN doing prenatal care. The thought of finally having my nights to myself after all those years was very tempting. But I couldn't bring myself to abandon those mothers who needed me."

"Did you ever regret your decision?" Faith asked.

"Not for a second. Those newborns' cries are music to my ears."

Faith slapped the porch rail. "Speaking of crying, that's what the guests will be doing if I don't get breakfast going. Shall I put some oatmeal on for you?"

"Not quite yet." Grace stifled a cough. "I'll come in in a sec."

Concerned, Faith slipped off Maeve's jacket and draped it over Grace. "Okay, but not too long. I'll let Merrill know you're out here."

"She really likes you, you know. And don't think I don't know about your little fireside chats." Feigning disapproval, Grace wagged an accusatory finger at Faith.

"Spying on us, are you?" Faith teased. But Grace had it right. Having bonded the night of Gage's troubling homecoming, Faith and Merrill had taken to sharing a glass of wine most evenings. Poor Ellie tried once or twice to stay up and chat with them, but bowed out yawning.

Faith hadn't expected to make new friends at The Mermaid's Purse, but getting to know Merrill had been an unexpected perk. "Your sister's great. We've just about decimated all of Maeve's wine, though," Faith laughed.

"I'd say you've earned it, seeing as how you've filled in for her. Anyway, I'm happy Merrill has someone to talk to," said Grace. "That's one of the things I'm thankful for today."

Faith swallowed. If this woman in the grips of a serious illness could find a way to be grateful, certainly she could set aside her own melancholy for a single day. "Me, too. Happy Thanksgiving."

The two women smiled at each other a moment, then fell quiet. Faith had decided to head inside when she spotted movement through the kitchen window. Sure enough, a second later, David and a yawning Gage joined them.

"Where are you boys off to so early?" Brushing flyaway hair from her face, Faith wished she'd at least cleaned her teeth before coming downstairs.

"Beach. Paddle out." Gage clomped loudly down the porch stairs on his way to David's jeep.

"Does Roxanne know?" Faith asked. *Shut up! Not your business!*

"She does," said David. "We're surfing now, then holding a Thanksgiving memorial for all the storm survivors," he explained. "Gotta go. Conditions are perfect." He scooped an armload of wetsuits from a side porch rail and caught up to the teen in the driveway.

"Don't you want breakfast first?" Faith called.

"Can't. Waves wait for no man."

"Or woman." The back door opened again, and Roxanne appeared, shrugging at Faith before making a dash for the car. "Don't worry," she called from the front seat. "We'll be back in plenty of time to help with the big feast."

Only vaguely aware of Grace's warm hand on hers, Faith gaped at the departing group. Not only had mother and son put aside their issues for the day, but Roxanne apparently had relented on Gage's grounding. Maybe it wasn't considered punishment if Mom came along?

With a tap of his horn, David skidded out of the stone driveway, surfboards jutting from the 4x4 like shark fins, Gage's fist raised triumphantly over his head, Roxanne turning to wave.

62

"He's just being kind to Roxanne." Grace squeezed Faith's arm. "And to the boy. I imagine this is a hard time for Gage, what with his parents splitting up, and then the storm." Grace's consoling tone made Faith feel like one of the midwife's laboring mothers.

"Of course. They'll have a blast," Faith managed before bolting into the house. Grace had clearly misunderstood her reaction; Faith merely had been taken aback by Roxanne's participation. But in retrospect, the mother's presence made sense. After her son's recent missteps, how could she bear to let Gage out of her sight? And the way Roxanne had been keeping herself holed up, the outing would be good for her. Perhaps she and David had even hatched a plan to get Gage to spill his guts.

David. Faith shoved a tray of sticky buns into the oven. Why on earth would Grace the baby whisperer think his exclusive early-morning surfing outing would bother her? If Grace thought Faith had expected a hand from David, she would remind her that she could easily pull off a lovely Thanksgiving celebration without any assistance from anyone—least of all a third-rate cook who toted his supplies around in a paper bag like a kid clutching a sack of candy.

After all, David was only doing what Faith had asked: teaching Gage how to surf.

Mollified, Faith cracked a dozen eggs into a cast-iron skillet for a frittata. But as the sticky buns scented the downstairs a buttery cinnamon, the aroma triggered a wave of melancholy so strong it thickened Faith's throat. She had never been sentimental about the holidays, so why this sudden surge of emotion? Growing up, it had only ever been her and Connie at the table to celebrate, Faith recalled as she filled pitchers with juice and milk for the breakfast bar. Connie's sticky buns stood out as one of the few Sterling traditions. Or had that custom commenced at a Hennessey holiday, her father partaking in the cloyingly sweet treats as well? Faith blinked away the unexpected sting behind her eyelids.

Not that mother and daughter had celebrated many holidays recently. Faith's chosen métier demanded her presence on every holiday. On these überdemanding occasions, customers pumped up on artificial cheer and family drama consumed and spent a great deal more than normal, to Faith's employers' delight.

But being a member of the Mermaid's Purse household made this Thanksgiving a very different holiday, Faith realized, slipping triangles of toast into Maeve's silver bread caddies. In the few short weeks since arriving at the inn, and in spite of the arbitrary line she attempted to maintain between host and guest, she had grown quite attached to its occupants: from Roxanne's tough love and Gage's painful teenage angst, to sweet, devoted Fred and the luminous Mona, to the determined pair of Pennsylvania sisters who had installed themselves in Wave's End to help (and who did not seem inclined to leave anytime soon).

And then there was David, whose enigmatic presence deeply unsettled Faith, as much as she had tried to deny this to Grace. And finally Ellie, now surprising Faith at every turn.

She never could have envisioned these attachments when she had packed her bag in haste those few weeks ago in Brooklyn, never imagined her heart lifting as it did now watching Ellie lead Mona by the hand to breakfast, Mona's hair neatly combed and pinned back with a rhinestone barrette Faith recognized as her friend's. Faith blew a kiss as Ellie carefully seated Mona across from a smiling Fred, whose bandage-free hands were folded in front of him. To Ellie's relief, he had recovered enough from his recent scare to allow Ellie close to his wife again.

"They truly are the sweetest, aren't they?" Ellie joined Faith at a freshly set table for two on the far side of the dining room.

"As sweet as you and Dennis will be in fifty years' time." Faith pushed a serving of frittata toward her.

"I don't know about that." Ellie poked at the food with her fork.

"Of course you do. When's the last time you spoke to him, anyway?"

"A few days ago, maybe? It's so stupid, Faith. I don't even remember what we fought about. I think this baby thing has me so freaked out I don't know what I'm doing anymore."

"It's Thanksgiving. Call the poor guy and give him some hope, will you? You can't hide out here forever."

"Look who's talking about hiding! I would have thought you'd be firing away on all burners in a new Manhattan restaurant by now." Ellie sipped her tea, then lowered her voice to a murmur. "Have you decided what you'll do when the inn closes? I mean, *if* it closes?"

"Stay until Christmas, either way. Since I don't have another job yet, I might as well hang around."

"But it's the holidays. Isn't that when restaurants need the most help?"

"I've been too busy to look very hard," Faith admitted.

"Well, why would you want to, given all the distraction here?"

"What are you talking about?"

Ellie tilted her head. "Oh, I don't know. A seriously cute surfer chef, perhaps?"

"Please. Don't be ridiculous. David's *so* not my type." How had both Grace and Ellie decided that Faith was drawn to David?

"How do you know? You don't date enough to have one. And anyway, who *would* be interested in someone who is nice, considerate, excellent cook, et cetera, et cetera." Ellie ticked off David's attributes on her fingers. "Those are *such* turnoffs. And let's not forget *hot*. You *hate* hot. Girl, have you seen that man's guns?" Ellie got to her feet and flexed her arms in a bodybuilder's stance.

"Stop. You look like you're about to give birth." Faith held her stomach and laughed at the hilarious sight of Ellie grimacing while clenching her fists over her expansive belly. "Okay. Stop doing that *now*. You're right. He's nice. *And* helpful in the kitchen. I'll give him that."

"You *could* give him a lot more—"

"Whoa. Stop right there." Faith grabbed Ellie's arm and gently pushed her back into her seat. "David and I are friends. That's it."

"Whatever, Faith. If I were you, I'd open my eyes. That's all I'm saying."

63

"More exotic spices?" Faith teased at the sight of yet another paper bag in David's hand when the surfers returned. In the spirit of the holiday, she had taken Grace's and Ellie's advice to heart, letting go of the morning's misgivings.

"Nope, totally native this time," David said, lingering in the kitchen. "Well, North Carolina native, anyway." He offered her the bag. "Candied pecans. My mom always made them for Thanksgiving."

Realizing how melancholy the holiday might be without his mother, Faith impulsively asked for David's help with the final preparations. He wasted no time pushing up the sleeves of his Ron Jon shirt and reversing his cap before getting to work.

Flushed and triumphant several hours later, Faith and David surveyed the fruits of their afternoon labor: two turkeys roasted side by side and now resting on the kitchen counter, resplendent in golden skins and redolent of Faith's rosemary-thyme rub; turkey drippings-enriched giblet gravy and cornbread stuffing; and ten pounds of peeled and quartered Yukon golds prepped in a lobster pot on the stove with chunks of chopped onion, ready for boiling, mashing and a dollop of some top-secret ingredient David so far had refused to divulge.

Then there were the casseroles of roasted yams, dusted with David's candied pecans, the offering that kicked off their collaboration in spite of Faith's resolve to work alone.

The rest of the menu reflected the guests' favorites, based on Faith's earlier poll. David took the initiative and heightened the glistening cranberry chutney, carefully recreated from Fred's instructions, with fresh ginger and orange zest. The pantry also kept four desserts safe from Pixie's inquiring paws: an apple crisp, for which Merrill and Grace had peeled and sliced several dozen Pink Ladies; Piquant's pumpkin chiffon mousse, contributed by Faith and served in Maeve's cordial glasses; a pecan pie put together by bartender Roxanne and fired with a generous splash of bourbon; and a tray of chocolate-chip cookies Ellie and Mona had lovingly labored over the previous afternoon.

Yes, Faith thought, surveying the spread, she and David had orchestrated quite the banquet. The boarders agreed, praising the delicious aromas they encountered as they returned from assorted afternoon activities: attending the traditional high school football game, serving a community meal for storm survivors, strolling a rare stretch of boardwalk untouched by Nadine.

Tanya and her aunt Hilda would arrive at any time. Faith looked forward to meeting this spunky relative.

Only Ellie was conspicuously absent. As she collected the guests for dinner, Faith found her friend alone in the living room listlessly checking her phone, wads of spent white tissues lined up beside her like wilting dahlias. "Looks like I waited too long," Ellie said dully.

According to Ellie, Dennis had declined her call.

"That's ridiculous," Faith said. "Dennis would never do that. I don't understand why you always jump to these conclusions. Now, blow your nose and come to the table. You wouldn't want Mona to see you all sad and teary, would you?"

Still sniffling, Ellie stood and followed Faith to the dining room, where boarders and guests had already assembled around one giant table assembled for this special occasion only. Presiding at its head, Connie spotted the two friends and patted empty seats on either side of her. "Just waiting for you two."

"Go ahead." Faith gently pushed Ellie toward the table, but stopped short of sitting herself.

"Everyone's waiting for you, Faith," Connie said.

"But I have to serve," Faith protested.

"Not today you don't. Come sit."

Reluctantly, Faith took her appointed seat, tongue-tied suddenly and perching stiffly on the edge of her chair. But as her fellow diners chatted and ribbed her about wearing her apron to the table, Faith begin to relax, and held one of Maeve's cut-glass crystal goblets for some of the Beaujolais nouveau Tanya was pouring. A few sips helped to dispel her anxiety, and Faith began to enjoy this new vantage point. By the time applause erupted at David's and Gage's arrival with platters of turkey, Faith had settled in her chair, her apron now hung over its back, content to relinquish control momentarily and leave the serving to them.

Having set down the meat, David and Gage retrieved the remaining casseroles from the kitchen, Gage practically salivating at the tempting array of food he carried.

When they were all seated (David beside Faith, a move Faith knew her mother had orchestrated), Connie cleared her throat. "I want to welcome you all to my first Thanksgiving at The Mermaid's Purse. I've never been around a table this grand for a holiday. It's . . . well, it's just lovely." Swallowing, she clasped Faith's hand. "I'm especially grateful to have my daughter with me for this one. And *all* holidays," she added, causing Faith to color.

"We've had many holidays together, just the two of us," Connie continued. "But I never would have pulled this off—and by *this* I mean a great deal more than this magnificent feast—without Faith. I'm forever grateful."

At the guests' applause, the blushing Faith bowed her head, fervently wishing her mother would wrap up her toast. But caught up in the moment, Connie continued.

"And though we'd probably rather forget the tempestuous night that brought us together, I want everyone to know"—Connie's voice trembled as her gaze rounded the table, lingering on each person—"how blessed and thankful I feel to be with all of you today. I may have won a bed-and-breakfast, but this"—she grabbed Ellie's hand as well as Faith's this time—"this is my real prize. I'll think of you as my family always. My special Wave's End family. And I'll never forget you."

Faith glanced up as her mother's voice cracked, glimpsing the shimmer of tears in Connie's eyes, her toast taking on a prophetic poignancy. How would her self-proclaimed new family react once they learned The Mermaid's Purse might close its doors? Faith wondered.

Roxanne raised her glass first. "To family. Bless you, Connie and Faith. We're so grateful you opened your doors to us."

"To family. To Maeve. To The Mermaid's Purse. To new friends." Tributes ran around the table, the clink of guests' glasses as delicate as the tinkle of wind chimes.

"To old friends. And new babies." Reaching across to tap Ellie's glass, Faith noticed her furrowed brow. All that worry couldn't be good for the baby.

In the meantime, Connie had invited Pastor Wilkins to say grace. After rising and leading the guests in the prayer, he asked their indulgence while he shared a Bible passage from Isaiah:

"'And the Lord will create upon every dwelling place of Mount Zion, and upon her assemblies, a cloud and smoke by day, and the shining of a flaming fire by night: for upon all the glory shall be a defense.

"'And there shall be a shelter for a shadow in the daytime from the heat, and for a place of refuge, and for a covert from storm and from rain.'

"Amen," the pastor concluded. "And amen to Connie and Faith, and to all the shelters and refuges in our communities, near and far."

"Amen," echoed the guests, heads bowed.

Gage broke the silence. "Is it okay to eat now, or is there more sappy stuff?" he inquired, invoking laughter around the table.

"Of course we can eat." David got to his feet. "Once we carve. And, Gage, you are my sous chef today. Stations, please." At the sideboard, David handed Gage a serving fork. "Stick it right there, dude. And don't move a muscle until I tell you."

Biting his lip in concentration, Gage anchored the breast of the initial bird while David sliced the meat onto a platter. Faith had to hand it to David: he had taken her suggestion to get closer to Gage and ran with it. She wondered if Roxanne had let him in on the worrisome investigation.

Meanwhile, the sumptuous sides made the rounds, the cooks explaining the dishes' various origins, David hopping up to refill empty casseroles from kitchen reserves. Conversation ceased as the guests consumed the feast with gusto. Faith was so hungry herself she had finished half her meal before noticing that Ellie merely pushed her food around her plate.

"I know you're upset," Faith whispered across the table, "but you have to feed that little guy, remember?"

"I know. I'm trying." Ellie managed a tiny bite of turkey, then set her fork down with a grimace. "I can't get any more down." She took a sip of water, then cupped her hand over her mouth.

Two seats away, Grace overheard Ellie's last comment. Ever attentive, the midwife leaned over Merrill to question her. "Are you feeling nauseated, honey?"

"Not exactly. It feels more like cramps."

Faith glanced up, alarmed. "Cramps? Why didn't you say something?"

"They only just started."

Panicked, Faith stood and slipped behind Connie to get to Ellie. "She can't be in labor, can she, Grace? If she is, we're in trouble, because her obstetrician's all the way in the city."

"Relax. I doubt it's labor." After setting down her napkin, Grace maneuvered to Ellie's side and placed a hand on the young woman's shoulder. "I'm certain it's nothing, but would you mind coming upstairs and letting me check things out? That is, if you feel comfortable with me," she added.

"I don't know . . ." An ashen Ellie looked up at Faith for reassurance.

"You should. I'll come with you." Faith helped Ellie to her feet. "It'll be fine."

"She's the best, Ellie." Merrill got up to hand Grace her cane.

Meanwhile, at the far end of the table, Mona sensed trouble. "Baby," she cried, rocking back and forth. Fred moved Mona's water glass preemptively and held his wife tightly to calm her. Despite her discomfort, Ellie paused to reassure her charge. "The baby's fine, Mona. See?" And as she had the day the two women met, Ellie placed Mona's hand on her abdomen, instantly calming her. Mona leaned her head against the bulging belly. "Baby's sleeping," Mona whispered, eyes closed.

"That's exactly right." Grace gently disconnected Ellie from Mona. "Let's go check out your little slugger, shall we?"

"I'll be back in a sec, Mona. Don't worry." Ellie stopped to kiss the top of the snow-white bun she had wound for Mona after the woman's nap, then followed Grace out of the dining room, Merrill and Faith at their heels.

"Are you sure you're up to this?" Merrill murmured to her sister at the bottom of the stairs.

"Up to this? I *live* for this. It's second nature."

With Merrill assisting Grace up the stairs, Faith helped Ellie a few steps behind, relieved that her friend appeared to be breathing easier. But before she reached the landing, Ellie cried out in pain, doubled over and sank onto the carpeted steps.

64

With difficulty, Faith helped Ellie upstairs and onto her bed, where she lay on her back, one hand on her belly and the other clutching her friend's hand.

"I'm scared," Ellie whispered. Her palms were slick with sweat. "What if something's wrong with the baby?"

"Don't think like that." Faith squeezed her hand. "Let's wait and see what Grace says."

The midwife entered, stethoscope draped around her neck. "Old habits. Never travel without it." Grace slipped its ear tips beneath the soft wool cap she wore that day instead of the baseball cap. "Now go," she said, shooing Faith out into the hall. "This won't take long."

Anxious and pacing, Faith did what she regretted *not* having done days ago: call Dennis, willing him to answer as the connection went from three rings to four.

Finally, he picked up. "Faith? Is that you?"

"Thank God. Where have you been?"

"With my family in Connecticut. Where else would I be?" Dennis sounded bewildered. And perhaps a bit drunk.

"Ellie's been trying to call you for hours. She thinks you're ignoring her."

"I would never do that. My little nephew got hold of my phone earlier. He must have messed with the settings. I only just now saw all of Ellie's calls. And now *she's* not answering."

"I know. She can't right now."

"Why not?" he asked, immediately suspicious. "Did something happen? Let me talk to her."

"I can't. She's with the midwife."

"Midwife? What's going on there?"

"Nothing. I'm sure we'll know something soon."

"*Something* is not nothing. Tell me what's happening. I can tell something's wrong. God! Why is Ellie even down there with you, anyway?"

Faith was about to tell him that his fiancée's coming to Wave's End was one of the best decisions she'd ever made, but Ellie's door opened at that moment and Grace stepped out into the hall, stethoscope around her neck.

"Is that the father?" Grace mouthed.

When Faith nodded, the midwife held out her hand for the phone. "If you don't mind, I'd like to speak to him myself."

65

Faith listened, astonished as Grace told Dennis the culprit was gas. The condition was quite common in pregnancy, Grace explained, and often became quite uncomfortable as the baby grew.

"Mother and son are perfectly fine," the midwife assured Dennis.

"I don't know how you do that for a living. My heart's still pounding," Faith said to Grace in the hall after handing off the call to Ellie. "Ellie's really okay, right? I mean, you wouldn't tell her she had gas just to make her feel better?"

Grace smiled tiredly. "Of course not. Ellie's fine—and will continue to be, providing she takes care of herself."

Especially now, Faith thought, picturing Ellie curled up and talking to her fiancé. Maybe Dennis was right. It might be best for Ellie to head back to Brooklyn and to him. While Mona might miss her terribly, she and Fred eventually would move to more monitored quarters, although the pastor had confided to Faith today that he had made no progress on that front. Maybe it was time to rally more resources for that search; of all the residents under this roof, Fred and Mona were most in need of a housing safety net.

In only a few months, Ellie and Dennis's baby would arrive, Faith realized with a start. Consumed with her Wave's End duties, Faith hadn't devoted a single thought to Ellie's baby shower. Hopefully, the new and improved, compassionate post-hurricane Ellie would understand the delay.

As pies, mousse and other sweets replaced the savory casseroles downstairs, Faith's dread of informing the inn's boarders crept over her again. Tomorrow would not be easy, she realized, getting to her feet. "What do you say we go down and have dessert, Grace? Everyone's probably dying to know how Ellie's doing."

"Thanks, but I believe I'll pass. I'm a bit tired." She stifled a yawn. "Either I'm out of practice, or it's all that tryptophan in the turkey."

"Let me help you to your room and bring you some dessert. How does a bite of everything sound?"

"Delicious. But I don't want to be a burden."

"Burden? If you hadn't been here today for Ellie, I don't know what we would have done."

"You would have managed. Babies have a way of telling you what they need, even before they arrive."

"So, Saint Grace saves the day again," Merrill teased, emerging from the sisters' bedroom with a shawl. "Come, my dear," she said, draping Grace's shoulders. "Let's get you comfortable."

As Merrill guided Grace to their bedroom, Faith went and sat at the top of the stairs, not quite ready to rejoin the diners, content to catch bits and pieces of dessert chatter floating up from the dining room below: Gage negotiating with Roxanne for a chance to meet up with friends, Connie engrossed in conversation with Tanya's aunt, Pastor Wilkins and Bruce sketching out the format of a community information night for storm survivors, and Fred gently chiding Mona to open her mouth for a final forkful.

Over these conversations floated a Bob Marley hymn of praise and thanks: David's kitchen work soundtrack. For today at least, they *were* together, one Mermaid's Purse family, and feeling all right, Faith thought, humming softly in accompaniment.

Closing her eyes, Faith wondered where this same group would be in a year's time. She hoped they would be gathered with loved ones around their respective Thanksgiving tables, with strong, solid new roofs over their heads to protect them. To fulfill that vision for her mother, her campaign would have to succeed, she realized.

"Mind if I join you?"

Faith opened her eyes to find Tanya climbing the stairs.

"How's the patient?" Tanya asked.

"Perfectly fine, thank goodness. How about you? Enjoying yourself?"

"Immensely. So much more personal than a restaurant. You have a lovely group of guests here."

"Maybe not for much longer."

"Speaking of that, I did catch my colleague this week after all. Unfortunately, in terms of the foreclosure, she said the bank's hands are tied, unless the homeowner can demonstrate a hardship—"

"Isn't the accountant stealing Maeve's money enough of a hardship?"

"The key word is *demonstrate*. Unless charges are filed, it's really Maeve's word against the bank's."

"And my mother's stake in all of this?"

"Again, if Walker is investigated, authorities might question the legality of that contract. I'm sorry I don't have better news. However"— Tanya dug into a pocket—"I did locate some information on loans available to small businesses affected by the storm. Given some of the damage the inn sustained, you might be eligible."

Faith took the papers Tanya offered. "Thank you. I'm glad you both could come today."

"Me, too. Keep me posted."

As Tanya headed off to collect her aunt, Merrill emerged from her bedroom.

"Think they left any dessert for us?" Merrill peered over the railing.

"Doubtful. Looks pretty picked over. Is Grace sleeping?"

"Yes, finally. She has a slight fever. I think she's a bit run-down. And a little pissed off at me."

"What for?"

Merrill sat down beside Faith. "Because I read her the riot act. Told her she's done a ton of good here, but she really needs to check in with her doctors and focus on her own recovery."

"And her reaction?"

"Of course she didn't want to hear it. Said the work at the church makes her forget her fatigue. But I'm worried. She hides it well, but Grace really has been dragging the last few days." Sighing, Merrill turned to Faith. "I think it's time for us to head back to Pennsylvania."

66

Grace's and Merrill's bags were already beside the front door when a yawning Faith came downstairs at six the next morning.

As it turned out, everyone—including Ellie, who radiated good health after last night's scare—assembled at breakfast to say good-bye.

"What's all this? The farewell committee?" Grace joked weakly as she came downstairs to breakfast, her signature baseball cap back in place. As everyone ate, Grace made the rounds, saying good-bye to each guest. When she got to Ellie, she cupped the young woman's face with her hands.

"Now, remember: no broccoli or Brussels sprouts. And send me a picture when that little slugger is born. I assume you and your young man sorted everything out?"

"We did," Ellie said. "We're good."

"Excellent. Because that little baby needs his mommy *and* his daddy."

Farewells made, Grace gazed around the dining room. "I'll certainly miss this place. You made us feel so welcome." She sought out Connie, who lingered in the rear of the small group. "I just realized we never signed your guest book. I'd like to do that before we go."

"Of course." Coming forward, Connie retrieved the newest registry from the pile so Grace could add her name. Grace then passed the pen to her sister, who in turn handed it to Ellie, and so on, down the line of guests.

When all had signed, Merrill took her sister's arm and led her outside. Gage followed with the women's bags, as instructed by his mother. As they headed down the steps, a car screeched to a stop in front of the inn, and Alicia, the church volunteer from Faith's day of sandwich-making, hopped out.

"I'm so glad you two haven't left yet," she called. "I have something for Grace." From a bag, Alicia extracted a birdhouse made of balsa wood, painted cornflower blue, with a glossy crimson door that matched its mailbox and a trio of tulips blooming in a three-dimensional emerald pot. "This birdhouse turned up after the storm. It's been in our lost and found for weeks now, and no one has claimed it," Alicia explained. "After Merrill told me your concern for the birds, I couldn't think of a better home for it than yours, Grace. Our bird lady."

Overcome, Grace accepted the gift. As she held it up for everyone to admire, a dusting of fine sand fell from it. "Perfect. It's filled with the Jersey shore!" Grace laughed. "I will treasure this. And find the perfect spot for it in my garden."

"And thank you, Merrill, for everything you've done," Alicia added. "We will miss you both very much."

"Don't worry. You'll see us again." Birdhouse under her arm, Grace rapped the black namesake hanging from the inn's mailbox with her knuckles. "Keep doing what you're doing, mermaid's purse," she said, with a wink at Faith. "We'll be back soon. There will be work to do here for a very long time."

67

Apologies for leaving so suddenly. Hope this covers things.

Faith's throat constricted as she read the sisters' hastily scrawled note, having discovered it wrapped around a wad of bills on Grace's nightstand, an amount more than covering several weeks of lodging.

With red tape slowing the release of Wave's End emergency housing funds, the sisters' departure officially reduced the Mermaid's Purse's trickle of income to zero, which made the women's gesture all the more touching. Though Connie easily could have filled this vacancy from the town's growing list of housing requests, the inn's uncertain financial picture gave her mother pause.

More pressure for this campaign to succeed, thought Faith, tucking the money into her pocket. They were scheduled to meet in the dining room after lunch, when Faith would unveil her plan to save The Mermaid's Purse. Ellie had come through with a gifted creative team to interpret Faith's concepts, and the designers had descended the week before for inspiration, photographing the inn and peppering Faith and Connie with questions.

Today, Faith sought feedback from her mother, Ellie and Bruce on the website the designers had created.

The moment was opportune, the inn tranquil with Fred and Mona napping, Roxanne braving Black Friday insanity to replace some possessions ruined in the storm, and David and Gage volunteering along with David's surfing posse in the ongoing community-wide cleanup.

When ten minutes had passed after their agreed-upon meeting time and Bruce still hadn't shown up, Faith opted to start without him. She opened the laptop Ellie had brought from the city and turned it around with a flourish to display the new website: Campaign to Save The Mermaid's Purse.

Connie and Ellie gasped, absorbing the elements of the home page. Intent on crafting an honest message from the start, Faith had designated an up-to-date photo of the inn as the page's focal point. A smaller photo of Maeve cropped from the *Beacon*'s recent feature appeared alongside, while a commanding cherry DONATE bar drew the viewer's eye to the top right of the screen.

Below the bar, viewers could click to take a virtual tour of The Mermaid's Purse, while underneath the video, a crimson thermometer tracked donations in hundreds of dollars.

"This looks great, Faith," Ellie said.

Squinting, Connie pointed to a link below the thermometer. "What are 'Naming Opportunities'?"

"Chances for donors to dedicate portions of the inn for themselves." Faith clicked on the link, and the screen displayed a list of the inn's common rooms as well as each upstairs accommodation, along with a "naming" cost for each. "So, for example, a person donating five thousand dollars could name the dining room for himself. Or herself. Or their dog, if they wanted," she explained. An entire floor could be memorialized at a substantial discount, she added.

Connie scanned the items on the list. "You mean to tell me someone can dedicate a step on the staircase?"

"Why not?" Ellie chimed in. "Other donation sites do that. A step is a bargain at the five-hundred-dollar pledge level. But if you think that's too low—"

"What about some items in the fifty-to-one-hundred-dollar range?" Connie suggested.

"Already done." Faith scrolled to the bottom of the lengthy list. "Here you go: 'Name a porch rocker for a hundred dollars.'"

"That sounds more reasonable." Connie counted aloud as she reviewed the list. "And if all of these items were accounted for—?"

"There'd be enough money to pay off the inn's entire mortgage, and then some," said Faith.

"Imagine being able to tell Maeve that," Connie said.

"Wait. That's not all." Faith clicked another tab, loading a "Memories of The Mermaid's Purse" page laid out around an image of a lush garden wedding. "We'll ask guests to share memories from their visits here, with pictures if they have them. I'll bet there's been at least one marriage proposal on the grounds over the years. And more than a few babies conceived. This was Ellie's idea, by the way."

"Nice touch, Ellie." Connie patted her hand.

Besides "Welcome" and "Memories" pages, the site would feature the inn's history, the story behind the fundraising effort, and a profile of Maeve, with each page linking back to a "Reservations" page to entice new business.

Leaving the laptop open, Faith rose and circled the dining room table, ticking off other proposed campaign elements like e-mail marketing and social-media outreach. Caught up in the campaign, Ellie's team had proposed a line of commemorative swag, but Faith demurred, citing the costs involved and preferring to focus on their core goal: raise a lot of money in a hurry.

"So that's what it looks like right now." Faith dropped into her chair, searching the women's faces for reactions. "And we never would have gotten here if it hadn't been for Ellie pushing the team the way she has, so thank you very much." Faith reached across the table to fist-bump her friend.

"Thank *you* for making me feel useful. I still feel awful about what happened with Mona, but helping to launch this campaign—well, I feel as though I'm making a contribution."

"And just what do you call that little slugger you're carrying around?" Connie teased.

Ellie rubbed her belly. "I guess he's not quite real yet. But being in the trenches here with you guys . . . well, it doesn't get much more real than that." She swiped at her eyes. "Sorry. Hormonal."

"You're forgiven. And keep in mind this is only the first draft," said Faith, taking back the laptop. "But if you like this direction . . ."

"Like it? I *love* it! Don't change a thing!" said Connie.

"Great. I'll tell the team to keep going with it. We'll show it to Maeve once it's polished."

"This is so exciting." Connie went around to Faith's side of the table for another look. "I can't wait to get the word out."

Clustered around the computer, no one noticed Bruce slip into the dining room.

"Sorry to be the bearer of bad news, ladies," he said. "But you just might *have* to wait."

68

"But Maeve hasn't even seen the website yet," Ellie protested.

"She doesn't need to," replied Bruce. "She doesn't want us to do this. That's why I'm late. She wanted to talk to me about it."

Or did you go there to intentionally poison Maeve against our idea? Rising, Faith squinted at Bruce, trying to figure out why he might want to scuttle their campaign. Certainly he wielded a great deal of influence; Maeve literally trusted him with her money and her life. Perhaps he truly had Maeve's best interests at heart.

On the other hand, Bruce could be dipping into Maeve's remaining savings at this very moment to prop up his ailing newspaper, and no one would be the wiser. If the bank foreclosed, he would still oversee Maeve's take. But if the campaign succeeded in keeping The Mermaid's Purse open, ownership would likely shift to Connie, eliminating Bruce's involvement altogether.

"But why is Maeve so set against it?" Connie asked. "Faith's plan is brilliant."

"I'm sure it is, but she's just flat-out uncomfortable asking folks for money," answered Bruce. "She's embarrassed. Said she's never asked for help in her life, and doesn't want to start now."

"But she shouldn't be embarrassed. It's not her fault," Ellie said. "That criminal accountant put her in this position."

"We all know that," Bruce said. "But Maeve has her pride. She said she took money from those good people already, every time they stayed at The Mermaid's Purse. She doesn't think it would be right to take it again."

Faith tapped her chin. "Bruce, does Maeve truly understand what's at stake here? Because if we do nothing, her beloved inn will go down in flames. She can't possibly want that."

Bruce exhaled heavily and crossed his arms. "She understands. I went over everything. All the documents from the bank. She's holding out for another option."

"Outside of a miracle, there is none." Faith wished she had been there to hear his conversation with Maeve. She didn't want to believe Bruce would conspire against Maeve, but something wasn't adding up. She rubbed her lower lip, helpless against her rush to judgment, a defense mechanism honed over years as a spectator at Connie's parade of dubious partners.

Finally, Faith could remain quiet no longer. "Why didn't you do something?" she burst out.

Bruce blinked in surprise. "Are . . . are you talking to me?"

"Yes, you. You're here almost every day. The day we came to visit. The morning after the storm. Every time we turn around, there you are. If you're such a master at predicting storms, why didn't you see this mess coming and do something to stop it?"

"I told you: I warned Maeve as best I could without betraying my sources." Bruce looked taken aback by Faith's accusation. He removed his glasses and rubbed under his eyes.

"Sources? Really? Maybe you were just hanging around to gather more color for your front-page story. So you could sell more papers, and keep your business from failing."

Speechless, Bruce looked to Faith's mother.

"Faith." Glaring at her daughter, Connie gripped Faith's arm. "You need to stop right now. You're being horrible."

"What are you really after, anyway?" Yanking her arm away, Faith sat down hard at the table. Unwittingly, Bruce had uncapped something deep within her: years of bottled-up vitriol and resentment against every man in her mother's life who had come before him. "Maybe it's not just the inn you're after. Maybe it's my mother."

"I said, that's *enough*." Connie's palm struck the table, the impact toppling a bud vase. "I'm sorry, Bruce. I don't know what to say. You've been nothing but kind, and yet it appears my daughter has temporarily lost her mind."

"You have nothing to apologize for, Connie." Bruce slid his glasses back on. "And, Faith, I can't think of a single thing I've done to make you feel this way, besides trying to help. That's what friends and neighbors do. I promise you, my intentions with Maeve, and with your mother—"

Faith snorted as Bruce glanced over her head at Connie.

"Are nothing but honorable," he continued. "And if any of that has offended you in some way, well, I don't know how I can fix that."

⟊

Ellie sat with Faith in silence for a while after Connie left with Bruce. Finally, Faith took a deep breath, holding it until her diaphragm protested in pain and she had to expel it. "Well, I guess I told him," she said weakly. "Oh, my God, Ellie," Faith cried, dropping her head into her hands. "What the hell have I done?"

"I think the question is how are you going to fix it?" Ellie said as she rubbed Faith's back.

After submitting to her friend's calming touch for a few moments, Faith sat up again. "I just wish I knew where that came from."

"I don't think it's a huge mystery. Obviously, you had some things to get off your chest."

Faith rubbed her face. "About my mother? That's for sure."

"Actually, I was thinking more of your father."

Faith stared at Ellie. "How is this about him? I don't even remember him."

"Exactly. He abandoned you. Okay, officially your mother left *him*, but he gave her no choice. *He's* where all this distrust comes from."

"So you think I'm projecting my daddy issues onto Bruce?" Faith massaged her lip while she considered this. "I suppose it's possible. But it still didn't entitle me to rip Bruce a new one. I'm sure he'll never speak to me again."

"He seems like a decent guy. He'll come around. As long as you apologize."

"Ugh. I'm too embarrassed to think about that right now. But as far as this place goes, I'm not giving up this campaign without a fight. No matter how Maeve feels. This inn is my mother's future. It's all she has. I didn't put my life on hold and come down here only to watch her hand over The Mermaid's Purse to the bank."

Rising, Faith scooped up the laptop and headed out of the dining room.

"Where are you going?" Ellie called.

"To have a little sit-down with Maeve. She needs to hear this whole thing from my perspective."

69

After navigating the maze of halls in the rehabilitation center, Faith eventually located Maeve sitting alone in the facility's solarium. She sat down at the table, asking Maeve about her recovery and making small talk, then cleared her throat. "Maeve, Bruce told us how you felt about the campaign."

"I come from a long line of hard workers. We don't ask for handouts."

"I respect that, but I thought you might want to have a look at it before you make your final decision. Will you at least let me walk you through what we've done so far?"

"I'm not too sure about all this technology," Maeve said.

"I'll handle that part. You don't have to do a thing but watch."

Reluctantly, Maeve agreed. "But only because you've made the trip to see me, dear."

"You'll see we've tried to be sensitive," Faith said, launching the site. "*And* honest." As she demonstrated the campaign, she watched Maeve surreptitiously, hearing the woman's breath catch when the "Memories" page displayed. "It might be nice to hear from some of your guests after all these years, don't you think?"

"Perhaps," was all Maeve would say. When they moved on to "Naming Opportunities," she balked. "The place might feel a bit like a museum, what with all those plaques with people's names hanging everywhere."

"They wouldn't be that intrusive. I promise. And remember," Faith said softly, her hand on the arm of the wheelchair. "If this plan works, *you* wouldn't be living there. My mother would."

"I suppose you're right. But still . . ." Maeve pulled a crumpled tissue from inside the sleeve of her sweater and dabbed her nose.

"I understand your reaction. And your pride. But, Maeve, there's not a lot of time. This campaign is our best shot at turning things around. If you don't let us do everything in our power to rescue the business you built, there won't be any more Mermaid's Purse. And that's something you might regret it for the rest of your life." Faith watched the tissue in Maeve's hand begin to quiver.

Emboldened, she pushed on. "If you don't fight, it would be like . . . like handing another victory to that swine, after he's already harmed you so deeply. You'd just be giving more satisfaction to a monster who tried to destroy you and everything that mattered to you, just to feed his miserable addictions."

Faith sat back, shocked for the second time that day by the intensity of her emotions. Even Maeve blinked at her in surprise. Months ago, Faith hadn't even heard of The Mermaid's Purse; today, she was pleading for its life.

Ellie was right. Something primordial *had* driven her to lash out at Bruce earlier. Saving the broken-down inn was the only way to rescue her mother. And maybe herself.

Ellie was reading a magazine with Mona in the salon, but she jumped up when Faith returned. "So, how did it go?"

Faith patted her pocket, where she had placed the paper Maeve had given her for safekeeping. "By the time I finished, Maeve gave us permission to name the darn toilets if we want to."

70

It was one thing for Faith to be smug with Ellie, and quite another to face her mother after her earlier outburst. She found Connie upstairs in their room.

"Don't apologize to me," Connie barely glanced up from her magazine when Faith entered. "Bruce is the one that needs to hear it."

"I know. I'll go and see him first thing tomorrow."

Connie set the magazine aside. "I can't help but feel some of your anger down there might have been meant for me."

"It wasn't. Not directly." Faith sat on the edge of the bed. "Let's face it, Mom. There haven't been a ton of stand-up guys in our lives. I guess I didn't really know what to do when I finally met one."

"You and me both, Faith."

"So tell me: Do you like Bruce? I mean, *like* him, like him?"

"I don't know yet. He's a gentleman, that's for sure. But I want to take things slowly for once. See if that makes a difference."

Faith smiled. "I think that's a good idea. I hope I didn't ruin things between you. Because that wasn't my intention."

"You didn't. Anyway, this inn is my priority at the moment."

"Right. The inn. On the bright side, I did get Maeve's blessing on the campaign."

"You did? That's wonderful! Bruce seemed so sure—"

"Well, Bruce underestimated my powers of persuasion. Anyway, the site will go live in a few days."

"Maybe it will be so successful we won't have bad news to tell the boarders." Connie pulled her sweater around her shoulders.

"I hope you're right, but we can't wait any longer to tell them, Mom. As soon as everyone's back tonight. They deserve to know."

71

In spite of the mouthwatering Thanksgiving leftovers David took it upon himself to concoct—turkey, brie and cherry-chipotle panini; sweet potato and bacon mash; wild rice, cranberry and cheese-stuffed peppers—Faith's anxiety over her mother's imminent announcement prevented her from enjoying a single bite.

Looking around the long table left in place from the holiday meal, Faith realized everyone had taken their same seats from yesterday, like family members at the dinner table—that is, everyone but Gage. According to David, the teen had refused a ride back from the cleanup, saying he'd catch a lift with friends. A subdued Roxanne periodically glanced at the door, Faith observed.

David also must have sensed Roxanne's anxiety, because he leaned over to reassure her, his dark head against hers. *Transference?*

Faith yearned to brandish her fork at him. *What about me? Can't you see I'm worried? That my insides are as wobbly as aspic, as slushy as the sorbet in the Blue Osprey's freezer the day we met?* Then again, how could he know? Until today, her emotions had been buttoned as tight as her double-breasted chef's coat. Maybe if she opened up to him the way she had to his father (but in a far less unhinged manner), she might elicit more of a reaction.

Meanwhile, next to Faith, Connie deliberately prolonged the meal, assiduously collecting every last crumb of pecan pie on her plate with her fork. Finally, after another meaningful look from Faith, Connie picked up her spoon and rapped it against her water glass.

David pushed back his seat. "Go ahead, Connie. We're all ears. Although I don't know how you'll top yesterday's toast."

Setting the spoon down, Connie paused a moment, positioning and repositioning the utensil beside her dessert plate. "I agree, David," she said finally. "Nothing could top yesterday. But that was yesterday, and today—" She paused, gnawing her lip. "Well, I'm afraid today is a very different story. It truly breaks my heart to say what I have to say."

In tears, Roxanne rose halfway through Connie's halting announcement and bolted from the dining room, before Connie could even soften the blow with a mention of the pending campaign to save the inn.

"How much time do we have before the bank takes over?" David asked.

"About four weeks. And don't worry, Fred." Connie reached across to cover the man's hand. "Locating a place for you and Mona is at the top of Pastor Wilkins's list. And a few others', as well."

"Thank you, Miss Connie. I don't suppose our Ellie can come along with us, could she?"

Brightening at the man's vote of confidence, Ellie tightened her grip on Mona, whose agitated rocking had commenced even before Connie had begun to speak. Though mostly disconnected from the everyday, the elderly woman's reactions often reflected a prescient lucidity and intuition that belied her confusion. It was as though Mona knew about the pastor's earlier phone call, when he told Faith that all area facilities with memory care were full to bursting at the moment, with waiting lists even, but that he wasn't giving up.

"I wish I could," Ellie said. "But I'll come visit you, wherever you are. With this guy." Ellie patted her stomach. "And we're not giving up hope yet. Tell them about the campaign, Faith."

Summoning all the cheer she could muster, Faith demonstrated the fundraising website to the silent diners, and fled to the kitchen immediately afterward. Wiping her sweaty palms on a dish towel, Faith leaned her forehead against the cool refrigerator door, where the calendar hung, the heavily circled foreclosure date a damning reminder. Faith's heart beat a cadence, a stopwatch ticking off the seconds until the December deadline.

What if the campaign missed the mark? What if the inn's target audience of past guests turned out to be perfectly content to memorialize The Mermaid's Purse exactly as it had been during their stay, preserving it as a lovely memory and nothing more—memories that wouldn't cost them a cent? What would that mean for the present residents? For the Wave's End families in shelters and seedy motels waiting for housing? For her own mother?

"So what does this foreclosure mean for Faith Sterling?"

Faith spun to find David carrying a plastic tub of dirty glasses. "Don't tell me you didn't know," she said, taking the tub to rinse the glassware. "Your father must have told you."

"He didn't. I swear. Scout's honor."

Faith waved away his two-fingered peace sign. "I don't think that's the right symbol."

"Don't avoid the question."

"Me? I'll survive. I'll head back to New York, eventually find a new job and apartment. But those poor people in there—" Faith loaded plates into the dishwasher. "I hate to think that their last memory of The Mermaid's Purse will be of us booting them to the curb."

"Aha! A little soft spot in that shell."

Shell. What had Grace said that day on the porch about the contributions of a mermaid's purse? "Of course a soft spot. How could I not?" Watching the boarders' dejected faces as Connie broke the bad news, Faith had felt as though she were putting her own family out on the street—which, in a sense, she was.

At that moment, she resolved to take every remaining meal in the dining room, elbow to elbow with the boarders. With her *friends*. To hell with boundaries. Her mother had gotten it right all along. This wasn't business as usual. The inn was a port in a storm, however temporary.

Frustrated with the unfairness of the situation, Faith slammed the dishwasher rack so hard it clattered against the appliance's rear wall.

"Whoa. What are you doing?" David detached Faith's hand from the rack, lacing his fingers lightly in hers.

"I'm . . . I'm just trying to do my job."

"Maybe you don't need to work so hard."

"But that's why I'm here. To help."

By now, David held both her hands and drew her closer to him, his gaze intense and disquieting. "Everyone here knows how much you care about them."

"I don't think they—"

"Trust me. I'm one of them."

"But I've been so awful. Making all these rules. And, oh, my God, what I said to your father today . . ."

"I'm sure he'll survive."

"No. You don't even know, David. I was like a crazy woman—"

"Faith. Please." Freeing a hand, he cupped Faith's chin and lifted it, giving her no choice but to look at him. "Do me a favor. Shut up." With that, he leaned in, his gaze seeking permission, Faith granting it by closing her eyes and surrendering to his sweet and savory kiss. He tasted of pancetta and brie and other ingredients from the meal he had just prepared. As his lips consumed hers, Faith struggled to remember the last time, *any* time, a guy had cooked for her.

None came to mind. Not because they hadn't offered, but because *she* always refused, the kitchen her domain, Faith too terrified to relinquish control. Too insecure to be nourished by someone else.

This time, she *had* let go. As David's kisses warmed her cheeks, her nose, her forehead, Faith realized she'd been letting go all along, since the first time she allowed David into her space, her world, accepting his paper bag spices. The day on the back porch, so engrossed in conversation with him she nearly burned her roasting vegetables. Salvaging the soup, with his help. From there, the potpies. Their Thanksgiving collaboration. His originality and resourcefulness tonight.

Too many cooks, indeed. Instead of the flameouts Faith envisioned, the letting go had felt delicious.

Faith lifted her head, her neck igniting as David nuzzled it.

Truly, truly delicious.

72

Finding the *Beacon*'s entrance locked, Faith sighed with relief. Turning away, she headed back to the car, grateful for additional time to finesse her apology to Bruce.

"Faith! Wait!"

At the newspaperman's call, Faith dropped her head, did an about-face and slowly walked back to the open office door where Bruce stood. *Okay, let's do this.*

"Hey, there," she said, too brightly.

"Happened to glance out the window and saw you. I take it you're looking for me?"

"Who else?" *Oh, Lord. Insert foot.*

"I'm working on tomorrow's issue. Come in if you'd like."

"Thanks. Listen," Faith began once inside, shoving her hands into her jacket pockets. "About yesterday: I was *way* out of line. To put it mildly. I had absolutely no right, no basis for saying those things."

"That's right," Bruce said. "You didn't. I run an honest business here, Faith."

"I know. I shouldn't have—"

"And yes, the days of this little community newspaper might be numbered, but I built the *Beacon*. I'd never resort to sensationalism just to sell papers. It may not compare to your fancy New York newspapers, but the *Beacon* has scruples. *I* have scruples."

"I know that." Faith gazed up at him. "I don't know what came over me. Ever since I arrived in Wave's End, it's as though Nadine turned my whole life upside down. And my mother's. Nowhere near the way the storm affected people here, of course," she hurried to clarify. "Just . . . emotionally. I'm trying to figure some stuff out. Please forgive me. I know my mother likes you, and that's good enough for me." Faith extended her hand, and Bruce shook it.

"Apology accepted. I like her, too. And because of that, as nasty as you were to me, I have to admire the way you stood up for your mother."

Faith grinned, leaning against the door frame. "Force of habit, I guess."

"And by the way, I was against this lottery idea from the start. Walker put that contest idea into Maeve's head, too. Probably saw more dollar signs. Unfortunately, it only resulted in heartache—aside from bringing you and your mother to Wave's End, that is." Bruce smiled. "I must say, my son seems to enjoy having you around."

Faith coughed at the mention of David, her face warming as she flashed back to their latest encounter. "Speaking of Walker, when do you think he'll turn up?"

"Actually, that's why I'm here today. The feds arrested him late yesterday at JFK Airport. I've been up all night writing the story. Let me give you a preview."

∽

Sitting at Bruce's desk, Faith read the headline intended for the *Beacon*'s next front page:

LOCAL CPA NABBED EN ROUTE TO CAYMAN ISLANDS; CHARGED WITH MONEY LAUNDERING, TAX EVASION

"Holy . . . Was I *right*, or what?" Faith crowed. "I told my mother that's where they'd find him. Does Maeve know?"

"Called her first thing. You would have heard from me the second I finished."

Faith read a little further, learning Walker faced up to twenty years in prison if convicted. "Now that they've got him, what are the chances Maeve will get her money back?"

"In time to avoid foreclosure? Slim to none. It may take months, even years, to recover the money he siphoned. She'll have to take a number. Apparently, this guy was in pretty deep with a number of clients."

"Still, we should go back to the bank with this news. Tanya said we had to demonstrate financial hardship. These charges certainly illustrate that."

"It's worth a shot. I'll stop by there first thing Monday. Do you want to join me?"

"Of course. But even if the bank grants a delay, I still think we should launch the campaign. Did Maeve mention she approved it?"

"She did. Said you were quite convincing."

"I was only thinking of my mother. And of the boarders, of course."

Bruce leaned over and hit a few keys. "That reminds me of another update I'm working on. The beach fires. The fire chief closed his investigation."

Faith shut her eyes. "And what did he conclude?"

"Here. Read it yourself." Bruce hit the return key, and the next headline filled his screen.

73

*FAULTY GAS LINE TRIGGERED BEACHFRONT
FIRE; ARSON RULED OUT.*

Faith spun in Bruce's chair to face him. "So that's it? No suspects? No arrests?"

"None. The salt water corroded the utilities, creating a fire hazard. In fact, most of the gas and electric at the beachfront will have to be ripped out and replaced, just as a safety precaution."

"But that chain they found . . ."

"Evidence kids had been messing around up there, for sure. There were some beer cans as well, apparently. But ultimately, nothing connected them to the fire." Bruce tapped the screen. "It's all there, if you want to read the details."

"No, thank you," Faith said, getting up. "That's all I need to know."

74

Her conscience eased, and bursting with the news of Gage's exonera-
tion, Faith bounded up the inn's back steps and into the kitchen, where
she found David prodding simmering turkey carcasses with a wooden
spoon. "Turkey soup! You read my mind. David, you'll never believe—"

"I'll believe anything, if you just come with me." Dropping the
spoon, David grabbed Faith's hand and pulled her out onto the dark
recesses of the porch. He proceeded to kiss her hungrily, sabotaging her
attempts to speak until Faith finally pulled away, laughing.

"Stop already," she said, leaning against a porch column. "I really
need to talk to you. I saw your dad today. I apologized."

"Good. Now you can stop beating yourself up about that meltdown
of yours."

"I'll need a minute for that. Anyway, he's a good guy. He told me
they got Walker."

"About time. Hope he gets what he deserves." Coming toward her
again, David reached for Faith's waist, but she sidestepped him.

"*Wait.*" She slapped him playfully. "He told me something else: that
the beachfront fire wasn't set. The gas line caused it." Faith watched him
closely for his response.

Exhaling, David leaned against the wall. "That's a relief."

"I *knew* it! You knew that was Gage's chain."

"I'm just glad he's off the hook."

"Did he tell you where he was that night?"

"No. But he swore he wasn't involved in any fire, and I believe him."

"Still, we have to make sure he's okay."

"Gage is fine. He's out of trouble." Approaching Faith again, David clasped her hands and attempted to nuzzle her neck.

"No, I mean *really* okay." Wriggling to thwart his advances, she angled her face toward his. "I have an idea. Will you help?"

"I already taught the dude to surf." David drawled, kissing Faith's nose lightly. "What's next, flyboarding?"

"I have no idea what that is, but this idea is strictly land-based. Are you in?" Faith yanked David's hands, gazing at him expectantly.

David sighed in mock exasperation. "If I say yes, woman, will you stop talking?"

∽

Starting the coffee the next morning, Faith felt her cheeks flush at the memory of last night's porch interlude. Surely her mother, or especially Ellie, would notice the change in her, spot the evidence of David's affections, even if Faith was playing it close to the vest for the moment.

But neither woman said a word. Fueled by the news of Walker's arrest, Connie and Ellie were already in full campaign-launch mode. The Save The Mermaid's Purse site was going live at nine o'clock on this final Sunday morning in November. They'd synched the launch with the delivery of an impassioned e-mail composed by Faith and blessed by Maeve to the inboxes of all prior inn guests.

"I can just imagine everyone sitting around drinking coffee and reading this," Connie said, rubbing her hands together.

At exactly 9:12 a.m., ignoring the piles of dirty breakfast dishes, Connie sat at the kitchen table glued to the laptop, eagerly awaiting the outpouring of support, while Ellie paced the dining room. Assigned by Faith to manage the launch logistics, Ellie tapped her Bluetooth earpiece, spouting real-time statistics from her site administrators in the city. The metrics on hits and opens and click-throughs and other digital benchmarks were completely foreign to Connie, but, judging from Ellie's broad smile and thumbs-up, their message had hit its mark. Their target audience had already swarmed to the fundraising site in very encouraging numbers.

Connie stared at the thermometer on the main page for evidence of activity. "It's not budging," she said worriedly when Ellie passed next.

"You have to refresh the page." Reaching over her, Ellie clicked the circular arrow at the top of the screen. As the page reloaded, the bottom of the thermometer bulb flooded with color.

Connie clapped her hands. "Look at that! We're already at five thousand dollars. *Five thousand*, Faith."

Faith covered her ears. "Don't tell me. It's too stressful. There's too much riding on this." She had remained in the dining room as long as possible to avoid hearing anything.

But when Ellie squealed over something on the "Memories" page, Faith found herself lured back to the screen in spite of her earlier resolve. Sure enough, one donor had already posted a remembrance, which Faith proceeded to read aloud:

"'So sorry to hear about your troubles.'"

"I thought you didn't want to know," Connie teased.

Ignoring her mother, Faith continued reading.

"'The first time I ever saw a beach or the ocean was when my family stayed at The Mermaid's Purse. I've brought my own family many times since. I will never forget that sight, or your lovely inn.'"

"That's so sweet," Connie murmured.

"So's her picture." Ellie clicked to enlarge the accompanying image: a sunburned young mother in a red swimsuit kneeling on the beach, arms around a towheaded boy playing with a plastic bucket and shovel. "I wonder if Maeve would remember her," she mused.

"How much? How much?" demanded Faith.

"Well, that's surprising." Sitting back, Ellie licked her lips.

"Five thousand? Ten thousand?" Connie pressed.

"No," said Ellie, her tone subdued. "No donation at all."

"That's okay. There will be others to make up for that one," Connie said confidently. "I'm going to call Maeve right now and let her know we're off to a good start."

Despite that disappointment, dozens of Mermaid's Purse memories popped up on the campaign site over the next few hours. The addictive page drew them to the laptop throughout the day, attracted like zombies to sweat to serially refresh the screen.

By evening, however, a disheartening trend had emerged: while posted memories and images piled up in earnest, donations inexplicably had stalled. Beyond the initial blip at the site launch, the thermometer gauge had not budged, and not a single naming opportunity had been claimed.

Faith did her best to reassure them. "It's too early to freak out. People aren't going to just hop on and make a twenty-five-thousand-dollar donation. They need to think about it. Move some funds. Be patient and give the campaign a chance to work."

75

Faith and Bruce met at the bank at nine a.m. on Monday morning. Once they presented evidence of Walker's arrest, including the naming of Maeve as a victim of his alleged criminal activities, the bank agreed to reexamine the inn's case. Under a process known as forbearance, the creditor could offer the inn up to six additional months to catch up on its payments, the bespectacled loan officer explained.

"That's wonderful," said Faith. "So Maeve now has until June?"

"Not exactly," he said. "We're just the local branch. Those decisions come from our corporate foreclosure division, after a formal review."

"But it's right here in black and white." Frustrated, Faith slid the *Beacon* across the loan officer's desk.

"I see that. We value Ms. Calhoun as a customer and member of our community, and we're pleased to see justice being served. But you both must understand. We have to protect our assets, especially in this turbulent period after the storm."

Faith and Bruce exchanged troubled glances.

"Tell you what," the officer said. "I'll do what I can to expedite this. I should be able to get back to you in a few weeks." Standing, he extended his hand.

Meanwhile, Faith and David indulged their furtive flirtation over the next few days, exchanging meaningful glances at mealtimes and stealing kisses in the inn's nooks and crannies when they thought no one was looking.

David questioned the subterfuge. "Why are we hiding? We're both adults."

"I know. It's just a bit weird with my mother here," she whispered one night after she had snuck down the hall to his room. They lay side by side, sharing his headphones to listen to his music. Connie was only an excuse; in truth, it had been so long since Faith had experienced the heady rush of blossoming romance that she wanted to draw it out and savor it.

"I feel like I'm back in high school," David mock-complained.

"When I was in high school, my mom was the one who brought the guys home."

They shared a laugh over that, and Faith's love of rap, which David found hysterical. Over that night and the next, they talked into the wee hours, discovering each other. Faith adored action films; David loathed them. As a kid, David blew through books about boy detectives; Faith preferred biographies and cookbooks.

David propped his head on his elbow to face her in the dark. "You did *not* read cookbooks."

"Yes, I did. My mother sold them door to door at one point. There were quite a few around the house."

And on and on.

"So . . ." David stretched, rolling over on his back. "Are we doing this?"

"You mean the campaign?" Faith deliberately misunderstood him. "We certainly are. We're already three days in."

"No. I mean *this.*" He wagged his finger inclusively. "Us. I like you, Faith. And judging from the last week or so, I'd say you like me, too."

"Of course I like you. But you have to admit: this is a weird setup."

"You mean the fact that we've barely advanced beyond kissing, and we're already living together?"

Faith laughed. "I hadn't thought of it quite like that. But yeah, that does make it hard to figure out where we go from there."

"How about . . . here?"

∽

While Faith would have preferred to seal herself away in a bubble with David, reality interfered. Another week passed, during which the Save The Mermaid's Purse online thermometer barely budged, and the mail yielded only a handful of checks amounting to a few hundred dollars. Also, the bank had yet to render a decision about the loan extension.

"I can see why they call it 'forbearance,'" Faith complained to David one afternoon as he left to pinch-hit in his friend's pizzeria. "I'm so fed up with worrying and waiting to see what will happen to this place I seriously could lose my mind."

"Please don't," David said, kissing Faith good-bye. "Everyone's already lost enough around here. Just try to think good thoughts."

Later, Faith, Connie and Roxanne had tea in the living room following yet another subdued supper. Painfully aware of their hosts' distress, the boarders had stopped asking about the fundraising campaign, albeit preparing for a possible foreclosure in their various ways.

Should that scenario occur, Faith was least worried about David. Philosophical about his business loss, he traveled light and landed on his feet. Bruce had repeated his offer of letting him stay at his place, David told her, although he appeared in no rush to take him up on that. Her main concern about David in the event of a move was whether he could maintain the connection he'd forged with Gage, which would depend heavily on where Roxanne and Gage ended up, Faith realized.

She had overheard Roxanne making a housing inquiry or two. But because strong post-storm demand quickly ate up the area's subsidized lodging, Roxanne's efforts had turned up only a couple of rooms in a sketchy motel in a neighboring town.

"How can I take Gage to a place like that?" Roxanne complained to Faith now as they sat on the couch. "And even if we did move there temporarily, he'd have to change schools, since it's in a different district. I can't do that to my kid again." Leaning forward, she kneaded her forehead with the heels of her hands. "It's hopeless," she said flatly.

Faith placed her hand on Roxanne's knee. "It's not. There must be something out there besides a crummy motel. What if you just paid for the housing outright instead of using the town subsidy? Would that give you more options?" she asked.

"Maybe, but I can't do that, because my 'loving husband'"— Roxanne's tone dripped with venom—"is restricting my cash flow."

"What? Can he do that? I'm sure a lawyer could—"

Roxanne sat up and faced Faith. "Don't you think I've thought of that? I *will* call a lawyer. But right now, I'm just trying to make it through the day without . . . Honestly, I'm overwhelmed."

"Is there anything I can do?" Roxanne's hair could use a washing, Faith noticed, as could her stained Metallica sweatshirt.

"I doubt there's anything anyone can do," Roxanne said, getting up. "I'm going to bed."

Faith stared after her, concerned about the woman's state of mind. Roxanne herself said she hadn't lost all that much in the storm, comparatively speaking. And surely she could find a temporary living arrangement by making a few more phone calls. But listening to her tonight, Faith realized Roxanne wasn't up to even that simple task.

"I'm worried about her, Mom."

Connie looked up from her tea. "I am, too."

"I think Roxanne is depressed, and that the uncertainty of the inn's situation is making things worse."

"What do you think we should do?" asked Connie.

Mother and daughter looked at each other across the salon. With Ellie's help, Faith had knocked herself out trying to resurrect The Mermaid's Purse, but perhaps now it might be prudent to concede they had run out of time. And options.

"I hate to say it, but I think we have to admit that this campaign failed dismally," said Faith.

Her mother paused before replying. "I think you're right," she said softly. "I'm sorry, Faith. I should have listened when you tried to warn me about this lottery idea."

Rare as these acknowledgments were from her mother, Faith derived no satisfaction from this admission as she took in her mother's slumped shoulders and downturned mouth. "Maybe so, but a lot of good came from it."

"I appreciate that, coming from you. And I meant what I said: never again. I promise."

Faith held her breath, anticipating her mother's next words, but Connie only drew a little *X* over her breastbone with her thumb.

"Cross my heart. No more contests," Connie finished, getting to her feet. "I guess I'll start researching flights back home. What's another ten years packaging potatoes?"

"Please, you two. Don't give up hope," Ellie said hoarsely as she entered the salon. "Not yet."

"Sorry, El," said Faith. "If nothing else, the campaign collected some lovely memories for Maeve. And chipped away a bit at that line of credit."

As she watched her mother head toward the stairs, Faith felt her phone vibrate in her back pocket and pulled it out to look at it. "Mom, wait. I missed a call from Merrill. Maybe she's calling to say she and Grace are ready to come back!"

A return visit by the upbeat sisters certainly would lift spirits around The Mermaid's Purse, Faith thought, retrieving Merrill's voice mail.

But upon hearing the message, Faith could only cup her hand over her mouth, replaying the recording on the remote chance she'd misunderstood, holding up a finger to quiet the chattering Ellie and Connie.

"Will Grace and Merrill come for Christmas?" Ellie demanded as Faith set her phone in her lap. "They have to. It'll be the last time we're all together. And tell Grace I promise the Slugger and I will make it through the entire meal this time." She laughed.

"I can't, Ellie. They won't be here for Christmas."

"Okay. Then we'll get them to come before." Connie came and sat beside Faith. "It will be nice to celebrate early."

"No, Mom. You don't understand. They can't come. It's . . . Grace. She's gone."

76

Her sister had gone quickly, and with little discomfort, succumbing to a low-grade infection that Grace's compromised immune system couldn't fight, Merrill had said in a voice numb with shock. She apologized for conveying the news via voice mail, but hoped they would understand there were many people still to be contacted.

"How can that be? Grace seemed fine." Ellie's tears splashed onto her rounded belly as the three huddled to listen to Merrill's message.

"Her resistance must have been pretty low after her treatments," said Faith.

"Then why did she wear herself out in Wave's End instead of staying home and taking care of herself?" Ellie blew her nose hard.

"Because that wouldn't have been Grace." Connie spoke softly. "Doing for others gave her a great deal of joy. Consider her life's work."

"All those babies," said Faith.

"I wanted Grace to meet mine." Ellie gulped.

Faith put her hand on Ellie's knee. "She would have loved that."

Per Grace's wishes, there would be only a simple, private memorial, but Merrill promised to get in touch with Faith as soon as possible after the service.

Stunned, Faith wiped her tears from the screen with the hem of her shirt. In Faith's two brief porch encounters with the late midwife, Grace had exhibited a quiet strength, a profound perception of the human spirit. How she would have enjoyed more opportunities to speak with the midwife to ask how she and Connie might move forward as they prepared to close the Mermaid's Purse's doors forever, to tell her how right she'd been about David.

"I swear Grace was with me today," Connie said quietly. She had moved to the armchair by the fireplace, the spot they had come to think of as Mona's.

"Mom." Faith's voice splintered. Over the years, her mother sometimes claimed to feel the presence of the departed. Usually, Faith tolerated it, but this loss hurt too deeply. All the visions and crystals in the world wouldn't bring Grace back.

"What do you mean, Connie?" Ellie asked.

"I was on my way to visit Maeve. I had been dreading the visit, feeling bad I didn't have better news to bring her. And then suddenly, the oddest thing happened: I was stopped at a traffic light, and something made me look up. And there, right in front of me, a mob of seagulls was headed straight toward the ocean."

Ellie sat up. "You think they were a sign from Grace?"

"All I know is, the birds were such a big part of the reason the sisters came here in the first place. You weren't here their first morning, Ellie, but Grace explained that when a disaster drives the birds away, it's a sign things have gone horribly wrong.

"Anyway," Connie continued, "as the seagulls took off this afternoon in this lovely *V* formation, a wave of hope washed over me. A feeling that whatever happened in the future, things would be okay. *We* would be okay," she clarified, looking at Faith. "Where else could that have come from but Grace?"

"That's beautiful, Connie," Ellie said.

"I know it's difficult, but we have to focus on moving forward. To the next season. It's what Grace would want."

Connie got up, went to Ellie and crouched in front of her. "I believe Grace will watch over you. She'll see you through this pregnancy and delivery. We'll see you through it. You'll have an easy time of it. You'll see."

⁓

The three sat a while longer in silence, finishing fresh tea Connie made for them. Finally, Ellie rose to go to bed, tearfully embracing each of them. Watching her friend head up the stairs, Faith took in Ellie's distinct waddle, her need to pause on the landing to knead the small of her back with her fist before tackling the rest of the stairs. Her friend would give birth in less than two months, Faith realized with a shock—one more reminder that if all else failed and The Mermaid's Purse shuttered its doors, the boarders would not be the only ones impacted; Faith and her mother would face their own housing crises, too.

Time marched boldly on, no matter how desperate the desire to slow it. Each day had to be savored.

Finally, Connie went to bed, too. Faith remained on the couch, giving her mother time to fall asleep. Then she headed upstairs, passing by her own bedroom and heading straight for David's, slipping inside to wait for him.

77

The news of Grace's passing further blackened the mood at The Mermaid's Purse, where the approaching foreclosure deadline had already overshadowed any thoughts of the coming holiday. In the kitchen, December's bull's-eyed date taunted Faith each time she passed it, until she could stand it no longer and tossed the calendar into a drawer.

In the days following the midwife's death, no one but Faith bothered to check the fundraising's site donations thermometer, where the temperature remained frozen at the five-thousand-dollar mark. Finally, she set up an e-mail alert for updates on any new donations and forgot about it, focusing instead on the two boarders most vulnerable in the event of a foreclosure: Fred and Mona.

At least Pastor Wilkins was keeping his promise to look in on the couple while he searched for another place for them to live, accepting Faith's invitation to dinner that evening.

"They're in the dining room, all ready for you," Faith heard her mother greet the cleric.

Roxanne and Gage had graciously agreed to dine a little later in order to give the elderly couple some privacy with their pastor.

"How soon do you think their pastor will find something for them?" David asked Faith, ripping a hunk of bread from a loaf on the counter. Her kitchen boundaries happily falling by the wayside, Faith had granted him carte blanche to invade her space as he liked.

"I have no idea. I hope it's soon, because if we have to close this place, those two will have nowhere to go."

"It's not as if The Mermaid's Purse is a safe haven for Mona."

"I know, but at least it's somewhat familiar. *We're* familiar, most of the time. And we're support for Fred. If they have to transition somewhere else in the interim, where no one knows them, I . . . I don't want to think about what might happen."

David's response to this was unintelligible, his mouth stuffed with bread he had soaked in the bowl of beef daube Faith offered. For the pastor's visit, Faith had decided comfort food was in order: a time-honored recipe of marinating inexpensive chuck overnight in Beaujolais, then bringing the mixture to a simmer the next day with garlic, carrots and celery, copious amounts of fresh black pepper, a Provençal bundle of bay leaves, thyme and rosemary, and a drizzle of olive oil.

The stew never failed to please—even this shortcut version, with dried spices substituted for fresh, and supermarket egg noodles filling in for homemade pappardelle. Faith set the cover back on Maeve's Dutch oven, which performed nearly as well as Piquant's heavy enameled cocottes.

"What will Ellie do if Fred and Mona leave?" David asked when he'd finished chewing.

"Head back to Brooklyn and get ready for the baby, I guess. She said she and Dennis would come for Christmas."

"And you?"

Faith glanced up in surprise. Since the night of their first kiss, they'd avoided any discussion of the future, falling into a comfortable rhythm, like playing house.

"That's the million-dollar question. I guess I need to figure out the answer before *then*." Faith opened the kitchen drawer and jabbed at the

December 31 foreclosure date on the calendar. "What about you? Any plans for after?"

David set his bowl in the sink. "Trying to cobble some things together. I'll stick with the catering while I see how it all plays out. But in the meantime, there's Christmas."

"I know. I wanted to plan a lovely send-off for everyone. But after Grace . . ." Faith covered her face with her hands.

"You still need to do that." Speaking softly, David gently pried Faith's hands from her cheeks, his touch buoying her, his warm brown eyes brimming with compassion. "Everyone needs this send-off. For closure. What if we did something simple, like an open house?"

"Right. With zero funds."

"Who needs funds? We'll tell people to bring a plate of something. Or a bottle."

"What people? We barely convinced the guests to post a photo, let alone—"

"I'm not talking about the inn guests. I meant people here in Wave's End. Maeve's friends, neighbors, fellow business owners. After the story my dad wrote about that accountant screwing her, they'll want to see her. Say good-bye to the inn."

"But Maeve's not well enough to come."

"Then she'll be here in spirit."

"Still, there's invitations—"

"Evites are free. Ellie could manage those. And with so many people present, it might turn up some housing possibilities for Roxanne and Gage. Maybe even for Fred and Mona."

"I suppose you're right."

"That's my girl."

Faith's neck flamed at David's throwaway use of the possessive. "So this is happening."

"Yes, it is. Wave's End needs a party. And The Mermaid's Purse should go out with her head held high."

78

In spite of Faith's trepidation, Connie embraced the idea of a final gathering. "Why not? Eat, drink and be merry. We'll be like the orchestra on the deck of the *Titanic*: we'll keep on playing, even as the ship is sinking."

With Bruce's help, they composed the list of invitees: neighbors, friends, business associates, church members. Affirmative responses to Ellie's whimsical Evite poured in immediately.

And then one morning during breakfast cleanup, Connie added a last-minute guest: Maeve Calhoun, now permitted to leave the rehabilitation facility for several hours at a time. Maeve's first social outing would be a return to her beloved Mermaid's Purse for the farewell party.

"It's bound to be an emotional day for her. It might be her last visit here." Draping a damp dish towel over the oven handle to dry, Faith heard her phone vibrate and went to check it.

"It will. But Maeve's cut from pretty strong cloth. She'll handle it all right." Connie started the aging dishwasher and raised her voice over the din. "It wouldn't be right to close the doors without letting her say good-bye."

"Hold that thought, Mom. I just got an alert from the fundraising site. Maeve just might get another chance." Faith set down her phone and retrieved the laptop from the dining room, carting it back to the kitchen and opening it to the Save The Mermaid's Purse page.

"Come look at this. Remember the 'Memories' page on the website? That woman in the red bathing suit? Mary somebody-or-other." Faith clicked and scrolled frantically until she located the photo. "There she is. Mary Alice Tilden."

"The one who wrote about bringing her family here year after year," recalled Connie, looking over her daughter's shoulder.

"Yes, exactly. Anyway, her son Charley, that boy in the picture with her, is all grown up now. He has loads of happy memories of staying here, too. He'd like to come and talk to us. He says he wants to help us save The Mermaid's Purse!"

79

The soonest their would-be benefactor Charley Tilden could come and discuss his interest in The Mermaid's Purse was the day of the inn's farewell party, Faith reported later that day.

"We can't change the date of the party," Connie said. "The invitations already went out. And not long after that, we'll have to leave."

"*If* we have to leave," said Ellie. "Maybe this is our Christmas miracle."

"Tell the man to come to the party. *With* his checkbook," Connie announced.

Listening to the two women, Faith had to smile at their fantasy of a philanthropic angel swooping down to rescue the inn from financial destruction. For her part, she resolved not to get her hopes up, continuing her more pragmatic approach of cleaning out the inn while preparing for the party. After much discussion with David, and having unearthed boxes of namesake memorabilia gifted to the inn over the years, Faith agreed the party would feature a mermaid theme.

In the meantime, they still needed to meet the day-to-day needs of their boarders, planning, preparing and clearing away of meals, and the laundry, housekeeping and errands that kept the inn going. If nothing else, she now had a broad array of experiences to add to her resume once she left The Mermaid's Purse, Faith thought, kicking off her shoes to relax on the salon sofa one evening. A few pages into one of Maeve's outdated magazines, Faith dozed off, only to wake disoriented sometime after ten, magazine on the floor beside her.

Remembering she hadn't defrosted anything for the next day, she padded to the kitchen barefooted to survey her freezer inventory, only to halt at the sight of Roxanne and Connie huddled at the kitchen table, their backs to Faith and a box of tissues between them.

Not wanting to intrude, Faith took a step back, watching and listening from the shadows of the dining room.

"I swore I'd never let him do this to me again," Roxanne whimpered.

Mitch. Did Gage's father ever quit? How had he antagonized Roxanne now? Faith wondered. Perhaps it was the girlfriend again, or money issues. But when Roxanne turned toward Connie, Faith spotted the angry purple bruise on her cheek and covered her mouth, realizing how volatile relations between the estranged couple had become. She hung back, holding her breath as Roxanne accepted an ice pack from Connie and pressed it to her face with a wince.

"You can't let Mitch get away with this," said Connie.

"I thought the separation would protect me. How stupid could I have been?"

"You're not stupid."

"Oh, yes, I am. As stupid as I was to think that if I made the right dinner, dressed the way he liked, made sure Gage did well in school, everything would be okay."

"It's part of the madness. You made the right choice, leaving him."

"Everything seemed fine today at the coffee shop until we started talking about this place possibly closing. Mitch got it into his head we should move back in with him. We started fighting about it in front of Gage, which made it worse, because my son would probably want us to live together again as a family more than anything in the world, besides finding Tucker."

As Roxanne wadded a tissue to her nose, a guilty Faith decided to make her presence known. But before she could move, Roxanne spoke again. "Anyway, when I refused, Mitch asked me where we planned to live after. I told him I didn't know yet, which is the truth. You all know how difficult this housing search has been for me."

"We can help you with that," offered Connie.

Roxanne readjusted the ice pack. "Then Mitch called me a liar. He accused me of keeping that information from him so he couldn't see Gage. I don't know where he *gets* these things. But I wasn't hiding anything. I swear."

"I know," Connie murmured.

"Thank you for not judging me. I always feel so much better after I talk to you."

How often *did* the two talk? Faith wondered from her hidden vantage point.

"I knew it was coming," Roxanne continued. "Even though Mitch promised *again* it was the last time. I can always tell, you know? His eyes . . . they change. It's like a switch. It's my fault, though. You'd think I'd recognize the warning signs."

"It's *not* your fault. These men mess with your head, making you feel like you did something wrong . . . like you're nothing." Connie bit off her last words. "It takes a long time to get out from under their thumbs. But you have to. And the first step is to stop blaming yourself."

"I know. I need to work on that." Roxanne stood and set the ice pack on the table. "I'm so sorry I unloaded on you. You've done so much for us already, opening this place to me and my son."

"Stop."

"Stop what?"

"Stop apologizing. Women like us develop a terrible habit of saying sorry way, way too much."

Women like us? What sorority included both Roxanne and her mother? Faith wondered. The day Faith found her birth certificate, Connie had admitted to her husband's drinking and gambling issues, to their constant fighting. But physical abuse? Her mother never mentioned that. Perhaps the revelation had been there, implicit, and Faith had chosen to ignore it, refusing to believe that the man who had helped to bring Audrey Hennessey into this world could be capable of physical violence.

"I don't want Gage to grow up with that kind of insanity," said Roxanne. "That's why I finally left Mitch. I tried to hide this from my son. But Gage sees it now. I know he does. And that . . . that devastates me, to the point where I can't cope with anything else."

As Faith grasped the depth of Roxanne's raw pain, she realized why even the thought of making a few phone calls paralyzed Roxanne to the point of inaction.

"I felt the same way with my daughter," said Connie.

Faith held her breath, hovering in the doorway, ashamed of eavesdropping for so long but terrified that if she revealed herself now, her mother might stop speaking so candidly.

"The sad part is, the children do see," continued Connie. "From a very young age. Faith was barely four the day she found me."

Found you where? Lightheaded, Faith leaned against the doorjamb for support.

"I saw the fear in her eyes that night," Connie said. "He had already done his damage, and started with his usual excuses and empty apologies. But when he heard Faith's bedroom door open, the coward ran out. I tried to clean myself up before she found me, but I didn't have enough time. I'll never forget that look on Faith's face as long as I live. That's when I went to the sheriff and asked for the order of protection."

Order of protection? Was this the same incident her mother had described to her? Faith longed to wipe her damp forehead with her sleeve, but didn't dare move a muscle.

"Did he give it to you?" Roxanne asked.

"Yes, he did." Connie's voice faded, then came back stronger. "And then the sheriff said something that just . . . well, it set something off inside me."

Faith relaxed slightly, knowing what was to come.

"What was that?" Roxanne whispered.

"He said . . . that an order of protection wasn't a bulletproof vest."

Bulletproof vest? Jerking to attention, Faith lurched into the kitchen. "Mom," she cried, the greeting lodging in her throat.

"Goodness, Faith. You scared me." Connie got to her feet so abruptly she had to grab her chair to keep it from falling. "I thought you'd gone to bed. I was just giving Roxanne some . . . some life advice," she stammered.

Meanwhile, Roxanne lowered her head, pulling her hair over her swollen cheek.

"Your ex did that to you?" Faith asked, placing her hand on Roxanne's shoulder.

Slowly, Roxanne nodded, her head still bent.

"Nobody deserves that. I'm so sorry, Roxanne. And Mom, what you just said . . . Why didn't we ever talk about what I saw that night?"

"I prayed you'd forgotten."

"Still, you could have told me the other day, when I found my birth certificate."

Connie led Faith to sit at the table. "And remind you of the horror I exposed you to the first few years of your life?"

"Knowing might have helped me to understand some things."

"What things? My failure as a mother? My serial attraction to the wrong men? I think they're both pretty clear."

"No, neither of those. But it might have explained why I have a hard time . . . I don't know . . . trusting people? It's so difficult for me to . . . to let my guard down. Let people get close. Especially guys." *Until I came to Wave's End.*

"And you think that comes from the way your father treated me?" Connie asked.

"Maybe. I don't know. Who knows how that affects a kid? Maybe living those first couple of years as someone else left some scars. Maybe somehow deep down I always knew what really happened that night, and it made me more guarded."

"I'm sorry, Faith. You did deserve to know. To have things out in the open. Stupidly, I convinced myself I was protecting you all these years. But now I see how it must have hurt you."

"I get why you would do that. But tonight, hearing Roxanne—" Grabbing a tissue, Faith glanced at Roxanne, who continued to listen quietly. "I'm sorry, Roxanne, but after hearing your story, I get what my mother went through. It fills in the blanks somehow." Hearing the truth earlier might have cast a different light on her mother, enabling Faith to comfort her occasionally, instead of always criticizing her, always judging.

How much Faith had judged, and how wrongly.

"Still, I regret it," said Connie. "The way I regret a lot of things. It's taken me too long to own up to this, even to my own daughter. But in spite of everything, taking you away that night is the thing I'm most proud of having done in my life."

Roxanne looked up. "I don't know if I can be as brave as you, Connie. I'm so . . . so tired."

"You can. For Gage." Connie smoothed Roxanne's hair. "And we'll help you, won't we, Faith?"

Faith nodded. "Of course. You're going to be okay."

"I promise you I'm right. Moon and stars," Connie said, with a vaguely defiant glance at Faith. "Faith hates when I say that; I suppose I've given her plenty of reason to. But when the two of us were on the run, that's the only thing that helped me focus: knowing at the end of every day, even when my life was falling apart, I could look up at the sky and count on the moon and the stars being there. Even on cloudy nights when I couldn't quite make them out. Because I knew the clouds eventually would clear, and I'd see the moon and stars shining brightly again, as though someone had set them there just for Faith and me."

Long after Roxanne had gone upstairs with a fresh ice pack, and Faith and her mother crawled into bed, Faith lay beside Connie, thinking about everything she had learned that night and wishing she had known the deeper symbolism of *moon and stars*. Had she grasped its profound significance, so much more to her mother than a cheap, gold-plated necklace, she might have thought to grasp Connie's hand under the arid desert sky. Instead, Faith's life had been dogged by a nagging unease fed by her mother's habitual searching—the yearning that drove Connie to enter contests, one sweepstakes after another, her eye on pie-in-the-sky prizes that might never materialize, never satisfy.

Except that this prize *had* satisfied, Faith realized, turning onto her side in the trundle bed. This hundred-twenty-five-dollar chance, for which her mother had sacrificed everything, had paid off in the most unlikely, extraordinary ways. Despite its dated décor and peeling shutters, The Mermaid's Purse provided the sort of shelter and sustenance for mother and daughter that had been missing their entire lives.

Elementally, the inn had done the same for their boarders. And though it could be too much to hope for, there might be additional riches deep within The Mermaid's Purse, theirs for the taking.

Maybe Charley Tilden's sudden attraction to the inn meant that their luck had turned.

Faith whispered into the night. "Mom, are you awake?"

Connie sighed. "Barely."

"Can I ask you something?"

"Of course. Anything."

"How did you come up with our new names?"

PART 6:
RECONSTRUCTION

80

"Seriously?" Faith sat up and switched on her bedside lamp. "You named us for a moving company?"

Connie shrugged. "I didn't have that much time to think about it. The sheriff needed our new names by the next day to complete the legal paperwork."

"So you just picked them out of thin air."

"You could say that. That night in the back of the pickup truck, you slept, and I watched the traffic on the highway," she said, sitting up and stuffing pillows behind her back. "There were mostly trucks at that hour, but then a moving van went by. Sterling Van Lines. And I thought to myself, What a good, strong name, with weight to it. I picked Connie for Constance Ford. You probably don't remember her, but she played a spunky mother on my soap opera."

"I don't, but Connie suits you. And I suppose as family names go, Sterling's not terrible." Faith hugged her knees. "And my first name? How did you come up with that?"

"Faith? That was easy. I remember feeling terrified and conflicted that night, wondering if I had made the right choice to leave, or if running away would only make the situation worse."

"It doesn't sound like things could have gotten any worse."

"I know that now. But that night, I wasn't so sure I could do it on my own. Do you realize, Faith: I was younger than you are now, and already a mother?" Connie folded an arm behind her head. "Anyway, I had no money, and no contacts where we were headed. So I prayed for strength. And for faith in myself. Then I looked down at you sleeping next to me, and it came to me. I would name you Faith. So your face would remind me every day to believe in myself."

"Aw, really?" Faith leaned her head on her mother's shoulder.

"Really. And you did, Faith." Connie patted Faith's knee. "You do. Although I could have named you Esmeralda and you still would have inspired me. That's why whatever happens with this place"—she stretched her arms over her head—"whether this Charley Tilden turns out to be the Mermaid's Purse's savior or we get our bottoms kicked to the curb, this whole experience will have been worth it, because I lived it with you."

"Don't you mean, 'for you'?"

"What are you talking about?"

Faith slipped out of bed and rummaged through her belongings until she found the pants she was looking for. "This," she said, taking out a paper from the pocket and unfolding it on the bed.

"Where did you get that?" Connie asked.

"Maeve gave it to me at the nursing home. And I must say, you have quite a way with words."

"It was from my heart. And I never expected you to see that essay, by the way."

"Well, I did. And I understand why Maeve picked you. She said you got to the essence of it." Faith picked up the paper and read aloud:

"'While I may not be your most experienced applicant, I can promise I am your most dedicated. In trying to provide a home for my daughter all these years, I've worked many, many jobs. Some worked out, and some didn't, but I learned something from every one. I've never been too proud to do an honest day's hard work if it would keep a roof over her head. My daughter has become a success in the hospitality industry in her own right, and I would like to follow her example. If you permit me to carry on the Mermaid's Purse tradition, I will work tirelessly, dedicating that effort to my daughter, who has been my shining star for my entire life, teaching me the value of hard work and perseverance.'

"Maeve told me that all the other essays went on and on about the beach and the ocean," explained Faith. "But she said when it really comes down to it, innkeeping is about the behind-the-scenes work that makes running the place look easy, makes the guests feel welcome."

Smiling, Faith folded the letter. "Congratulations on winning The Mermaid's Purse, Mom. I don't think I ever said that."

⟋♋

"Careful, Mom. You're getting crumbs in the bed," Faith said with a laugh.

"I don't care. These are so delicious. Why haven't you made them before?" Connie took another bite of the scone Faith had retrieved from the kitchen.

"Because I didn't have Maeve's recipe until now. Or her mother's recipe, I should say."

"Did she give the recipe to you along with my essay?"

"No, but she told me where to find it. It's been in the drawer of her mother's kitchen table all along."

"Isn't that funny. You'll have to show me how to make them. For after."

"Let's not think about that right now." Faith finished the last of her scone. "Anyway, they're easy. Just remember two things: First, soak the currants in boiling water beforehand to soften them up. And second, add just a pinch of salt to the dough. Any more, and they'll be tough. And use table salt, not sea salt."

"No problem. I never use that fancy stuff. All right. Let's see if I've got it: salt and water?"

"Yes. Salt and water. Remember what Bruce said that first day: you don't want to mess with Maeve's scones."

"Yes, he did say that, didn't he? But if this inn ends up being mine," Connie said, licking her fingers in the moonlit bedroom, "I suppose I *could* mess with them, couldn't I?"

81

Much later, Faith fell into a restless sleep, dreaming of the flatbed's icy metal as her four-year-old self peppered her mother with questions: Why did they have to leave the shelter when she had just started to make friends? Why did that lady in the next bed—a woman who in Faith's dream looked remarkably like Roxanne—cry when they left? Where would they go? Her mother tried to shush her, hunting for the scrap of paper with the name of the shelter where they were going, and coming up empty-handed.

Faith (Audrey, then) had begun to cry, and, desperate to soothe her, Connie-then-Rita suggested a game they played often at home. They would toss a coin to decide which direction to go in, and Audrey would get to choose: heads for east and tails meant west.

She had sat up then, excited to play this game she knew so well, a contest that frequently netted Audrey her favorite television show or dessert. In her heart, Audrey knew her mother always vetted both options before offering her daughter a choice. But this: this was bigger. Her mother had never asked her to weigh in on such an important decision. Her mother held up the nickel, then tossed the coin high in the air. Audrey heard it land with a plink on the metal floor, and her mother searched for it, worried, on her hands and knees. After several minutes, she still hadn't located the coin, and Audrey's heart began to race.

At that point in the dream, Audrey-now-Faith woke, her heart pounding through pajamas soaked with perspiration. Had her subconscious produced the memory of that night, or had Faith simply reconstructed it from bits and pieces gleaned from her mother? Either way, the dream's lack of resolution, the questions and responsibilities it raised, deeply unsettled her. Without that coin, mother and child in flight were rudderless, with no guidance as to the path they should travel, or expectations that lay ahead.

Without that coin, how would Faith know what to do?

82

Waiting outside the gates of Wave's End High School with David, Faith rose on tiptoe, peering over the masses of students pouring out of the school. "Wait, I think I see him. His hair kind of sticks out in the crowd."

David waved wildly. "Yo, Gage. Over here."

The teen shuffled over, glancing over his shoulder nervously. *Probably doesn't want his friends to see him with us*, Faith thought.

"What are you guys doing here? Is my mom okay? My dad?"

"They're fine," said Faith.

"Okay, so then what's up? Am I in trouble?"

"*Should* you be?" asked Faith.

"No, but . . ."

"Good. Then we're kidnapping you," said David.

"For what?"

"You'll see," David replied. "Hop in, bro."

❧

Sated by the fast food meal consumed at their first stop, Gage stared as they pulled into their next destination. "Whoa. Is this for real?"

"Sounds pretty real to me." David winced as he got out of the car.

"And my *mom* said this was okay?"

"Yes, she did. And *my* mom, which is just as critical," Faith answered. "Come on. Let's check it out."

Inside the animal shelter, they could barely hear themselves over the barking. Strolling up and down the aisles, they stopped at each crate to look inside, petting the snouts of any dog or cat that showed interest.

"There's so many dogs here. How are they going to find homes for them?" Gage asked.

"Our numbers have almost doubled since the hurricane," explained a volunteer, overhearing. "In some cases, the dogs wandered away during the storm. In others, people had to give up their pet when they went into temporary housing after their homes were damaged."

"That's so sad. How am I supposed to pick just one?" Dropping down to the floor, Gage went nose to snout with Bam Bam, a Labrador retriever.

"Because Connie will have a fit if you come home with more than one," said David.

"Not to mention Pixie," added Faith. "That cat is not going to know what hit her."

"This guy seems to like you." When David sat down next to Gage, Bam Bam obligingly licked the hand he offered.

"Anyway, you don't have to decide today," Faith said. "We can just have a look around, maybe play with a few of them."

"Are you kidding me? We are *so* deciding today. I'm not leaving here without a—" Gage cocked his head. "Wait a minute. That can't be."

Scrambling to his feet, Gage ran down the row, David and Faith following as the teen clutched first one crate, then another, peering into each. "I know that bark," Gage insisted. "I know he's here. Tucker, where are you? Tucker? *Tucker!* Holy . . . Guys, here he is! I found him!"

∽

The shelter volunteer was less surprised by the reunion than David and Faith were. "You'd be amazed how often this has happened since the storm." In Tucker's case, a family found him immediately after the hurricane, but, unable to care for the Irish setter any longer, had dropped Tucker at the shelter a few days before.

"Tucker." In the back seat, Gage buried his head in the dog's rust fur. "Don't even try to get away from me again."

Up front, Faith sniffled, even catching David blinking repeatedly.

On the ride home, Gage playfully shoved David's shoulder from behind. "And if you tell the other guys I was crying, I'll beat the crap out of you." However, this threat didn't keep Gage from sniffling while Tucker lapped his tears. "I can't believe I found you," he repeated.

When they stopped at the pet store for dog food on the way home, Faith tapped Gage on the shoulder as he contemplated the array of leashes. "What do you think of this one?" From her purse, she uncoiled Tucker's original leash.

"What the—" Gage grabbed the leash. "How did you get that?"

"It wasn't that hard. Once the investigation closed, I stopped by the firehouse. Since it was no longer needed as evidence, the fire chief had no problem giving it to me."

83

The Saturday of Maeve's mermaid-themed party on the weekend before Christmas dawned crisp and monochrome, a bite in the air but minus the threat of snow. The farewell festivities would start at three o'clock; Charley Tilden had a previous engagement and would arrive around five, Ellie reported.

Faith, David, Connie and Ellie rushed around all day putting finishing touches on the food, drink and decorations. Meanwhile, Roxanne laced sea foam streamers through banisters and chandeliers. She strung cardboard conchs, starfish and of course mermaid's purses on fishing filament and looped them over buffet knobs, coat hooks and plate racks. She wove fairy lights through an old fishing net David unearthed in the garage, draping the net over a dining room mirror.

At five minutes to three, the inn's residents gathered in the front hall to greet Maeve, who would arrive momentarily with Bruce.

"You told Bruce about Tilden, didn't you, Mom?" Faith asked.

"No, I didn't. I assumed you did."

"It doesn't matter," said Ellie. "I'll fill him in once he gets Maeve here."

When the front door finally opened, an incandescent Maeve maneuvered her walker into the front hall. Joy wreathing her face, she studied every detail, as though returning to The Mermaid's Purse after a very long absence instead of just about seven weeks of recuperation.

Connie wrapped Maeve in her arms. "Welcome back."

"Oh, my." Maeve beamed at her welcome committee. "It is so wonderful to be back here." Elbowed by Roxanne, Gage stumbled forward to present Maeve with a foil trident.

"It's a symbol of power. To go with our theme." Gage blushed furiously as Maeve reached out and patted his cheek.

"You must be Gage, the young man I've heard so much about," said Maeve.

"That's him, all right." Taking Maeve's coat, Connie ushered her into the dining room, where the invited guests had assembled. In twos and threes, dear friends and many of the local merchants stepped up to greet her, complimenting her on how well she looked. Connie remained by Maeve's side, introducing her to the few guests she didn't know, including Tanya and her aunt Hilda. Faith had invited the two at the last minute when Tanya called to say she'd be visiting that weekend.

"My aunt was so excited to come back here," Tanya said, taking Faith aside. "Thank you for inviting us again."

"And I can't thank *you* enough." Beyond digging into the foreclosure, Tanya had helped in another area. With Roxanne's permission, Faith had reached out to Tanya, who immediately connected Roxanne with a local attorney specializing in spousal abuse, as well as a support group. "Donna is a good friend and a terrific lawyer," said Tanya. "She'll take good care of Roxanne."

Faith fervently hoped that with Tanya's connection, and the support from her Mermaid's Purse family, Roxanne would find the energy and the courage to fight for herself and her son.

As the party progressed, Faith watched the guests consume the food with gusto. Despite the potluck invitation, she and David had nevertheless competed to interpret the whimsical mermaid theme, tapping their respective restaurant suppliers for donations. For his part, David concocted mermaid cocktails, layered rainbow confections in alcoholic and nonalcoholic versions, hand-rolled sushi, and crab and cucumber canapés.

Not to be outdone, Faith whipped up butter-poached shrimp cocktail, starfish finger sandwiches, and an undersea vanilla mousse tinted emerald and served in individual compote glasses of Maeve's. Crystal bowls of miniature fish crackers and gummy fish popped gold and ruby against nautical-striped beach towels Connie had draped on the dining room tables.

Caught up in refreshing drinks and refilling food platters, Faith found that the two hours until Charley Tilden's arrival flew by. Motioning for her mother and Ellie to join her, she slipped to the front hall to wait for him, breathing deeply to quiet her nerves, reminding herself nothing would likely be decided during this introductory discussion. But then her pragmatism went out the window, replaced by butterflies: How wonderful would it be if today's meeting could extend the life of The Mermaid's Purse?

Tanya wandered over, one of David's signature cocktails in hand. "I love what you've all done here today. All that's missing is a mermaid. Although I've read that unlike their animated versions, some of those creatures could be downright cunning." Taking in their serious faces, she set down her drink. "You all look a little nervous. What's going on?"

"We're about to have a meeting," said Faith.

"In the middle of Maeve's party? With whom?"

"The son of one of the inn's guests. He reached out through our fundraising site and offered to help," answered Faith.

"Really? And just who is this so-called savior of yours?" Tanya asked.

"Tilden. Charley Tilden," said Connie.

Closing her eyes, Tanya leaned against the wall. "No. Please tell me you're joking. Do you have any idea who that man is?"

"No, but I have a feeling you're about to tell us," Faith said.

"Oh, Faith. I so wish I didn't have to. Charley Tilden is one of the most prominent real estate developers in Manhattan."

"So then he's loaded. How is that a problem?" Connie asked.

"The problem is, he's also reviled. Tilden made his money by being an unrepentant slumlord. The ass—I mean, *Tilden* forced tenants out of the buildings he bought so he could build luxury condos."

"How do you know all this?" Connie asked.

"Because I did a lot of pro bono work representing those ousted tenants."

"But if he builds luxury condos, why would Tilden be interested in The Mermaid's Purse?" Faith asked.

"Because he's a snake. He's always ahead of the market. He knows coastal property values are depressed after the storm. The vulture is probably swooping in and buying up real estate up and down the East Coast."

"But Tilden told us he stayed here as a kid," said Connie. "He made a point of saying how much he loved it."

"*Yecchh.*" Tanya pretended to stick her finger down her throat. "Emotional blackmail. Doesn't surprise me a bit. That was simply his entrée to you."

Faith sank onto the steps. "So that's it, then. Tilden was our last hope."

"Sorry. I was stuck talking to the mayor," Bruce said as he joined them in the hall. "So where's this benefactor Ellie mentioned? From your face, Faith, I gather he's a no-show?"

"Worse. He's a slumlord," she answered.

"I'm so glad no one mentioned anything to Maeve," said Connie. "I guess it will be up to the bank now to decide what happens to this place."

"Could the bank sell the inn to Tilden, Tanya?" Faith asked.

"That's possible. Hopefully, if the bank gives you more time, Tilden will get antsy and move on."

"In the meantime, somebody should probably cancel our meeting with him," said Ellie.

"I'll do it." Faith got up and smoothed the front of her shirt. "After building up our hopes the way he did, nothing would give me more pleasure than to tell him the deal's off."

⁀◦

Having washed her hands of their would-be benefactor, Faith headed to the dining room to serve dessert: colorfully iced cupcakes arranged into a free-form mermaid. An S-shaped coral swirl served as her flowing mane, an emerald horn of plenty defined the lower body and fins and two strategically placed lavender cakes designated the décolletage. The entire sea creature shimmered under a coat of sugary crystals.

Passing the tray, Faith eventually reached the exhausted Maeve, who was saying her good-byes as Bruce waited to take her back to the nursing facility.

"You've thrown me such a lovely party," she said, clasping Faith's hand. "All of you working so hard—on this day, and on that computer idea of yours. And after all I put you through: my foolish idea about the lottery, my trusting that accountant of mine. I don't deserve this, after all the grief I've caused."

"Of course you do," Faith said. "You built the inn into what it is today. And in a crazy way, through all of these hard times—the storm and your accident and the foreclosure—my mother and I learned some things about each other. Such as how resilient we are, for one. I'm grateful for that."

Faith handed Bruce a container of leftover mermaid cupcakes to give to Maeve's nurses. "And now, Maeve, I must get back to work. In case you haven't heard, my boss is a slave driver."

As the crowd began to thin, Faith busied herself stacking empty plates and wiping down tables, not thinking anything of it when the front door opened once more.

"Hello!" a familiar female voice rang out. "Have you any vacancies?"

84

Connie, Ellie and Faith flocked to the front hall to welcome the new arrival.

"I'm sorry to intrude. I've just been thinking about you all and—" Merrill stopped short, taking in the bedecked banisters, the glittering fishnets. "Oh, my. You're having a party. I can come back another time—"

"Don't be silly. You're staying." Linking her arm in Merrill's, Faith led her to a dining room table. "It's so wonderful to see you. We all . . . we're just so sorry, Merrill. The news about Grace was such a shock."

"Thank you. Your flowers were lovely, by the way." Merrill looked around the decorated dining room. "Staying here made Grace so happy. You guys made her happy."

"As you did us. Here: eat." Connie set a plate of party leftovers and a glass of chardonnay in front of Merrill. "I know you're both missed at the church," she continued. "Did you hear they're still holding the dinners? Even though the power's back on and people have found temporary places to live, they still come and eat together. Those meals have become something of a support group for the storm's survivors. A lifeline."

"I'm glad to hear that. It felt special to be a part of that with my sister."

Connie glanced at her watch. "You know, if you stopped over at the church now, you might be able to catch the end of the meal."

"Tomorrow, maybe. I'd planned to stay the night here. That is, if you have a room for me?" Merrill glanced around hopefully. "You know the Abbott sisters. We never plan ahead."

Connie assured Merrill they could make room for her.

"Anyway," Merrill continued, "when I looked up the inn address to send a thank-you card for the flowers, I saw everything you've been trying to do: the memories, the fundraising. It shocked me. I had no idea things were so bad. I knew I needed to come right away."

"We're so glad you did," said Ellie.

Merrill reached over and squeezed her hand. "If only Grace could see you. You look more radiant than ever. I never expected to lose my sister this soon, but hearing from the mothers of all of the lives my sister helped to usher into the world . . . "Merrill sniffed and bent her head. "Well, it does ease the pain a little."

"It sounds as if Grace left quite a legacy with all of those babies," Connie said, handing her a tissue.

"She certainly did." Folding the tissue in her palm, Merrill cleared her throat. "But that's not the only one my sister left. Which is why I needed to come here tonight."

85

"So there it is." Merrill's voice shook as she refolded the page from her sister's will and slid it back in the envelope.

"We couldn't possibly . . . ," Connie said, shaking her head in disbelief.

"It's just . . . too much." Faith attempted to digest all the zeros in the amount Merrill had just read to them.

"It's not too much. It's exactly what Grace wanted," Merrill said. "And it's all very legal."

"How could she have known about the foreclosure?" Connie asked.

"I don't know. Perhaps she overheard something while we were here? But Grace was very intuitive. She sensed you were struggling. And she found the work you do here to be very special, and wanted to see it continue," Merrill finished.

Her sister had designed her extremely generous bequest in a very specific way that Merrill learned about only after Grace's passing. The money, which would be placed in a trust for Merrill to administer, would permanently reserve the second-floor rooms at The Mermaid's Purse, with the stipulation that they initially be used to lodge Wave's End residents left homeless by the storm.

"So that means Roxanne, Gage and David can stay." Connie sagged with relief.

"Yes, it does. For as long as they need to. And any others, as well." Merrill managed a smile through her tears. If and when residents returned to their homes, she continued, the rooms could then be offered to other individuals in financial or emotional difficulty and needing lodging. Grace left it up to Merrill to vet each applicant.

"So those people would live at The Mermaid's Purse rent-free?" Ellie asked.

"Yes, with one caveat." Each beneficiary would be required to pull their weight at the inn somehow, with jobs determined by the inn management. "Grace didn't believe in handouts. She wants the guests to have some skin in the game."

"As well they should," agreed Connie. "But what if the inn closes?"

Grace had covered that possibility by stipulating that should The Mermaid's Purse close its doors or be offered for sale, the monies would revert to a separate foundation she established to provide low-cost prenatal care.

"Grace is an angel," Ellie whispered.

"That kind of talk would make my sister uncomfortable. She lived simply and saved well. It was her mission in life to help."

"Her help couldn't have come at a better time. Isn't that right, Faith?"

Faith massaged her lower lip, bowled over by Grace's generosity, yet nagged by the nonnegotiable bank cutoff just days away. "I'm beyond grateful to your sister, Merrill. How soon would we be able to take advantage of the funds? I know these things take time to sort out."

"If you're concerned about the probate period, my pragmatic sister took that into account with the other part of her bequest." Merrill fished in her purse. "She gave this to me before she died. Asked me to deliver it in person when the time came."

Connie's eyes widened at the amount of the check Merrill offered.

"She knew the estate would take a while to come through," Merrill continued. "Is it enough to tide you over?"

"And then some." One hand on her heart, Connie held the check out in the other for Faith and Ellie to see. The donation would more than cover the mortgage payments in arrears, and several more going forward, until they could access Grace's bequest. The check would keep them solvent until at least spring, Faith realized.

"And Grace never told you her intentions?" Connie asked.

"Not a thing. Except to say Faith would understand. Something about the shell on the mailbox?" Merrill's brows crinkled into a frown. "Does that make any sense, Faith?"

Faith nodded, recalling the tap of Grace's cane against the mermaid's purse. "Yes. It makes perfect sense."

"So what do you say?" Merrill wiped her cheeks.

"I'd say . . ." Faith glanced over at the check in Connie's lap one more time. "Well, I'd say The Mermaid's Purse is back in business!"

86

After setting up the women with a celebratory round of mermaid cocktails to toast Grace's memory and generosity, Faith left them to tidy the kitchen.

To her surprise, she found the entire area in perfect order, serving trays drying in the dish drainer and stacked containers of leftovers in the refrigerator. Also chilling was a robust bowl of romaine brimmed with Kalamata olives, grape tomatoes, hard-boiled eggs, capers and leftover crabmeat, ringed with red onion slices and avocado slices.

Only one person could have readied this perfect light supper for the boarders, complete with a chunk of feta for crumbling and cubed bread for croutons. *David,* Faith thought, closing the fridge door. She realized she hadn't seen much of him all afternoon. This must have been where he had been hiding himself.

Reopening the fridge, she grabbed a bottle of chardonnay, then a pair of wineglasses from a shelf, and headed upstairs. Absorbed in conversation, the women barely looked up as she passed.

Faith found David exactly where she expected he would be: sprawled on a settee on the second-story balcony, staring up at the night sky and feet resting on the railing, still in his eternal shorts and flip-flops despite an outdoor temperature hovering around forty degrees.

"Aren't you freezing?" she asked as she kissed him.

"Not anymore, now that you're here." David accepted the wineglass she offered. "Are we toasting the successful party?"

"You could say that. And the celebration's not over yet."

David listened, mouth falling open as Faith filled him in on Grace's gift. "So I still have a roof over my head."

"If you want it."

"Oh, I want it. Here's to keeping this crazy place open."

Clinking her glass against his, Faith sat beside him, snuggling against his shoulder.

"Wait until my father hears," David said.

"And Maeve." Connie and Merrill would visit her tomorrow and tell her, Faith added.

"I suppose this makes your mother the official Mermaid's Purse innkeeper."

"I suppose it does. It at least keeps her employed for the immediate future, which is a huge load off my mind." She rested her feet on the railing alongside his. "I admit I had my doubts about this in the beginning. But watching her these last couple of months, I know she's up to the task."

"Maybe it's because you finally allowed yourself to see her that way."

Faith turned to him. "What do you mean?"

"Let's be honest here. You get a *little* bit of a rush from being in charge. Now hold on," he said as Faith set her wine down hard on a side table. "Don't get all defensive. It's just that I know how she feels."

"Do you? Are you saying you feel like *I* control *you*?" Sitting back, Faith crossed her arms.

"Of course not. I'm talking about me and Bruce. I've lived in his shadow all my life."

"My mother never lived in my shadow," she scoffed. "And your father seems very proud of you."

"I think he is, today. I'm just saying we can't escape the roles our family assigns us. But then, you won't have to play the responsible daughter much longer, will you? With that money, Connie can hire a real staff, and you can go back to your exciting life in New York. *If* that's what you want."

David got up and leaned against the railing, raising his glass to her. "I've enjoyed getting to know you, Faith Sterling."

Enjoyed? Confused, Faith got to her feet. Was he dismissing her? She had been so relieved about the foreclosure solution she hadn't thought about the options it offered her. Was David so ready to blow off this thing between them, whatever it was? "You're forgetting I don't actually have a job at the moment. My boss thinks it might be a year before the seaport is up and running again."

David ran a finger around the rim of his glass. "There *are* other restaurants," he said slowly.

"I know." So she had just been a fling for David. Otherwise, he wouldn't be suggesting she move on. Why had she wasted her time with him? This was what happened when she allowed those lines to blur. "Manhattan's a big place," she said airily. "There are tons of jobs. Xander said he'd put in a good word for me."

"I'm sure he would." David set his glass down beside Faith's. "But what if you didn't have to look as far as the city?"

Now Faith was totally bewildered. "What are you talking about?"

"I'm talking about reopening The Blue Osprey." David pulled some papers from his shorts pocket. "I got the breakdown from the insurer. With some state money, and some help from my father—" David held up his hand to stop Faith from speaking. "I know. Don't even say anything. I've decided to let my dad cosign a loan."

With Bruce's backing, and a top-notch construction crew, he could reopen the damaged restaurant by summer, David explained. "My dad thinks it will be good for community morale if I do that. And it will send a message to vacationers that Wave's End will be open for summer business."

"That would be great. But what does all this have to do with me?"

"I've been thinking: given how well we collaborate in the kitchen, maybe you would consider coming on board. As a creative partner. I have to admit it, Faith. I'm really impressed by your talent."

Faith rubbed her lower lip. It was one thing to surrender to a fling with this man, and quite another to leap into a business arrangement with him. "Are you really serious about this? Because we have very different culinary styles. And I've seen that kitchen, remember? It's so small we could end up killing each other."

"Which probably would scare the customers away," he said, smiling. "Seriously, I've considered that. The new kitchen will be much bigger after the remodel, and open to the dining room, like a brasserie. We could sit down together, rework the menu. There are some local favorites I want to hold on to, but with so many New Yorkers here in the summers, I'd really like to take the food up a notch. Maybe do some wine pairings. Bruce is working on getting a seasonal liquor license . . . sorry, I'm getting ahead of myself."

"It's fine. I can see how excited you are."

"This is what it comes down to." He refolded his papers and stuffed them in his pocket. "I think we could do amazing things together in the kitchen. Beyond that . . . well, the sky's the limit."

What did that mean? Turning away, Faith gazed up into the heavens. When she had first climbed the stairs, the night had been spectacularly clear, but now wisps of translucent cloud blurred the night stars. *Moon and stars.* She gulped a lungful of wintry air. "I'm very flattered, David."

"Then it's settled."

"I didn't say that. So much has happened here tonight. I need some time to digest everything."

"Take whatever time you need. The remodel's going to take a few months." He stood behind her, his arms circling her waist, and nuzzled her hair. How simple it would be to accept his proposition and explore their chemistry outside the confines of The Mermaid's Purse.

"On the other hand, if there's anything I can do to persuade you . . ." Gently pulling aside the neck of Faith's sweater, David proceeded to kiss the length of her collarbone. She shivered, less from the exposure than from the scorch of his mouth on her bare skin.

"Hey. You're not playing fair," Faith protested weakly, leaning her head back. But what *was* there to think about, really? She couldn't deny their mutual attraction. And from a career standpoint, most chefs would give their right arm for the opportunity David had just dangled in front of her: to get in on the ground floor of a new, or renewed, restaurant.

David would make out on this deal as well: without being overly boastful, Faith knew she brought a certain culinary cachet to David's modest eatery—not to mention her New York following.

As David's efforts moved to Faith's other shoulder, a nagging thought reduced their searing effect a degree or two. What if David had been flirting with her all along in order to butter her up for this proposition? What if he was wooing her well-honed skills to polish his restaurant's reputation?

Abruptly, Faith straightened up and adjusted her sweater. "I'll sleep on it," she said curtly, crossing her arms across her stomach.

"Okay," he said slowly. "Hey?" he asked, turning her around. "Did I do something wrong?"

Faith shook her head. "No. Just . . . long day."

Nodding, David stared at her a moment before gathering the empty bottle and glasses and heading inside.

⁓

Only when one hundred percent certain David had gone to bed, Faith slipped back inside, drained from the day and craving sleep. Downstairs, she wandered the rooms in search of her phone, finally locating the device on a dining room table. As the screen came to life, she grinned at the endless stream of emojis from Xander: row after row of palm trees, martini glasses (no doubt he had indulged in a few of these himself, judging from this message) and bikinis, followed by silverware, shell-fish and three different models of boats thrown in for good measure. *Wherever you are, boss, hope you're having fun,* she thought, scrolling and scrolling.

Finally, Faith arrived at the text portion of Xander's message:

Hey, right-hand chef: Are you down for winter in MIAMI? Pop-up location too sweet to pass up. Need you in kitchen NOW to heat this UP!

87

No one understood Faith's decision to go to Miami, least of all David. She tried to explain it to him on neutral territory, over lunch at a fast food restaurant.

"That's ridiculous." He threw down his napkin. "You can't deny we have something here."

"What exactly do we have, David, beyond playing house and cooking a few meals together?" Unable to admit David's offer had terrified her, she trivialized their connection, seizing on Xander's proposition and the chance Miami offered as an escape. She needed to get away and figure out how she felt about David without the pressure cooker of a long-term commitment.

His face darkened. "That's not fair. You know it's more than that. You just don't want to give this a chance."

"I don't even know what 'this' is." She dipped a French fry in mayonnaise. "Anyway, I just told you. I am giving us a chance. I'll be back in a few months, once I help Xander get back on his feet. He gave me my start, you know. I owe him that much." Hadn't she had almost this exact conversation with David's father not so long ago?

"Right. And doesn't the guy still owe you, like, ten grand?"

Faith pinched her lip, regretting having confessed the loan to David. "By my helping him, he'll be able to pay me back faster."

"That is truly twisted logic."

"That's your opinion. But I can still help you from Miami. I can track the construction progress by video chat. And proof the menus by e-mail. It's not as though the restaurant will be open before I get back."

"And what about your mother?"

"What about her? You heard Roxanne. She's ecstatic to take my place." Gage's mother had been shadowing Faith in the kitchen the last few days, turning out a mean pulled pork and macaroni and cheese for dinner the previous night.

And with Grace's financial support, Faith could now leave Wave's End without feeling she'd left her mother in the lurch.

David sat back against the molded booth and surveyed her. "I guess that's it, then."

"I guess so."

"Hmm." He tapped the tip of a plastic straw on the tabletop. "Could I ask you to do one thing before you leave?"

88

David's wetsuit landed in Faith's lap with a plop.

"You promised," he said. "Now, zip yourself into that. Don't worry. It's a cold-water suit."

Glaring at him, Faith took the hooded suit and climbed out of the jeep, shivering as she quickly stripped down to her long-sleeved T-shirt and leggings. As she stepped into the damp wetsuit, she held her breath against its dank, fishy odor. "Surfing in January: is this your idea of a compatibility test?" she called.

David laughed as he lifted the surfboards out of the car. "You could say that. Come on. Grab a board."

Still grumbling, Faith picked up a board, surprised by its lightness, and followed him to the water. She surveyed the surf, so picturesque when viewed from the jeep a moment ago and now so intimidating as she prepared to enter, waves swelling and thundering onto one another nearly in slow motion. Feeling a tug, she looked down to see David fastening the board's Velcro cuff around her ankle. "That'll keep you connected. Now, follow me."

"It's cold," she complained as she waded in behind him, gasping as the waves washed over her.

"You'll warm up in a second. Now, pull yourself halfway onto the board belly down, like this, and paddle out with me beyond the break."

On her stomach, Faith cupped her hands as David demonstrated, navigating alongside him to more tranquil waters.

"Okay, now show me how to get up," she demanded.

"Not yet." He shoved her board lightly. "Paddle back and forth a few times, following the shore. The way I just showed you."

"Really? Didn't we already cover this?" Sputtering, she followed his instructions, paddling north, turning around well before an imposing jetty and stroking furiously back to David. "So I paddled. What's next?"

"I'm not feeling the love here." He grabbed her board to steady it, and the two bobbed in tandem. "Nice out here, isn't it?"

Faith stuck her tongue out at him, a gesture David missed because he had already turned away to demonstrate "duck diving": pushing the surfboard down and then undulating one's body like a sea horse in order to duck under a wave.

Faith hastily mimicked the maneuver.

"I get the picture," she said.

"Remember it. You'll need it if you get stuck. Okay, so how to stand: first, get up on your knees, like this."

Following his example, she knelt on her board.

"Next, you start out low." David crouched like a cat on its haunches, feet planted beneath his shoulders, and effortlessly raised himself upright. "Now, you try."

Eyeing him dubiously, Faith tentatively planted one trembling leg then the other on her board, frozen in the doubled-over position and fearing she would tip into the sea at any second. "Okay. I'm up. I'm feeling it."

Staring into the gray-blue water, she panicked at the speed with which it carried them from shore. "What if I can't get back?"

"You'll get back. You're doing great," David encouraged her from behind. "Now, just stand all the way up. It's all about the weight transfer. Press your feet into the board and pull yourself up from your center."

"Easy for you to say. And I can't *see* you, by the way." Anxious, Faith fell onto her knees again.

She heard the slap of David dropping to his board, then saw him paddle into view.

"It's no use. I can't do it." Frustrated, Faith ripped the strap from her ankle and flung it into the water.

"Yes, you can." Calmly, David retrieved the cuff and handed it to her to reattach. "Try again. Like this." He repeated the motions he had just shown her. "Now, focus on the shoreline," he said once upright. "That'll help your balance."

"'Focus on the shoreline,'" she mimicked, glaring at him.

"Come on, Faith. Give it another shot. You don't strike me as a quitter."

"I'm not. I did everything you told me. And I can't do it."

"You can, if you stop trying to control the situation and just go with it."

"Right. So we're back to the control-freak thing."

"We're not. Just stay in the moment. Surfing is about looking where you want to go. Trust me."

I'll trust you, all right, you damn yogi with all your feel-good bullcrap. Gritting her teeth, Faith tugged down the sleeves of the wetsuit, certain David had designed this exercise expressly to punish her for leaving.

I will do it this time if it kills me. Slowly, shakily, she rose up on her knees again, then, squinting at the beach, planted her feet and hauled herself halfway to standing, trying hard not to think about her rear end sticking out behind her, only a few feet from David.

"Just a little more. You've almost got it," he encouraged.

Overhead, seagulls circled and squawked.

"Don't rush me," she protested. Calling on every one of her core muscles, she willed herself upright. "Look! I did it! I'm surfing!" she cried, stretching her arms wide. David was right: having a focal point did limit the wobbling. Where was he, anyway? Faith glanced over her shoulder, anxious for his approval. The ill-timed movement knocked her off balance, however, and Faith tumbled backward into the water, where she felt the reproving yank of her leg rope. *Now* that apparatus made sense.

Surfacing, Faith spun in search of David, who lounged on his board a few yards away. "I did it. Did you see me? I stood up!" Faith punched the air in triumph.

"Yes, I did. Good job, Gidget." He splashed her playfully. "Not bad for your first time."

"First of many. I'm hooked. Now show me the rest." Repositioning her board, she hauled herself onto it and paddled toward him.

"*Now* do you see what I'm talking about?" he asked.

"I do see." She got to her knees. "And I'm psyched to try again. Let's go!"

In response, David turned his board toward shore and rode the next wave onto the beach.

"Wait! Where are you going?" she yelled. Faith paddled furiously, hopping off in waist-high water and carrying her board the rest of the way. "I don't get it," she said, yanking off her hood. "I finally get the hang of it and you're done?" She shook out her hair, spraying David with seawater.

"Yeah, I'm done." David stood, cradling his board under his arm.

"You realize I'm leaving for Miami tomorrow. We won't have another chance until spring."

"Exactly."

"What's that supposed to mean?"

"I accomplished my goal," he said, unzipping his wetsuit.

"Your goal." Faith dropped the board and crossed her arms. "And what might that be?"

"To whet your appetite enough to leave you wanting more."

89

David insisted on taking Faith to the station, where she would catch her train to the airport. Doubt had racked her ever since David's surfing lesson, the tantalizing primer that provided another satisfying window into his psyche—a window he had abruptly slammed shut.

Had Faith opted to stay in Wave's End over the next few months, she might have had the chance to pry it open again. But she had already made her decision: her plane for Miami left in a few hours.

"I'm coming back. I promise," she said again. "At that point, we'll still have plenty of time to get things ready for the season."

To further convince him, she devoted long hours in the days leading up to her departure to going over the Blue Osprey's menu from top to bottom. The two stayed up late in the inn's kitchen to prepare the favorites he insisted should remain on the menu for the locals. Though it wasn't the moment for Faith to suggest some signature plates of her own, she did share a few ideas.

They arrived at the station a few minutes before her train would arrive. "I have something to show you," she said. She extracted a sheaf of papers from her purse and handed it to David. "There's a mock-up of the new menu for you to review. Trying out some new fonts. I've left all the favorites like we agreed, and added one or two dishes of my own. Placeholders," she emphasized, leaning over his shoulder to review the pages with him. "Tell me which ones you like and I'll send you recipes to try. And feel free to tweak them with more secret Caribbean ingredients," she teased, trying to lighten the moment.

Ignoring the levity, he shuffled through her papers, pausing at the last one. "What have we here?"

"Just another refinement I thought of."

He stroked his chin. "That's a pretty major refinement."

"I know. I just wanted to put it out there. You only have the chance to do these things once. I hope you'll think about it while I'm gone."

"Right. Think about it." As David fiddled with the brim of his baseball cap, a faint whistle blew in the distance.

"Yikes. That's my train." Faith planted a breezy, intentionally platonic kiss on David's cheek. Then she scrambled out of the car, grabbing her bags before he could assist her, and strode toward the knot of people boarding the airport express train. Feeling David's eyes on her, Faith turned and waved from the platform; once seated, she stared out of the window until the tracks wound out of Wave's End and turned David into a distant dot that eventually disappeared.

90

Tanned but tired outside Newark Airport, Faith dodged returning snowbirds while searching for her ride. The four punishing months at Huracán, Xander's ironically monikered South Beach eatery, had sapped her, and she savored the temperate May air on her cheeks. The sweltering sorcery of the Magic City had failed to cast its spell over her. By the time the art deco destination had emptied of its winter residents, Faith ached for the Northeast's comparative torpor. She left her boss to manage the waning days of his lucrative pop-up, whose profits would help resurrect Piquant.

"Will I see you again in New York?" Xander had asked Faith that morning over farewell mimosas at a Miami Airport bar. He faced a good six months of renovations before he might bring his seaport restaurant back to life, he estimated.

"I honestly can't say right now. I promised David I'd be in Wave's End for the summer season."

"*David, David, David.* What's that man got that I don't?" Xander teased.

"I'll say this much: you two couldn't be more different."

"Well, I hope you bring him good luck, as you did me. You're like 'The Opener,' Faith: sweeping in to get a restaurant off the ground, then disappearing. Maybe there's a reality show in there somewhere."

"I'm pretty sure I've already seen that one. My true reality is that I'm allergic to commitment."

"Then I'm especially glad you stuck with me." He slid a check across the table toward her. "It's not everything, but it's a start. I'll get you the rest as soon as I can."

"I know you will." Her glass empty, Faith slipped off the bar stool to hug Xander. "Promise me you'll try to make it down to The Blue Osprey for a meal this summer. I know a cute bed-and-breakfast where you can stay—and I'll get you a friends-and-family discount!"

"Faith! Over here!"

Faith would have walked right by the pewter minivan, were it not for the arresting magnetic sign affixed to its side:

DISCOVER THE RICHES OF
THE MERMAID'S PURSE AT THE JERSEY SHORE.
OUR DOORS ARE OPEN FOR BUSINESS!

"Please tell me you didn't get rid of Maeve's station wagon," Faith said, embracing her mother.

"Of course not. Bruce just thought a van would be more practical and fuel efficient for future guests."

Apparently, Bruce still wielded his influence, even as Maeve's role receded, Faith thought as she got in the car. How ironic: less than a year ago, Faith had retrieved her mother from the airport, bent on talking her out of her prize. Today, Connie would deliver her to a new beachside business.

"What do you think of our uniforms?" Connie proudly tapped the embroidered black shell logo on the pocket of her polo, with the words *The Mermaid's Purse* stitched beneath it.

"Bruce's idea, as well?" Faith asked.

"No. Mine," Connie chided. "With some input from Roxanne. There's one for you, too, even though I'm guessing you'll be too busy at The Blue Osprey to wear it."

"You're probably right. But thank you for thinking of me."

"And I know you were expecting David," Connie continued as they exited the airport. "He said something came up at the restaurant at the last minute."

"I know. A wine vendor. He texted me." David's tepid excuse had disappointed her. Despite her draining work schedule, she'd devoted many a Miami midnight and dawn to their collaboration, and couldn't wait to see David and their redesigned restaurant in person. And yes: after four months of soul-searching, she could freely admit that she had sorely missed the surfer chef, he of the crumpled brown bag of Caribbean spices.

Today Faith would learn whether David's feelings mirrored hers. Perhaps he hadn't forgiven her for decamping to Miami. Or maybe he'd moved on to someone else.

Faith turned to her mother. "So, how's Roxanne working out?"

"Fantastically. That woman is a natural in the kitchen. With a little hand-holding from David, of course."

"*Hand*-holding?"

Connie glanced sideways at her daughter. "I didn't mean that literally. Anyway, what did you expect, after you left the poor guy high and dry?"

"I didn't leave him—"

"And by the way, The Mermaid's Purse hasn't been the same without you two canoodling."

"Canoodling? Who canoodled? And who *says* that, anyway?"

"Plenty of people. And you don't have to worry, Faith. Roxanne's mind is on other things." Having finally filed for divorce, Gage's mother had secured a winter rental in Wave's End starting in September. "She'll still be working for us, but those two really need a place of their own." Roxanne also would commence a culinary program at the county college after the summer season. "Tanya is helping her line up some financial aid."

"I guess we're lucky I bumped into Tanya on the bus that night," Faith said.

"And you'll be bumping into her a lot more, I imagine," Connie said as they exited the parkway. Faith already knew Tanya's aunt Hilda had moved into The Mermaid's Purse shortly after Faith's departure. With plenty of money of her own, Hilda refused Grace's charity and insisted on paying her own rent so that another storm survivor could benefit.

And after Tanya tracked down the ne'er-do-well contractor, Hilda launched a post-Nadine referrals hotline to steer survivors toward reputable services.

Other new arrivals since Faith left for Miami included a young couple with an infant, and a middle-aged husband and wife who had taken Merrill and Grace's room (Faith thought it sweet her mother still referred to the sisters' accommodations that way) while they figured out what to do about their Wave's End home.

With little traffic on this weekday and all their catching up, the ride passed quickly, and mother and daughter soon found themselves on the town outskirts. "Do we have time to drive by the water before Merrill gets here for lunch?"

Connie glanced at her watch. "I guess so, if we're fast. I'm so glad you were able to talk her into that dedication service for Grace."

Faith had been working with Merrill to determine the most fitting way to commemorate the late midwife's generosity. At first, Merrill balked at any recognition, insisting Grace preferred her gift remain anonymous. There would be no plaques inside the inn bearing her sister's name, she said.

After thinking about it for a while, an idea had come to Faith, and she had gotten Merrill on the phone late one night from Miami to discuss it.

"What do you think about a birdbath?" Faith suggested. "After all, Grace worried so much about the storm displacing the birds. That they might not find their way back home to the beach afterward."

As Merrill pondered the idea, it occurred to Faith that each of them had been displaced—if not physically by Hurricane Nadine, then by the random nature of life's circumstances.

And somehow, the timeworn Mermaid's Purse had evolved into exactly the sort of dependable home base each desperately needed: a comfortable, protective nest while everyone found their feet and spread their wings.

That home base, that nest, would endure, all thanks to Grace.

A birdbath in the garden would be the perfect tribute, Merrill agreed.

The birdbath was the reason for Merrill's visit to Wave's End today. After lunch, she and Connie planned to scour area gardening centers for the perfect terracotta birdbath.

Faith rolled down the window, gulping lungfuls of salted Jersey air scorched with the tang of hot tar from ongoing roadwork. Contractors' trucks and vans crowded many blocks, and the whine of electric saws filled the air in a cacophony of revival—the sound of a community of survivors returning to daily living, one piece of Sheetrock at a time.

"So much progress since I left Wave's End," Faith commented.

"Yes, but still so much to be done." Promised government recovery funds arrived in trickles, Connie reported. Her new boarders had shared horror stories of lost paperwork and wildly inconsistent insurance settlements.

"Thank goodness for the volunteers. Like them." Slowing the van, her mother pointed to a team of young adults in orange shirts. Their equipment trailer read **DOVES MISSIONS: DEDICATING OUR VALUES**

EVERY SECOND. "That group came all the way from Ohio with their own equipment. They sleep in the church basement. And refuse to accept a dime. That gives you hope, doesn't it?"

∞

Back at The Mermaid's Purse, her mother parked the van next to Maeve's trusty station wagon. "Go on in," she urged. "I'll catch up."

Outside, Faith took in the inn's new roof and freshly painted shutters, the clipped shrubbery, the porch steps that no longer groaned under her weight—all thanks to the improvement loans Tanya had told her about. After these nominal enhancements, The Mermaid's Purse appeared to stand a little taller, a little more welcoming, on the main road in Wave's End.

No sooner had Faith opened the door into Maeve's comforting kitchen than an aproned Roxanne came around from the dining room, with Tucker trailing her.

"It's so good to see you," said Roxanne, giving Faith a hug. "Taking over for you has been quite the adjustment."

"Not as much of an adjustment as a new baby, I'll bet," called someone from inside the kitchen.

91

Fully expecting to meet the new boarders Connie had mentioned, Faith was stunned to find Ellie in the kitchen, patting the back of the infant on her shoulder.

"Greyson, meet your aunt Faith." Ellie spoke softly as she handed over the baby. "And if you wake him up, I will cheerfully kill you. Your godson is *not* the greatest sleeper."

"Who cares? He's gorgeous," Faith whispered back. None of Ellie's social media updates had done her son justice. Smoothing the baby's chestnut sheen of hair, she nuzzled his scalp, inhaling his tantalizing olio of talcum and Ellie's Coco Mademoiselle. "Mom, come here and look at delicious Greyson," she whispered.

"I love how you did that, Ellie." Connie joined them in the kitchen, slipping a finger inside Greyson's fist.

"You mean his name? How could we not? Grace touched our hearts. And, Faith, when I heard Merrill was coming the same day you were getting back, I couldn't resist coming. Not to mention I get a little stir-crazy by myself in the apartment all day."

Ellie and Dennis had refused Ellie's parents' offer of a nanny, Faith had been surprised to learn from her friend.

"Look, he's out like a light now. I'll put him down." Ellie expertly snapped open the stroller that had been leaning against the kitchen counter, then took her son from Faith and laid him down.

"I still can't believe you're here," said Faith.

"I have to be honest," said Ellie. "This isn't just a social visit. I heard about Grace's dedication, and I wanted to be in on the planning. I have an idea."

"You should know Merrill really doesn't want a fuss," said Connie. "She's very happy with the birdbath alone."

"I know. And I respect that. At the same time, I hope she'll at least listen to what I have to say."

∼∾

Ellie waited to explain her proposal to Merrill until after the women had finished lunch, rocking the just-fed Greyson in her arms.

"Dennis and I feel that both Grace and The Mermaid's Purse are very special to us. If it wouldn't take away from Grace's ceremony, we'd love to exchange vows here in the garden that same day, with just a small group of family and friends. *If* that's okay." Ellie sat back in her chair, watching Merrill intently.

After a moment passed with no response from Merrill, Faith reached over and took her hand. "If this is too much for you . . ." she began.

Sniffing, Merrill gazed down at her lap.

"I'm so sorry." Ellie shifted Greyson to her shoulder. "I never should have suggested the idea. We'll figure out another—"

"Stop." Merrill rose and stroked the baby's back. "Your idea to be married that day is the sweetest thing I've ever heard. Grace would have loved it."

"Really?" Relief flooded Ellie's face. "So does that mean yes?"

Swiping away tears, Merrill nodded, and Ellie clasped her hand. "Thank you so much, Merrill. I can't wait to tell Dennis."

"Congratulations! I had no idea you guys were even thinking of a date." Faith got up to embrace Ellie. "Does that mean the designer dress fits?"

"Actually, I changed my mind about that. I'm keeping most things a lot simpler than I originally planned."

"Speaking of simple, we're planning a small tea that day after Grace's dedication," said Connie. "Your family is welcome to join us."

"That's very sweet, but although the ceremony will be intimate, we'll probably have a larger crowd at a reception afterward. Maybe a hundred. I don't want to impose that group on you. I'll admit we haven't quite figured out that part yet."

"Faith, maybe David can suggest some local venues," said Connie.

"I have a better idea." Faith widened her eyes at her friend. "Ellie, what if David and I hosted your wedding celebration at The Blue Osprey?"

92

No sooner had she spoken the words than Faith regretted them. What had she just proposed? She hadn't even seen David or the renovated restaurant yet, and had just committed to hosting a wedding reception in less than three weeks' time—for a hundred guests!

"Oh, that's perfect!" Ellie cried.

"David will have the final word on whether we can be ready," Faith backtracked. "I know he's waiting on a few inspections. And then there's silverware, and linens, and loads of other details to finalize." She and David were meeting later that day to divvy up the work checklist.

"Oh, I really hope you will be! If anybody can pull it off, it's you two."

Heading to the restaurant in Maeve's old wagon, Faith wished she felt as confident as Ellie, who had gone along with Connie and Merrill on the birdbath hunt. Approaching the inlet, her palms dampened at the prospect of finally touring the renovated restaurant—*and* seeing David in the flesh for the first time in months.

Panicked, she pulled over a few blocks before the restaurant to decide on her demeanor. She'd left things so awkwardly, kissing David's cheek in such a sisterly fashion when she left for Florida. If she kissed him today, he might read too much into the gesture. But didn't she *want* him to?

Maybe a hug instead. But should it be full-on frontal, or a more constrained one-armed version? *Ugh.* If only she hadn't damaged their easy, satisfying rhythm by decamping to Miami, she wouldn't be having this dilemma.

Faith checked her face in the car mirror, swiping on some lip gloss. Her rare hours off in the Miami sun had flushed her cheeks and streaked her ponytail with caramel. She reached up to tighten it one last time, then, on a whim, yanked out the elastic, letting her hair fall over her shoulders in waves before driving the final blocks to the restaurant.

On the way, she passed the site of David's farewell surfing lesson, a teachable moment about so much more than duck diving. She had often replayed that fleeting but triumphant on-top-of-the-world instant in her mind while melting in the Miami swelter.

Yes, he had whetted her appetite. By insisting she experience surfing, David had achieved his goal, leaving Faith hungry for more. More like famished, actually. And though there were plenty of surfing opportunities in South Beach and no shortage of available chefs, Faith had pursued neither.

It turned out there was only one beach for Faith: the battered sands of Wave's End, where fate had deposited her one balmy fall day. The resilient town had left its imprint on her, like the foamy filigree at the surf's edge studded with seaweed and sea glass and, on rare occasions when the tide cooperated, an occasional mermaid's purse, that caretaker of sea life.

And along with that beach, perhaps there was only one chef for Faith as well.

Still, why should she care how she looked in front of David? They would soon be sweating side by side in the kitchen. She was overthinking this, she decided.

In the end, David made it easy. Outside the restaurant accepting a delivery, he turned at the bleat of Faith's horn and, recognizing

Maeve's wagon, bounded down the block, yanked open her door and pulled Faith out of the car and into a bear hug so unyielding it left her breathless.

"Welcome back, partner!" David smiled broadly. "About time you showed up."

93

"Oh, my goodness, David. It's gorgeous." During David's grand tour of The Blue Osprey, Faith soaked up the fruits of their collaboration, which came alive in the restaurant's newly stuccoed exterior, its beige-and-cream striped awnings, the lush potted palms.

Gone were the dated yard-high corded pilings at the entrance, where a blue plaster osprey once had perched, now replaced with contemporary gas lamps. Instead of picnic tables on a concrete apron, the exterior dining area now boasted bronze cast-iron four-tops with salmon umbrellas and swiveling bar stools arranged on a brick patio. Strategically situated outdoor sofas framed copper fire pits, inviting conversation.

"Meet with your approval?" Inside, the sleek update continued, with David's original dining room tables and chairs rejuvenated by mahogany stain. Faith gasped at the most striking modification: per David's vision, the bistro-style floor plan offered diners glimpses of their meal-in-progress over a granite half wall, bronze sconces illuminating the prep area. "No more cursing in the kitchen," he kidded.

For their joint work area, he had splurged on streamlined work-tops and appliances: eight-burner stove, double-wide Sub-Zero freezer, single-deck brick-lined gas-and-wood-fired pizza oven. There was even a salamander, a grill equipped with high-temperature overhead gas heating.

Faith gulped. David—and Bruce—had spared nothing with this redesign. "It's amazing," she said. "You'd never believe it was the same place."

"I know. Except for this." David led her to a far wall and pointed to the small brass plaque affixed at waist height.

"'October 29, 2012,'" Faith read. "That's when Nadine hit."

"Here's the waterline," he said, rubbing the plaque. "I never want to forget it. That day changed everything for me, Faith."

David looked at her, and Faith moistened her lips, waiting for him to expound on that thought, the most telling thing he had said since she'd arrived. But he only wiped his hand across a tabletop, turning up his dust-coated palm. "But we move on. Anyway, we've got tons more work to do before we open."

"Right. And barely any time." She should not have expected anything more.

Turning away, Faith raised a finger in the air, her lips moving silently as she circuited the dining room.

"What are you doing?" David asked.

"Quiet. I'm counting."

"I can tell you right now: eighty-four seats, not including outside."

Faith turned to him, hands on hips. "What are the chances we can fit an even hundred?"

94

Chalk it up to everything he'd survived in the seven months post-Nadine, but David didn't bat an eye at the prospect of hosting Ellie and Dennis's wedding reception.

"Bring it on," he said. "It'll be a great soft opening for us. Let everyone know we've bounced back."

And somehow, in scarcely three weeks, the couple's nuptials came together. Ellie and Dennis tackled entertainment, tuxes and transportation, while Ellie's mother, Ingrid, worked her formidable city contacts to procure dresses and invitations on the compressed timetable.

"What did Ingrid say about your downsized wedding?" Faith asked Ellie one night on the phone.

"It bothered her initially, but she got over it. I think the storm mellowed her, too."

Privately, Faith believed it was because Ellie had matured enough in recent months to stand up for the wedding she and Dennis desired instead of submitting to the elaborate, stuffy church-and-ballroom affair of her mother's dreams.

Food-wise, in keeping with their pared-down theme, the couple opted for finger food only, selecting fresh, fun, locally sourced offerings reflecting the locale. Their fete would kick off with a raw bar brimming with Cape May salt oysters surrounded by crab claws and shrimp.

Main selections continually passed during the party would evoke a gourmand's boardwalk stroll: skewers of sizzling shrimp wrapped in crispy prosciutto, cilantro-studded crab cakes, tacos layered with butter-poached lobster, tuna sliders with wasabi mayonnaise, individual balsamic-drizzled roasted-tomato-and-mozzarella tarts, cones of Asiago-dusted French fries, tiny pots of corn chowder.

For the couple's custom cocktail, guests could avail themselves of palate-cleansing shots of vodka-infused fresh-fruit sorbet.

And finally, supplanting the wedding cake would be deep-fried *zeppoles*, dusted in confectioners' sugar or dunked in chocolate, served alongside chocolate-chip ice cream sandwiches filled with locally made frozen custard.

One by one, the remaining wedding details fused at The Blue Osprey. There was still one slight hitch, however: it was now the day before the wedding, and the new sign for their restaurant still hadn't been hung.

Though Faith tried not to worry, she wanted their restaurant to be one hundred percent photo-ready for guests' social-media feeds and the publicity they could generate.

"Don't worry. It'll be there," David assured her for the third time.

Merrill arrived for the weekend festivities that afternoon, and volunteered to be Greyson's official baby-minder during the reception. "For Grace," she said simply.

Ellie, Dennis and Greyson were staying at the inn, along with Faith. David had offered his room for use as the baby's nursery, saying he'd be spending so much time at the restaurant he'd barely be there anyway and could bunk with Bruce if necessary.

"Things are different now," David explained to Faith as they unpacked cartons of table linens. Collaborating on the restaurant renovations over the past few months had brought him and Bruce closer together, he said. "Maybe it *was* a good thing you took off for Miami. My father might not have gotten so involved otherwise."

Faith agreed about time's power to heal. During her months in Miami, she had missed her mother and the bond they'd forged during their months together at The Mermaid's Purse. She was proud of the way Connie had warmed to the challenge of running the inn, a zeal that intensified as Connie and Roxanne shifted into high gear to ready the inn for the twin celebrations.

For the thirty or so guests at that evening's wedding rehearsal, Connie and Roxanne turned out a simple but elegant early summer dinner, starting with a refreshing watermelon, feta and arugula salad, and followed by roast loin of pork with fig jelly, creamy scallion-studded polenta and roasted carrots served with cumin yogurt. Gage confidently supervised several friends recruited as servers for the evening. Hair slicked back and dressed in black pants and white button-down shirts, the teens self-consciously shuttled plates and drinks to and from the kitchen without a single mishap. Gage appeared smitten with a certain fresh-faced blonde, whose high ponytail bounced like a show pony's as she moved around the dining room.

"He's doing great," Roxanne whispered into Faith's ear. "He even made the surfing team, thanks to David. You've got a great partner there. I hope you know that." With a squeeze of Faith's shoulder, Roxanne excused herself to supervise the arrival of dessert: at Ellie's request, a reprise of the bosomy cupcake mermaid, her mane accessorized with a scrap of snowy netting for the occasion.

Deciding she could do with more champagne, Faith went in search of the bar, finding Bruce in charge of dispensing drinks. Though he long ago had accepted her apology for her lunatic outburst, Faith still colored as she held out her flute.

"Great to see you, Faith. Your mother's happy to have you back."

"It's good to be back. Thanks for all your support with the renovations. The place looks fantastic. David couldn't have done it without you."

"Nor without you. Here's to new beginnings in Wave's End." Bruce raised his drink.

"I'll certainly drink to that." Sipping her champagne, Faith glanced around the dining room. "Isn't it bizarre to think that Nadine started all of this?"

"She certainly made her mark. They're retiring that name, you know."

"Who is?"

"The weather powers that be. They keep lists of hurricane names. A name can be repeated every seven years."

"So why not repeat Nadine?"

"Because when a storm is so deadly that the future use of its name on another storm would be insensitive, they can strike that name from the list. They voted, and Nadine is no more." He shook his head. "You know, it's ironic. I looked it up once. Nadine means 'hope.'"

"It's not about the name," said Connie, joining them. "It's about the pain and emotions it dredges up."

Bruce regarded Connie then, a look of such concern that Faith realized he knew everything. This conversation was no longer about the storm, but about a mother rewriting history, making a wrenching choice to abandon an old traumatic life and forge a new one, with new identities.

"To Connie and Faith Sterling." Bruce raised his glass.

Faith lifted her glass to theirs.

"We'd like to toast to that, too, if you'd be so kind as to pour us each a drink."

Faith turned to see David in the front hallway, patiently assisting a stooped Fred into the dining room. Faith's eyes misted, remembering her mother's call one early April evening to let her know of Mona's passing, a couple of months after the couple moved into an assisted-living facility. "She went very peacefully in her sleep, as she sat beside Fred," Connie had related.

At least Mona had a chance to meet Greyson, an encounter preserved in a handsome walnut frame on the inn's mantel.

"Are we good?" Faith asked David as she embraced Fred.

Knowing she referred to the still absent sign, David gave her a thumbs-up. "Good as gold."

95

As Ellie's wedding day dawned, Faith paced the inn's back porch, sipping coffee while she waited for David. The morning's fresh, dry air was free of the torpor and humidity that had weighed it down all week. Overhead, a pearl sky rimmed rosy coral teased of the imminent sunrise. So far, all signs pointed to the weather gods smiling down on the happy couple later that day, just as Ellie had predicted they would.

Did anything ever *not* go that girl's way?

Swallowing a large gulp of coffee, Faith decided that whatever urgent restaurant matter of David's required her rising at this ungodly hour, it would have been worth it to witness the birth of this glorious day.

Countdown, she thought, closing her eyes and breathing deeply to dispel her mounting anxiety.

At the sound of a car sinking into the rock driveway, Faith opened her eyes, expecting David. Instead, her mother pulled up in the old wagon.

"Hi, honey," Connie greeted her as she strolled up the walk. "Didn't expect you to be up so early."

"Big day. David supposedly needs my executive decision on something. Where have you been? Oh, my God, is Maeve okay?" The former innkeeper had been living on her own in a small inland apartment for the last few months, and Faith knew Connie checked on her often.

"Of course. She's fine. You thought I was with Maeve?" Connie did a poor job of hiding her smile.

"But if you weren't with her . . ." Faith put two and two together. "*Ohhhh. I get it.*"

Connie squared her shoulders. "Yes, honey. I'm coming from Bruce's. We've been together for a while now. He's a lovely man, and we're very happy." Toying with a strand of hair, she searched Faith's face. "This time feels different. It really does. Are you okay with it?"

Faith hesitated. How often her mother had spoken those words: about her contests, her men, the chances she took. But today, things were different. The tide had shifted.

For the first time, Connie had asked for Faith's opinion. *My mother sincerely cares what I think.* The irony was Connie no longer needed Faith's advice. Far from the desperate, naive woman Faith had driven down to Wave's End last fall, her mother had earned her stripes, as an innkeeper and, dare she say it, as a friend. And certainly Bruce had proven himself a solid port in a storm. "I think it's wonderful, Mom. Bruce is great."

Connie reached out and coiled Faith's ponytail, letting it fall on her daughter's shoulder. "Thank you for that. I know you had your doubts, but I've never had a man treat me as kindly as he does."

"You deserve it. It's what I've always wanted for you." She had spent so much of her life protecting her mother, shielding her and cleaning up her mistakes. But when Faith finally had stepped out of her way, Connie had figured things out on her own. The sight of her mother so content and self-assured, with an equal partner at her side, freed Faith to pursue her own future without worry. "We're adults who should accept one another's choices and support each other without judgment. So enjoy each other, but promise me one thing: no more secrets from now on!"

Connie squeezed Faith's hand. "I think I can manage that."

Behind them, David's jeep rolled into the driveway.

"I've got to run." Faith hugged Connie fiercely. "I'm really happy for you, Mom."

Climbing into David's jeep, Faith jerked her thumb toward the porch, where Connie stood waving. "Did you know about that?" she asked David.

"My dad and your mom? Worst-kept secret in Wave's End." Backing out of the driveway, David rested his arm behind her. Faith held her breath, feeling his warmth through her T-shirt but resisting the urge to sink against it. "I haven't seen my dad this happy since—" David dropped his head on the pretense of shifting gears. "Well, let's just say it's been a long time."

"Do you suppose it's serious?"

"They're adults, Faith. Let them enjoy it, whatever it is. Just drink your coffee."

96

"So, what's this dire restaurant emergency?" Faith asked.

"You'll see." David turned onto Main Street, and the two talked over a few logistics during the rest of the short drive. Gage was being given a shot as a busboy today. The fresh fish for the wedding meal had been delivered late last night; David had gone back after the rehearsal dinner to slice tuna for the sliders and devein the shrimp.

"You should have said something. I would have come back and helped. Hey, where are you going?" They'd been so deep into the day's details she hadn't noticed the circuitous route David was taking to the restaurant.

He patted her knee. "Relax. It's a beautiful day. We'll get there."

While most of Wave's End slept, Faith stared out the window at the passing string of bungalows. Near the inlet, many had a barren, stripped-down look as their owners embarked on reconstruction.

"Sometimes when I look around, I wonder how much business we'll have this summer," said Faith.

"It might be a slow start," he admitted. "But that will give us time to find our rhythm in the restaurant."

"Assuming you can *find* the place," she teased. Faith didn't know the beach town all that well, but it did appear David was driving in circles. "Can you hurry it up, please? We have a wedding in a few hours, in case you've forgotten."

A few moments later, they circled onto Dolphin Terrace, the road running alongside the restaurant. Slowing the jeep as they passed the eatery's south wall, now repainted a soothing ochre, David paused at the stop sign.

"Hang on. This is a pretty auspicious day, and I want to remember every detail of our opening," David said.

"*Re*opening," she corrected. "Which could turn out to be our closing if we don't get in there and get to work. Can you please park this thing?"

Inching the jeep out into the intersection, David made a wide left turn onto Ocean Terrace. "So, what do you think?" he asked.

"What I think is"—Faith bent over to retrieve her coffee mug and notes from the floor of the jeep—"if we want to wow these wedding guests, we better get our butts in gear, like, yesterday." Out of the car now, Faith crossed the beachfront road, ticking off last-minute items to David, making it almost halfway across the street before she froze and stared up at The Blue Osprey.

97

Or rather, the restaurant *formerly* known as The Blue Osprey, because the weather-beaten, hand-lettered nameplate had vanished.

A magnificent new sign dangled above the restaurant's retooled outdoor dining area: a lustrous eggshell oval hanging from a scrolled iron bracket, its gleaming gold letters meticulously carved into the wood spelling out the restaurant's name.

It was this last detail that took Faith's breath away—not because David finally had seen to its installation, because she knew he would, but because the sign no longer read THE BLUE OSPREY.

Rather, in simple and elegant script, were these words:

Moon
&
Stars
Bistro

98

Faith could only stare up at the sign in amazement. David had followed her rendering of the locket perfectly—almost too perfectly, she thought. Taking a step back, she felt herself wobble, then David's strong arm clapped around her waist, steadying her. She leaned into him without hesitation this time, grateful for the support.

"It's what you wanted, isn't it?" he asked softly.

"Exactly. But when I showed you my design at the train station, you never said a word." She couldn't tear her eyes from the sign, where the three words nestled in the curve of the crescent moon and a trio of stars twinkled above.

During that briefest of conversations, and during all of the restaurant discussions that followed, David said nothing about her proposal to change the Blue Osprey's name.

And Faith had been just as happy to let it go, deeply regretting her suggestion, a brainstorm that had struck during her final emotional days at The Mermaid's Purse. Who was she to imagine David might change the name of his beloved restaurant? The new understanding between Faith and her mother had nothing to do with him.

She, Saint Faith of the Boundaries, had seriously overstepped her own. She would simply save her idea for a future endeavor.

That's what made today's unveiling so much sweeter—because her business partner had put his faith in her and placed Moon & Stars Bistro in lights—quite literally in lights, she realized, once David had reached inside the restaurant entrance and flipped on a rooftop spotlight that shined down on the sign.

"But The Blue Osprey. That was your baby. Aren't you sad to see it go?"

"Of course. But it's only a name. And we'll make a *new* name for ourselves with this one. It symbolizes hope, a fresh start. Hey, you're not upset I did this without you, are you?" David stepped close to stroke Faith's damp cheeks.

"How could I be upset? It's beautiful. It's perfect." She stared up at the sign again. "It looks exactly like—"

"I know. Your grandmother's locket." Turning her face toward him, David kissed her, closing the months-long divide between them, taking her back to that hopelessly low point in the Mermaid's Purse's kitchen, after telling the boarders about the foreclosure.

Dazed, Faith dropped onto one of the patio stools. "How did you know about the locket?"

"When I told Connie about your design, she showed it to me."

"My *mother* was in on this?"

As if on cue, the front door opened and Connie appeared. "I certainly was. And I know this morning we agreed to have no more secrets, but this one was already a done deal."

She had slipped out again as soon as Faith left her that morning and raced to the restaurant for the unveiling, she explained now.

Connie turned to survey the building's new façade. "I have to say, when he showed me your design, I was a little surprised that, given its history, you wanted to memorialize it in your new restaurant." Connie reached into her pocket and produced the necklace in question.

"That history doesn't define us anymore," Faith said. "You said as much when you explained to me how you chose our new names. As far as I'm concerned, from this point forward, *moon and stars* is all about the future. About possibilities."

Choked with emotion, Connie couldn't respond.

"I'm so proud of you," Faith continued. "For the way you've helped Maeve and Merrill, and Roxanne and Gage, and Fred and Mona, and Ellie and Dennis, and the new people and . . . well, everybody. Including me. *Especially* me." Her voice cracking, Faith took the necklace from her mother and fastened it around her neck. "It's time to change this story."

Having quietly observed the two for a time, David stepped up and wrapped an arm around each of them. "And perhaps time to prepare for a wedding?"

"Holy—" Faith glanced down at her watch. "You're absolutely right. We've only got a few hours to finish."

David smiled. "Don't worry. I knew this might distract you this morning, so I called in some reserves for the front of the house."

"Reserves?" Faith frowned. "Who could you possibly call on such short . . ."

Overhead, the Moon & Stars's spotlight blinked several times before the front door opened again. Faith gasped at the tall, tanned man in a chef's apron stepping onto the patio.

"Xander!" Faith fell onto her former boss and mentor. "What are you doing here? You said it would be impossible to make it this weekend."

"Your partner swore me to secrecy," Xander replied. "And seriously, did you ever think I'd miss your grand opening?"

"But what about Piquant?" She knew Xander had already engaged an architect to jump-start the seaport renovations.

"Under control for the moment. After everything you've done for me, I wanted to be here. And after today, we'll be square." He patted his pocket.

"See? Isn't this nice, Faith?" Connie asked. "With Xander here to help David, you can come back to the inn and primp with Ellie."

"Are you kidding? And miss the opportunity to work with these two pros? Not a chance." Faith linked arms with the two men. "I promise I'll be back in plenty of time to get dolled up. Moon and stars."

99

At the appointed hour, Faith and Ellie waited in wedding finery in the Mermaid's Purse kitchen, listening for their cue. In the garden, a keyboard's tinkle mingled with the expectant hum of the assembled guests and floated up through the kitchen screen.

On tiptoe, Faith peered out the window. "It's going well so far, don't you think?"

"I do."

"Make sure you say that outside," Faith cracked, eyeing the crowd in the yard and noting David's arrival with satisfaction. Her business partner cleaned up well, she thought, watching him clap the groom on the back and admiring the black shirt and sport coat thrown over his chef's pants—also black for the occasion. She turned to comment on this to Ellie when her friend sniffled beside her.

"Wait! The bride's not allowed to cry." Faith grabbed a napkin from the counter and dampened it. "You'll ruin your makeup."

"I can't help it. This is so emotional, coming full circle here with you. I feel like it's the end of an era." Ellie obediently gazed skyward, allowing Faith to dab at her eyes.

"Don't worry. We'll still see each other loads. Remember, I'll need to check on my godson." Pronouncing Ellie's countenance perfect, Faith positioned herself at her friend's back and fluffed her veil one final time, the diaphanous fabric landing in a frothy cloud against Ellie's classic linen sundress.

"There: all set."

"Thanks, Faith." Ellie's hand flew to her throat. "Oh, no! My something borrowed! They were supposed to be my grandmother's pearls. My mother must have them."

In the backyard, the final keyboard notes faded, and the celebrant solemnly invited the guests to take their seats.

Faith thought fast. If she ran outside to ask about the pearls, Ingrid would need to come back inside and retrieve them, delaying the ceremony, which wouldn't be a problem as long as Ellie didn't mind. Or might there be a simpler solution? Reaching back, Faith unclasped her own necklace. "Will this do?" she asked, offering Ellie her moon and stars locket.

∽

At the heraldic strum of a guitar, Ellie's father offered his arm to his daughter, and Faith stepped out onto the porch. The late-afternoon sun bathed her face as she paused at the top of the stairs, drinking in the sight of the small group of well-wishers beaming back at her.

The storm had lashed these people together, fostering relationships as unexpected as the treasures the East Coast tide continued to return month after month, items presumed stolen by Nadine: bundles of love letters, a cat's bowl, a wedding ring.

These expectant faces spanned life's continuum, from newborn babies, to partners discovering each other in the dusk of life, to those nearing the end of their journey and reflecting back with wisdom.

And now, the wedding! As the couple exchanged vows, Faith noticed the crystals on the bride's borrowed locket reflect the waning sunlight with Ellie's every movement, including their celebratory kiss. Officially married, Ellie handed her bouquet to Faith, then reached out to Merrill for the sleeping Greyson and shifted him to her shoulder. With Phillip guiding his wife and child, the family followed Merrill to Grace's birdbath, whose base wore a band of sunflowers for the occasion. In accompaniment, the guitarist strummed a plaintive acoustic "Blackbird."

Humming along with the Beatles ballad, Faith felt her chest tighten, recalling how the superstorm had plunged Wave's End—and countless other communities—into the hopeless dead of night, a darkness that stretched into weeks and months. The devastation *had* broken wings and crippled spirits, but also had provided a moment for the survivors to arise, supported by the Graces and the Alicias and an army of volunteers as they reconstructed their nests.

As the music ended, Merrill picked up a watering can and slowly filled the birdbath with water, the onlookers' silence amplifying the gentle gurgle. She then set the can on the ground, staring into the water's reflection before plucking a sunflower petal and tossing it in. With that action, Faith sensed a lightening of Merrill's burden, her executing of Grace's wishes a critical and healing step.

Heads in the crowd were bowed reverentially when suddenly the snoozing bundle on Ellie's shoulder wriggled, and Greyson signaled his presence with a lusty yell.

"My goodness. I'm so sorry." Flustered, Ellie clutched Greyson to her chest and rocked him. "He must be hungry. I'll take him inside."

"Don't be silly," Merrill said. "Grace always said a baby's cry was the most beautiful sound in the world. I know she's smiling right now." Merrill took the fussing Greyson from Ellie and walked away, and the couple followed. The guests took this as a signal to disperse, swarming Ellie and Dennis in a ragged receiving line.

Lingering at the birdbath, Faith peered at the water's still surface. A moment later, her mother's face reflected beside hers.

"So beautiful," Connie said.

"They really are a stunning couple," Faith agreed.

"I meant you, silly." Connie flicked the water with her fingers, rippling their reflections and making the two of them laugh.

"Grace must be happy. Now, all we need are some birds." Faith craned her neck at the sky.

"Congratulations, Ellie and Dennis!" At Gage's yell, the crowd turned toward the back porch where the teen now clutched a white wrought-iron birdcage festooned with sunflowers. "Sorry, they just got here."

"I think you're about to get your wish, Faith," Connie observed.

As the pair watched, Gage lifted the latch on the cage, releasing a pair of snowy doves that soared above the crowd, who cheered and captured the birds' flight into the clouds on their phones.

"Pretty cool, huh?" Gage descended the porch steps to mingle with the spectators, gloating with pride over his stunt.

"That was amazing, Gage. Where do the doves go?" Connie asked.

Shading his eyes, he squinted into the sky. "They fly right back to their loft. Their handler said they have a homing instinct."

"It's a perfect way to celebrate this day," Faith said as Gage turned away to chat with another guest. "If only the doves had dunked themselves in Grace's birdbath."

"That would have been a nice touch," answered Connie. "But we could use it for something else. How about we make a wish?" Burrowing her hand deep in her skirt pocket, Connie produced a penny and held it up. "What do you say, Faith? How will it land: Heads or tails?"

Faith frowned at her mother. "For a wish? I think you just toss the coin in. No heads or tails."

"My goodness, Faith. Must you always be about the rules?" Connie teased. "Just pick one, for old times' sake: Heads or tails?"

Heads or tails? Faith stared at the coin, instantly transported back to that long-ago night in the pickup truck, recalling that life-altering ride through the desert on her mother's lap as vividly as if it had happened yesterday—a journey with a lot of bumps and detours, but one worth making.

"All right. But only because I can tell you won't let this go until I do. And this time, *I* get to toss it." Taking the coin from her mother, Faith laid it flat on her palm. "I call—"

But just as she was about to fling the penny into the air, David appeared at her elbow.

"Hate to rush you," he said, "but we should head over to Moon and Stars before the crowd."

At the delicious sound of her new restaurant's name, Faith shivered with satisfaction. Accepting David's outstretched hand, she flung her mother's penny high into the air, then turned and strolled away with her new partner, unconcerned with the coin's ultimate flight, secure in the knowledge that, despite the squalls certain to cloud her horizon in the future, her immediate destiny, her moon and stars, were—for this moment in time, at least—perfectly aligned.

AFTERWORD

This story is a work of fiction. However, in 2012, a storm of similar magnitude devastated the East Coast, killing thirty-seven people and destroying close to 350,000 homes. Although Hurricane Sandy forever altered the topography of countless neighborhoods, the destruction also triggered an extraordinary surge of community and compassion. With reconstruction ongoing at the superstorm's five-year mark, this story is intended to honor Sandy's survivors for their resilience and determination to rise above disaster.

QUESTIONS AND TOPICS FOR DISCUSSION

1. Though *At Wave's End* is entirely a work of fiction, a major hurricane devastated the East Coast of the United States at around this same time. Talk about the role of the hurricane in the story, and how it transforms the characters. Are descriptions of the storm and its aftermath authentic? Did reading about the storm lead to a new understanding or awareness of some aspect of natural disasters that you might not have thought about before?

2. What do the novel's opening pages tell you about the relationship between Faith and her mother? How does this relationship change over time?

3. Did you like Faith Sterling as a person? What does her chosen profession say about her?

4. What kind of mother is Connie Sterling? How would you describe her parenting style?

5. Talk about the significance of "Moon and Stars." What meaning does it hold for Faith, Connie and David?

6. Early on, we meet Faith's best friend, Ellie. During the novel, Faith bonds with Tanya, Merrill and Grace. How do these female friendships affect Faith, and how important are they to the story?

7. How does the author use The Mermaid's Purse, a run-down bed-and-breakfast, in the story? What does the inn represent for each of the characters? How is Faith transformed by her stay at the inn?

8. Of all the boarders at The Mermaid's Purse, which one(s) did you like the most?

9. Connie wins The Mermaid's Purse in a lottery. Would you ever enter a contest like that? What would be the pros and cons to consider?

10. Is Faith's initial assessment and treatment of Bruce justified?

11. How is Faith transformed by the conversation she overhears between Connie and Roxanne?

12. It is often said that too many cooks spoil the broth. How does David's presence in the kitchen affect Faith? Is the evolution of their relationship believable? Why is David so keen to take Faith surfing?

13. What did you think of Faith's reaction when she finds her birth certificate? Was Connie justified in keeping this information from her?

14. There are more than seventy food references in the novel. What does food represent in the story? What did you think of Faith's menu selections? Which was your favorite?

15. Faith works hard to save the inn. What does the inn's future represent to her? If you had been a past guest at The Mermaid's Purse, would you have been compelled to contribute?

16. Why do you think the author wrote this? What is her most important message?

17. What did you think of the ending? Would you want to read more about any of these characters, and if so, which ones?

ACKNOWLEDGMENTS

A writer's life may be solitary, but it takes a supportive team to place a book in readers' hands. For their contributions along the way, I offer my deepest thanks to these individuals:

My agent Elisabeth Weed for her perennial encouragement.

My unparalleled Lake Union team, including Danielle Marshall, Kelli Martin and Gabriella Dumpit, who make collaboration a pleasure.

My developmental editors Susan Breen and Marianna Baer, each an accomplished author in her own right, who challenged me to dig deep for Faith's sake.

My early readers for their forthright and unflinching reviews, including Jennifer Clark Callinan, Karen Cassano, Mita Chatterjee, Molly Donovan Foster, Ellen Easton, Judi Feldman, Carrie Godesky, Teresa Cooper Kislik, Deirdre McGuinness, Jenifer Morack and Lisa Vlkovic.

Members of my retired book club—dear friends who once again proved to be *less* than retiring with their feedback, which I deeply appreciated: Angela Flarity, Susan Kuper, Lisa Muir, Ginny Stewart and Nancy Swanson.

All who helped to polish this story, including Sara Addicott, Nicole Manager, Alyssa Matesic, Monique Vescia and Laura Whittemore.

My childhood friend Deborah Albury, whose dream of taking a chance on a New England bed-and-breakfast inspired Connie's flight of fancy.

My daughters, Molly and Nora, and my new son-in-law, Bob (yay—another writer in the family!), for their faith and reassurance.

And finally, to Maurice: my port in a storm, my Moon & Stars.

ABOUT THE AUTHOR

Photo © 2015 Benjamin Russell

The author of the novel *Deliver Her*, Patricia Perry Donovan is an American journalist who writes about health care. Several years ago, she began writing fiction, and since then, her work has appeared in literary journals such as the *Bookends Review*, *Bethlehem Writers Roundtable*, *Flash Fiction Magazine*, *Gravel Literary Journal*, and *Hippocampus Magazine*. The mother of two grown daughters, she lives at the Jersey Shore with her husband. Connect with her on Facebook at www.facebook.com/ PatriciaPerryDonovanBooks/ and on Twitter @PatPDonovan. Learn more at www.patriciaperrydonovan.com.